The Mosquito Fleet

A Tale of the West Indies Squadron

Andrew Costa

Copyright© 2021 Andrew Costa

All Rights Reserved

ISBN: 9798777993236

Book 4 of "The Sullivan Saga"

Cover Images:

Front Cover; "USS Wasp vs. HMS Reindeer" by John Clymer, US Marine Corps Art Collection.

Back Cover; "Battle Lake Borgne" by Thomas Hornbrook US Naval Academy Museum, Public Domain.

Interior Images:

All interior images are in the Public Domain unless otherwise specified.

Cover Design by Cathy Wolf

The rendition of "The John B. Sails" is taken from that first transcribed in Harper's Monthly Magazine in 1916, and is in the Public Domain.

For my wife Kim

Acknowledgements

I would like to thank the following people for their help:

My father Mark, my wife Kim, Jennifer Guenther, and Andrew Brown for agreeing to read drafts of my manuscript at different stages and supplying me with valuable editing and feedback.

Mrs. Cathy Wolf for her work on the cover design.

Author's Note

Readers will note that some words and phrases are spelled phonetically when used in dialogue but not in text, i.e. Boatswain will be rendered as Bosun. In addition, British characters will use the distinct 'Leftenant' pronunciation of Lieutenant in dialogue. A further note on pronunciation is required for the word 'huzza.' Typically, this word is spelled and pronounced in the modern era as 'huzzah,' but contrary to popular belief during this period it would actually have been spelled 'huzza' and pronounced 'huzzay' similar to 'hurray.' Furthermore, the term 'regulars' refers to professional soldiers or the standing US or British Armies, as opposed to 'volunteers' which were militia.

During the Napoleonic Wars, the main theater where British and French troops engaged each other was in Spain and Portugal. Because of its location in the Iberian Peninsula, it was dubbed 'The Peninsula War' by the British, and when referring to service there, it was common practice for British soldiers to simply call it 'The Peninsula.' Readers will also notice several references to British officers "purchasing" a commission. At the time of the novel's setting, the British Army had a complex system whereby wealthy individuals could purchase an officer's rank, particularly infantry officers as artillery and engineering officers required special training for their technical branches.

In addition, the spelling of Puerto Rico will be anglicized to the period correct 'Porto Rico' for English speakers.

Glossary of Naval and Military Terms

Schooner- Sailing vessel with non-square rigged (triangular) sails on two or more masts.

Brig- Two masted "square rigged" (meaning square sails) sailing vessel (often overlapped with Sloops).

Sloop (of War)- Square rigged, three masted ship with less than 18 guns.

Frigate- Any square rigged, three masted ships "rated" between sixth and fifth, that is carrying between 20 and 44 guns on a single gun deck.

Ship of the Line- Square rigged, three masted ship having two or more gundecks, rating between fourth and first (between 50 and 120 guns).

Larboard- A period term used for referring to the left side of a ship, officially changed to 'port' in the 1840s to lesson confusion with starboard (meaning the right side of a ship).

Foremast- The forward mast.

Mainmast- The middle or largest mast.

Mizzenmast- The rear mast.

Forecastle- Pronounced 'Foc'sle', a raised deck above the gun deck at the bow of a ship.

Quarterdeck- A raised deck above the gun deck at the stern of the ship. On a ship with a Spar Deck (a single deck linking the forecastle and the quarterdeck) or on a ship too small to carry a raised deck, it referred to the after section of the ship's deck surrounding the ship's wheel.

Fighting top- A platform partway up the mast used by Marines as a sniper's nest.

Carronade- A short barreled, short range cannon, typically firing a heavier 32-pound shot and mounted on a sliding rather than rolling carriage.

Commodore- A title given to the senior Captain designated in command of a squadron and later the title for the rank of a single-star admiral in WWII.

Master Commandant- US Navy rank between Lieutenant and Captain, which evolved into the modern rank of Commander, which already existed in the Royal Navy.

Lieutenant Commandant- An unofficial title given to any Lieutenant in command of a ship not requiring a Captain or Master Commandant, it evolved into the modern rank of Lieutenant Commander.

Midshipman- Modern equivalent is the rank of Ensign, they were cadets or officers in training, often under the age of 18 sometimes as young as 12.

Sailing Master- A Warrant Officer (between commissioned officers and non-commissioned officers) responsible for navigation and handling of a ship.

Boatswain- Pronounced 'Bosun'. Senior NCO in charge of deck operations.

Coxswain- Pronounced 'Coxsun'. NCO in charge of the Captain's boat.

Ensign- An army rank equivalent to the modern 2nd Lieutenant. No relation to the later naval rank of Ensign.

Rounders- A bat-and-ball game that in the United States evolved into Baseball.

Whist- A card game popular during the Napoleonic era.

Beat-to-Quarters- When going into action, a Marine drummer would beat a tattoo calling all hands to their action stations. Modern equivalent would be "General Quarters" or "Battle Stations."

Letter of Marque- A license granted by a government to private citizens to act as privateers in time of war.

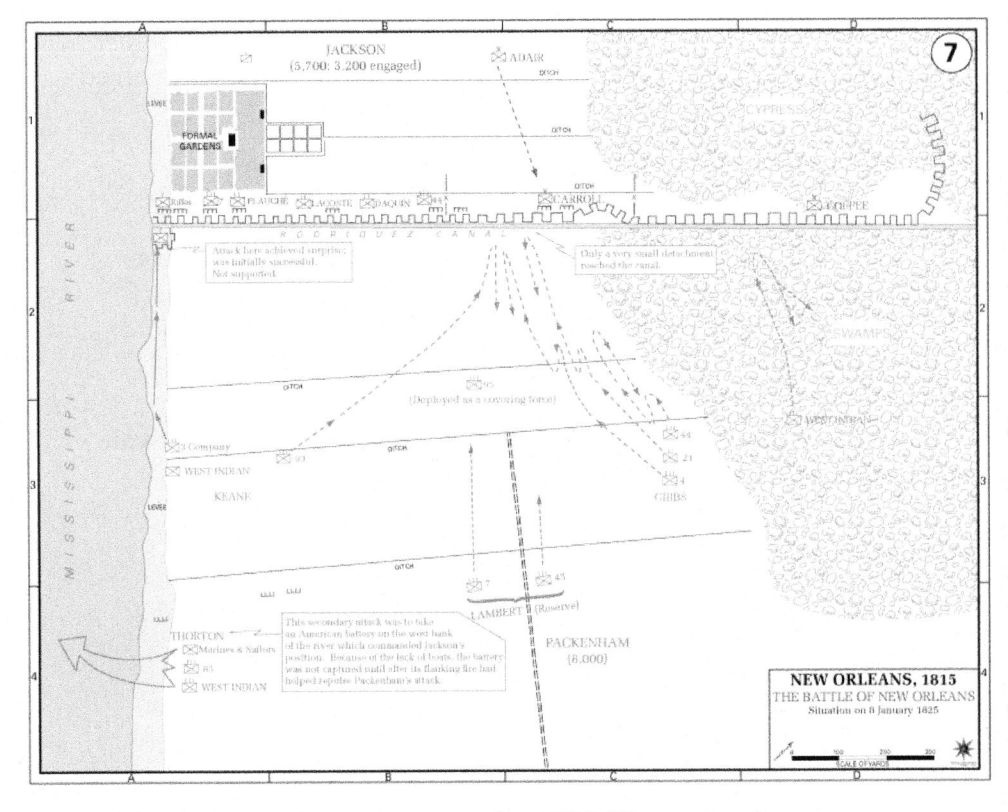

The Battle of New Orleans. Map credit: US Military Academy

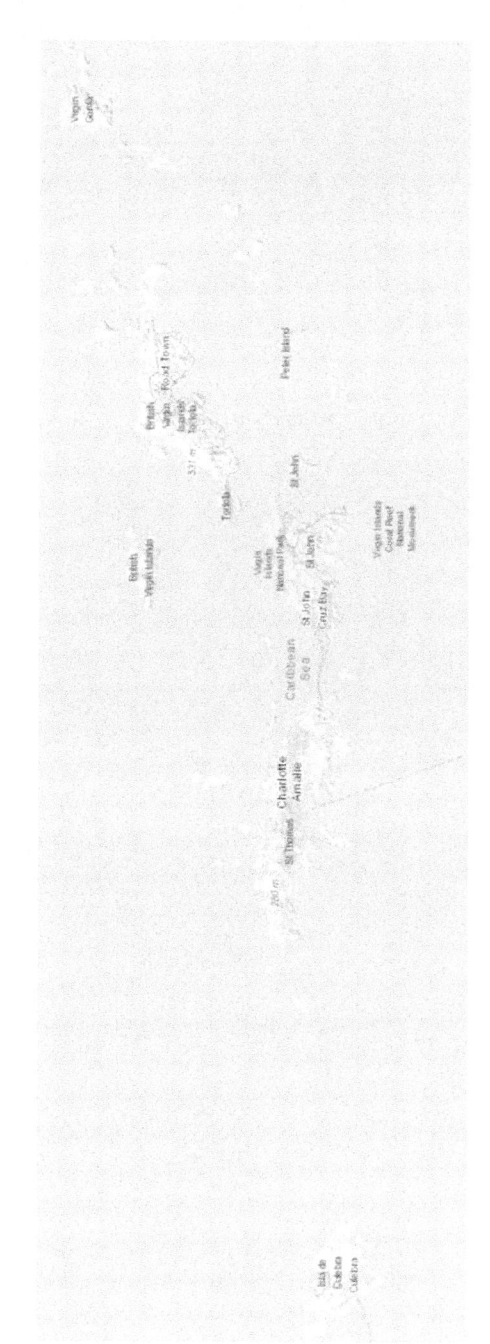

Leeward Islands.　　Map credit: US Geological Survey

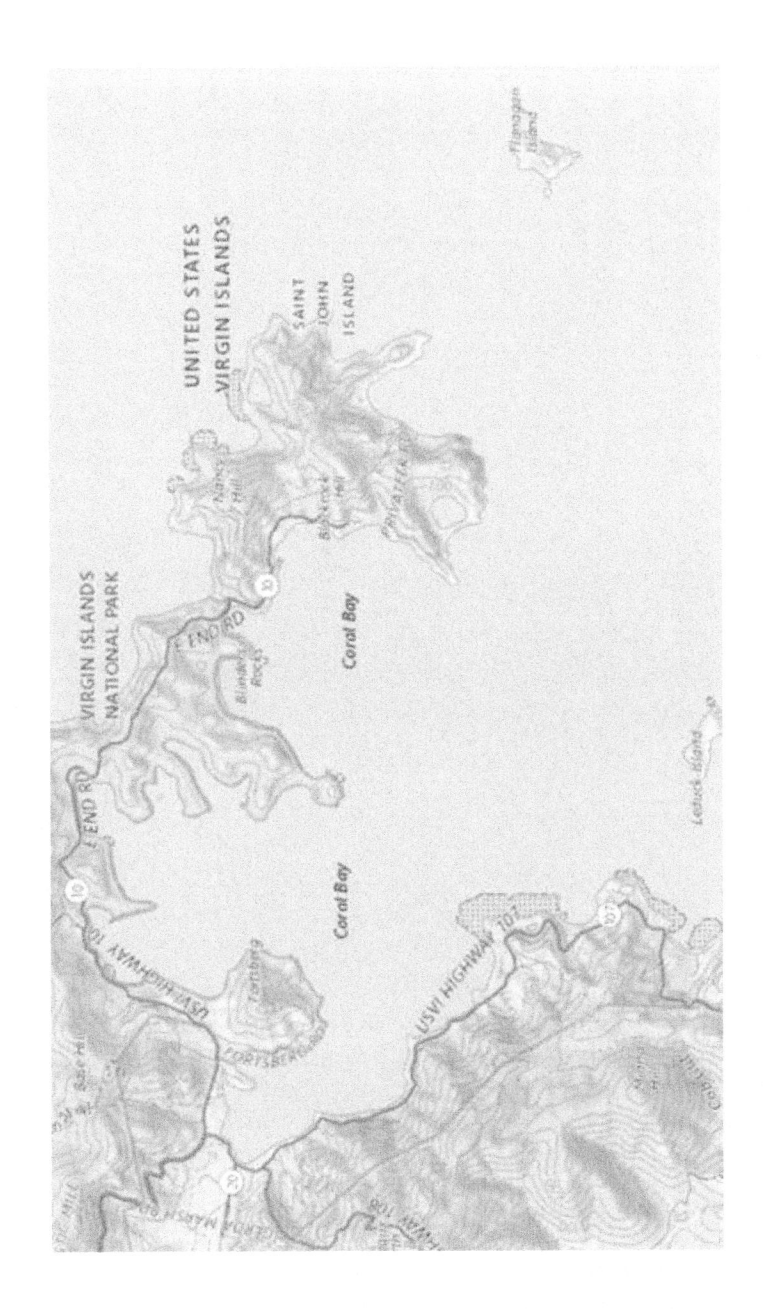

Coral Bay, Saint John. Map credit: US Geological Survey

Prologue

October 1814, USS *Wasp* in the Sargasso Sea, approximately 150 miles south of Bermuda.

The brig had been shadowing them for two days. Master Commandant Johnston Blakely had been at war long enough to know when a ship was following him, and the commander of the sloop USS *Wasp* was certain this was the case.

The *Wasp* had parted company with the last of their prizes in September. At various times the crew thought the mystery ship they had spotted was the *Atalanta*, but Blakely had ordered the Midshipman whom he had given command of the prize to make for Savannah. Blakely was headed for the Caribbean to continue his raiding of British merchants, and the heavily trafficked sea lanes in the West Indies were sure to be rich with targets.

"They gained on us during the night," the Sailing Master said to Blakely absent-mindedly as they both watched the ship over the aft railing.

Blakely took another look through his spyglass. Focusing on the brig, he noted the ship had set full sail, and was angled perfectly to catch as much wind as possible to drive her forward. *She's faster than us*, Blakely thought as he closed his spyglass.

"He's being awfully careless with so much canvas flying in this wind," the Sailing Master went on. The breeze had strengthened with the onset of daylight, and clouds were forming behind them to the east, sure signs that a storm was closing on them.

"He might be careless, or he's a deft sailor," responded Blakely. "He's handling her too nimbly to be a fool."

The Sailing Master looked at him. "Shall I make a course correction, Sir?"

Blakely shook his head. "No. We'll never shake him in daylight. We'll have to wait for dark instead. Set more sail and keep us ahead of him until nightfall."

Blakely then retired below to his cabin. As the day wore on he would take furtive glances out his cabin windows to see how far off the trailing ship was. He poured over charts and navigational calculations but determined that they were quite far from land of any sort, and would be for several more days at the least.

Outside the glass panes of his cabin windows, the sky grew increasingly ominous. The storm, possibly the makings of a late season hurricane, advanced upon the Wasp rapidly. The swells grew heavier, and Blakely noticed a distinct increase in the force of the wind.

Sweeping up a boat cloak, Blakely put on the waterproof garment and headed back on deck. Eschewing his cocked hat, he tugged a woolen knit cap over his ears, and turned his shoulder to the chilling wind. He walked back to the Sailing Master who was standing with his arms crossed near the ship's wheel.

"Any change?" Blakely asked him.

The Sailing Master glanced over his shoulder to the northeast, then shook his head. "I've watched him unceasingly. I've never seen such seamanship. He's been as close-hauled to the wind as he can get, and he's been gaining on us."

Blakely glared at the mystery ship over the aft rail. He then looked at the sky, growing concerned over how dark it had become.

"Come two points to larboard," he told the Sailing Master. He looked down at the ship's compass near the wheel. "Make your course south-southwest. We need to get around the edges of this storm that's brewing."

The Sailing Master frowned. "He'll be able to close the distance much more quickly than if we stayed on a more westerly course."

Blakely's face made an uneasy expression. "I know."

The Sailing Master sighed, but silently concurred that the more immediate danger to the ship was the oncoming storm rather than their pursuer.

"Rig up lifelines on deck," ordered Blakely, anticipating heavier seas. "Keep the idlers below and remain at full sail as long as you dare to keep that interloper off of our tail. When the wind finally gets to be too much, shorten to storm sail."

The Sailing Master nodded and barked out the orders to the Boatswain. With the deck in capable hands, Blakely returned below to his cabin, hoping to gain some sleep before he returned to take the evening watch. Despite the ever-increasing howling of the wind, he eventually drifted off in his hammock.

Hours later he was startled awake by the ship's steward rousing him.

"Sir! You're needed on deck!" the man said, shaking Blakely's arm.

Blakely jerked upright and rolled out of his hammock, throwing on his knitted cap and boat cloak. He hurried up the hatchway and was hit across the face by a blast of wind that nearly knocked him over. Steadying himself, he stumbled in the dark until he grabbed hold of one of the lifelines he had ordered rigged up and made his way aft towards the ship's wheel.

"I shortened to storm sail an hour ago, Sir," the Sailing Master shouted over the wind, his eyes little more than slits as he squinted to see through the slashing rain. "I'm not sure of the main topgallant in this wind," he said, pointing up the mainmast.

Blakely looked up the mainmast at its uppermost tier. The mast had been damaged in their last engagement with the HMS *Reindeer*, and while the crew had repaired it as best they could, everyone wondered if the ship could handle more strain in such hazardous weather.

"What of that brig that was following us?" he asked.

The Sailing Master shook his head. "She was still following last I saw just before the light faded," he said.

"She could still be following us," said Blakely, his instincts telling him there was something ominous about their pursuer. "I'll send word to have the lanterns doused in my cabin. We can lose him in the dark."

The Sailing Master almost laughed. "If he's still following us in this weather, he's a madman!"

The Sailing Master went below and Blakely took the watch. Holding tight to the ratlines near the ship's wheel, he stood shivering as rain lashed the deck. As the *Wasp* pitched and heaved in the heavy seas, he looked off into the darkness around him. Every now and then he would think he saw a shape, the outline of their ghostly follower, but he would blink and the mirage would be gone.

Doubt gnawed at Blakely constantly, as he could only wonder at the determination of a captain that would continue to chase them through the storm. *And in a brig, no less*, he thought as his eyes caught another blur through the rain. *How was he able to gain on us in a brig? They're nowhere near speedy enough to keep pace with us.* The skill of his opponent unnerved him, and he prayed they would be able to lose them in the darkness.

Even with the weather having turned foul, Blakely thought the ship was handling the situation well. The waves, while rough, were manageable, and the wind had not gotten worse from what he could tell, and he was hopeful that they would be able to ride the storm out. The crew continued about their tasks, staggering across the deck as waves washed over them, and braving the ratlines as the wind threatened to rip them out of their grip. Yet none showed fear of their predicament, though there were plenty of complaints, and in true Navy fashion they carried on with complete determination.

Having stayed on watch the whole night through, Blakely started to feel relief when he noticed the sky was slowly turning from black to grey. Though dawn would be impossible to observe given the cloud cover, the return of daylight meant that the hard part of riding the storm out was nearly over. It even seemed as though the wind was lessening and the waves flattening out.

He turned to look over his shoulder, just to be sure they had given the mysterious brig the slip, when a hand yelled out a warning. Blakely whipped his head back around to starboard, just in time to see a large wave crash against the *Wasp's* hull.

The impact of the wave sent the ship lurching to the left. One of the starboard cannons slid backwards and snapped the lines holding it in place. The great gun then tumbled backward across the deck and slammed into the backstay-plate that tied down the rigging holding the main topgallant mast steady. The backstay plate was smashed to pieces, and the backstays began to uncoil.

As Blakely saw the lines going slack, he felt a lump catch in his throat as he remembered the Sailing Master's warning about the topgallant. "Secure that rigging!" he bellowed, pointing to the limp hanging lines. A hand nearby heard him and started making for the backstay-plate, slipping on the deck and continuing to scamper on his hands and knees. Before the sailor could reach it, the ship was buffeted by a gust of wind, and Blakely heard the creaking of wood. He looked upward and saw the topgallant mast begin to bend, then snap at the brace that had been put in place to repair it. The topgallant mast fell into the sea beside the ship, and the *Wasp* lurched back to starboard as the mast pulled the ship downward. The upended cannon now rolled back across the deck as well, crushing an unfortunate seaman against the starboard rail.

"Get axes! Cut it loose! Cut it loose!" screamed Blakely as he ran to the rigging. Crewmen rushed over bringing any cutting instruments they could find. Desperately the men hacked and sawed at the rigging to break it loose before it rolled the *Wasp* over. After what seemed like hours but surely had only been minutes, the last coil of rope was cut and the sloop righted with a jolt.

Blakely and his men stood there in the rain, holding onto the rail watching the severed topgallant mast bobbing away on the waves. In only moments all sense of optimism had left them.

"Your orders, Sir?" asked the Sailing Master, who had come back on deck from below.

Blakely quickly surveyed his battered ship. The Wasp was damaged, but no longer in immediate danger. The sloop's speed and maneuverability were compromised, however, and in the storm, there was no telling how her stability might be affected.

"Clear the deck of any remaining debris," Blakely ordered. Turning to address the Sailing Master directly he said, "Get some men aloft to set more sail on the fore and mizzen masts. We'll need them in order to maneuver and to gain some speed to clear us out of this storm."

"Aye, aye, Sir," the Sailing Master replied without reservation, then barking an order to several Boatswain's Mates.

The crew set to work immediately, first securing the loose cannon, and hastily burying the crushed seaman over the side. Some of the hands went aloft and set more sail as had been ordered. The *Wasp* powered over the wave troughs with the extra canvas, still on the southerly course that Blakely had set the day before. The Sailing Master had the carpenter and his mates get to work on additional braces for the remaining topgallants, as well as start fashioning a replacement for the mainmast.

By noon the weather was beginning to clear with the wind losing strength and the rain becoming only a drizzle, though the seas were still heavy. Blakely allowed himself to breathe a sigh of relief, believing they had managed to skirt around the edge of the storm. All they had to do now was maintain their course and they would be able avoid the British controlled Bahamas and reach Hispaniola to effect more extensive repairs.

"Sail ho! On the starboard quarter!"

Blakely closed his eyes, gritted his teeth, and swallowed hard. Without turning around, he instinctively knew it was the phantom brig. He balled his hands into fists, angry at himself for thinking they had escaped danger.

"It's that brig, Sir," the Sailing Master said. His eyes we a bit wide, as he was thinking the same as Blakely. They could not run and were in no condition for a fight.

"If we couldn't put them behind us before we lost the topgallant, we can't do it now," he went on, though he did not need to. "I don't think we can keep out of range until dark neither."

Blakely turned to look at their pursuer. He glared malevolently at the brig as he saw it bounding over wave crests in the distance. "When we can't outrun them any longer, beat to quarters."

"You know we can't outfight them with our maneuverability crippled," the Sailing Master started. "They're already upwind as it is."

"I know!" Blakely snapped at the man letting his frustration out. He took a breath and calmed himself down. "We don't have a choice, so we might as well go down fighting."

"Yes, Sir," the Sailing Master answered, and he returned to his work.

The men worked faster to get the ship repaired, hoping to have a new topgallant crafted and installed in enough time to help them steal another night to lose the phantom in the darkness. Blakely admired their determination, but he knew it was too late. They would never be able to hoist a top mast, and get it rigged, in such heavy seas before the brig bore down on them. With every passing minute, the ship closed on their stern, and Blakely was able to get a better look at her. Strangely, he noticed she flew no ensign, though he was still convinced she was British.

It had finally stopped raining and there were even some breaks in the cloud cover. Blakely checked his watch and it showed half-past three in the afternoon. Taking a look over the stern he saw that they were now within range of the brig's bow chasers. If it had been an hour later, they might have been able to keep them just far enough behind until nightfall, but now it was too late.

Returning his watch to his pocket, Blakely let out a sigh. He then looked up at his men and bellowed, "Beat to quarters!"

The Marine drummer beat the tattoo and the crew ran to their guns. The men began to load the cannons and they all had the same thought on their minds. Would the guns fire? The rain and waves had made it impossible for the cannons to be kept dry on the open deck, and while the gunpowder might have been stored below in canvas bags, the vent holes were likely too wet for the priming charges.

Blakely took up position on the starboard rail. The brig was going to pass them on that side, which put the Americans at a further disadvantage seeing as the starboard battery was down one gun.

The brig had refrained from firing her bow chasers and crept slowly alongside the *Wasp*. Looking over the rail, Blakely could scarcely see a handful of men on deck, others no doubt out of sight behind the rail. He saw a man near the ship's wheel, wearing a cocked hat in the fore-and-aft style of a Lieutenant, with sandy side-whiskers. The man stepped up to the rail of the brig and grabbed hold of the ratlines, hoisting himself up. He looked over the *Wasp*, then turned his head to someone on deck and simply nodded.

The side of the brig exploded in a volley of cannon fire. Solid shot slammed into the side of the *Wasp*, crashing through the rails sending splinters slicing into the crew. Blakely looked down the length of the deck and saw three men had fallen, missing limbs or half their torsos smeared across the deck.

"Return fire as you bear!" Blakely screamed. The gunlayers yanked on the lanyards to trigger the cannons, but the flintlocks clicked without firing. A few of them tried again, only for their guns' flintlocks to click uselessly once again.

Blakely gulped with the realization that the fight was over before it even began, and wondered how his opposite number had managed to keep his own guns dry. Knowing the situation was hopeless, he saw no reason in senselessly sacrificing his men.

"Strike the colors," he told the Sailing Master. All of the crew gave him bitter looks, but they knew why he had done so.

Turning away from the reproachful eyes of his men, Blakely picked up his speech horn and prepared to hail the brig. Before he could speak, a volley of musketry crackled from the fighting tops of the brig, and some of the crew fell to the deck having been hit.

"Why do you still fire?" Blakely screamed at the brig's officer through the speech horn. "Damn your eyes! Can't you see we've struck our colors?"

The officer glared icily at Blakely over the small span of water between their ships. Raising a speech horn of his own he answered, "Strike if you wish, but it will not save you." He then lazily flicked two fingers in the direction of his gunners, and the brig's cannons fired again.

Chapter 1

December 14th, 1814, on the Mississippi River near New Orleans

Lieutenant Patrick Sullivan sat on a cotton bale, leaning against the rail of the small ship taking him downriver. Against his spine he felt the unfamiliar sensation of the vibration of a steam engine. To go along with the constant vibrating was the constant metallic clanking coming from the engine compartment, and the rhythmic splashing of the paddle wheel propelling the small craft forward. For a man who had spent the better part of his life at sea, this new method for traveling on water was as if the world had been turned upside down.

Patrick craned his head over his shoulder and looked over the rail at the riverbank, marveling at how quickly the scenery was passing him by even when running with the current. He gazed at the weeping Spanish Moss and bald cypress trees lining the Mississippi for a few moments as they sped past him, before turning his attention back to the book he was reading. He scowled and angrily wiped off bits of coal dust from the pages of his copy of Herodotus's *The Histories*. Looking up at the tall smokestack protruding from the center of the ship, he scowled again seeing the stream of black smoke puffing from the top of it. He had been picking bits of coal dust out of his hair and clothes ever since they had boarded the ship at Natchez, and it was irritating him to no end.

Leaning back and crossing his leg over his other knee, he propped the book up and tried to tune out the vibrations and the noise. It did not help that he had already read *The Histories* before two summers earlier, but he had not had time before embarking to find another book. He managed to struggle through two pages before hearing the sound of footfalls on the deck approaching him.

"This truly is a remarkable ship, Sir," said Midshipman Phillip Spencer. The blonde haired twenty-year old flashed one of his customary smiles, showing off his perfect teeth, and sat down next to Patrick. "I was just below with the engineer. I can't say I understood much of what he was saying, but it was very illuminating to see how it all worked.

Patrick glanced at the younger man, then back to his book. "You should probably study up on the mechanics of it now. I wouldn't doubt before long that they'll find a way to make every ship a steamship."

"Do you think so, Sir?" he asked, still with boyish amazement at the technological wonder they were passengers aboard.

Patrick nodded. "You can be certain of it. With speed such as this, you can be sure the Navy will want to find a way to mount cannon on them. It'll change the future of warfare. Imagine being able to move on the ocean without any regard for the direction of the wind? Seamanship, tactics, everything would be different."

"But think of the amount of coal a ship would need to be ocean-going," Spencer countered. "A steamship would need to be massive in order to carry enough, or they would need to stop frequently at ports to replenish their stores."

Patrick shrugged. "Technology improves with time, Phillip," he said. Holding up his copy of Herodotus, he waved it and continued with, "I recall reading in another book that the Ancient Greeks had a steam powered device, but it was only used as a trinket. It may have taken us almost two thousand years, but we have finally harnessed it for industrial purposes. There's no telling what we might be able to accomplish now that we have."

Spencer winced as he caught a coal fragment in the eye, and he rubbed desperately to get it out. Looking back at Patrick with one eye bloodshot and red, he said, "I do hope some inventor finds a method that doesn't leave coal dust getting everywhere."

Patrick wiped more coal dust off the pages of his open book and replied, "On that I agree."

With his eye successfully flushed of the coal fragment, Spencer stretched his arms and leaned back against the rail, resting his head on his hands. "I so wish these steamships would allow for swifter mail delivery. I loathe not being able to contact anyone at home."

Patrick smirked and let out an ever so small chuckle. He knew what Spencer truly meant was that he had been unable to receive any love letters. The Midshipman had somehow been courting a pair of sisters simultaneously and had bemoaned leaving them behind in Washington City. He had talked of the pair constantly and seemed very much in love with both of them, agonizing over the inevitable moment he would be forced to choose between them. It had provided Patrick with a small amount of amusement on their long voyage from the capital.

The pair had left the District of Columbia shortly after the British had abandoned their effort to take Baltimore. They were under orders to reach New Orleans before the British fleet, and make contact with a defector who had played a role in convincing the enemy to break off their campaign in the Chesapeake Bay, and who would hopefully provide further information. Setting out heading up the Potomac, Patrick and Spencer raced across the country using the continent's rivers, traveling down the Ohio, and then the Mississippi, as attempting to sail past the British blockade and around Florida would have been nearly impossible.

"I'm sure you'll be able to send your ladies a note once we reach New Orleans," he told Spencer. "They'll be sure to write back at once. At least you've had some contact with those you care for."

Spencer's normally cheery expression turned a bit dour, and he bit his lip for a moment trying to find comforting words.

"I've no doubt you'll see her soon, Sir. She would not have told you to come to New Orleans if she did not intend to meet you."

Patrick let a small smile tug at the corner of his mouth, and he gave a slight nod of appreciation. Spencer was one of the few people who knew that the spy they were to contact was in fact Patrick's wife, Anna. He had not seen her since the Battle of Baltimore, where she had delivered falsified intelligence to the British fleet, which evidently convinced them any further attack would be futile. The British warships had weighed anchor and left the Chesapeake Bay almost immediately following their bombardment of Fort McHenry, giving Anna no time or pretext to return ashore. Before she had left though, she had instructed him to meet her in New Orleans, as that was the next destination for the British.

Patrick had naturally been in a state of anxiety ever since. There was always a certain undercurrent of doubt in him when it came to his feelings for Anna. As she was a spy, he was constantly in a state of suspicion that her feelings for him were not genuine, and that he was being played by a pretty face. He tried to suppress those fears as she had never done anything yet to betray him and had given the

Americans valuable information on the enemy's plans and dispositions, aiding in the defense of Baltimore.

Patrick also worried constantly about her safety. The British naturally had no knowledge that she had become a double agent, and if they were ever to discover this, she would be executed. There were other dangers he could not foresee, and he would only be calm once she was finally in his arms again. Even then, he worried that their romance may have been only something of fleeting passion. They had eloped in haste before she left, and he wondered if their time apart might reveal if they truly loved each other.

"I'll be confident once I can finally make contact with her," Patrick said to Spencer. "Hopefully she'll find me."

Patrick returned to concentrating on his book as Spencer leaned back against the rail. This lasted barely a few more moments before Spencer spoke up again.

"Do you know anything about the naval officers at New Orleans, Sir?"

Patrick tried not to growl at the Midshipman. Spencer was an excessively talkative person, and while it sometimes helped to alleviate the boredom, he could at times be annoying.

"I am not well acquainted with Commodore Patterson, though I recall both he and Master Commandant Henley as being old Tripoli hands. At the time he was a Midshipman and not much older than you. There's also a Lieutenant Thomas ap Catesby Jones commanding a flotilla on Lake Borgne."

"Ap, Sir?" questioned Spencer.

"Yes, it's a Welsh inflection I believe. It would seem Lieutenant Jones is a bit of a traditionalist."

Spencer's face brightened as a thought came to him. "I hope the Lieutenant having the same name as Mister Jones is a good omen. Perhaps you'll get on well with him."

Spencer had been referring to Patrick's best friend, Tom Jones, who had been killed while serving with the militia defending the District of Columbia that August. Tom and Patrick had known each other since coming to the United States following the Irish rebellion of 1798. The two had worked together as merchant sailors during their teenage years, then were pressed into the Royal Navy for a brief spell, after which they had escaped and signed on with the US Navy, then fighting the Barbary Pirates in North Africa.

"It's a common enough name," answered Patrick bitterly. He was still coming to terms with the loss of his friend, and it was painful being reminded of him. "It will be important to gain a good rapport with the other officers though. We've seen how dangerous having senior officers at loggerheads can be."

The American war effort had been beset by difficulties between commanders through the length of the conflict. Patrick had personally seen such a situation nearly devolve into disaster at the Battle of Lake Erie, where his immediate superior had refused to support Commodore Perry as his ship battled the entire British squadron single-handedly, out of a hunger for personal glory. Rivalries at the highest echelons of the Army had seen successful leaders such as General William Henry Harrison pushed aside, while incompetents retained important commands. Some of this had been caused by the pernicious machinations of General James Wilkinson, who had been manipulating the Secretary of War at the behest of Spain. Patrick and Anna had uncovered his treason and made it known to Secretary of State James Monroe, who in turn presented their evidence to President Madison. Sadly, the incriminating documents had been lost when the British burned the Executive Mansion. Upon his appointment as replacement Secretary of War, Monroe was fortunately able to begin righting matters with the Army now that it was free of Wilkinson's influence.

Patrick felt the deck shift as the steamship began to make a turn to port. He looked up and saw their craft was rounding a bend in the river. As the cypress trees on the left bank receded, he then caught sight of their destination ahead. He gave Spencer a quick two thumps on the arm to alert him, and the Midshipman poked his head up to take a look.

"Oh, that is a lovely thing to see," said Spencer, relieved to at last be at the famed city. "Have you ever been to New Orleans, Sir?" he asked.

Patrick chuckled. "Once, a long time ago. It was still under Spanish control then, so no later than 1802 certainly. I must've been sixteen or so at the time." He studied the outline of the buildings clustered along the waterfront and made note of the distinctive church spires which he clearly remembered. Other memories now came back to him, and he chuckled again. "Tom got into quite a bit of trouble that time." He glanced sideways and noticed Spencer's puzzled expression. "Mister Jones was quite a trouble-maker in those days. And might have even been able to put you to shame when it came to carrying on with the ladies."

Spencer's eyebrows went up at the comment, as he had only known Tom Jones as a hard-working family man, albeit a bit rough around the edges. "What happened, Sir?" the Midshipman asked.

Patrick smirked. "Well, I wouldn't want word of his escapades getting back to Mrs. Jones, so I'll just say it involved swindling the owner of a gambling den, and the daughter of a judge."

The steamship chugged along, only slowing when it closed in on the riverside docks. With an ease of handling impossible with a sailing ship, their craft sidled up right alongside the dock. A deck hand threw a line over the side, and a longshoreman caught it, tying it off. The captain of the ship then blew the whistle to bleed off some steam.

Patrick covered his ears until the unfamiliar shriek died away. He then picked up his seabag which had lain at his feet and tucked his book away in it. Spencer also shouldered his sea bag, and the pair waited for the gangplank to be lowered. Once the longshoreman had secured the gangplank in place, Patrick and Spencer bounded across, finding themselves at the edge of a large square with a cathedral on the other side.

"Might I ask where to find Commodore Patterson's headquarters?" Patrick asked, turning back to the longshoreman. The man, who was very unkempt with greasy clothes and heavy stubble, pointed down the dock at a sailing vessel. He then uttered something in a nigh undecipherable accent presumably descended from French, which Patrick thought translated to, "You're looking for that Navy ship over there."

Patrick nodded, thanked the man, and waved for Spencer to follow him. The two walked at a brisk pace, and as he approached, Patrick spotted the name *Louisiana* adorning the nameplate of the ship they had been directed to. He then strode up the ship's gangplank.

A Marine guard was waiting at the gangway. He touched his musket across his chest in a salute, seeing that Patrick was a superior officer. Patrick set his sea bag down, returned the guard's salute, then gave the customary salute to the ship's ensign flying off the quarterdeck. He saw a Midshipman, who in turn saw him, and Patrick presumed the young man was the officer of the watch.

Patrick saluted a third time and asked, "Lieutenant Sullivan, requesting permission to come aboard."

"Granted, Sir," replied the Midshipman, seemingly surprised by the presence of a new officer. "Your business, Sir?"

"Reporting to Commodore Patterson. I just arrived in New Orleans."

The Midshipman nodded. "Aye, Sir. He's below in his cabin. I'll have one of the men escort you."

Patrick left his bag with Spencer, who also requested permission to come aboard, while one of the hands on deck led him below to Patterson's cabin below deck. When they reached the cabin door, the hand gestured to it, then gave the enlisted man's knuckled salute, and returned to his duties on deck.

Patrick knocked on the cabin door. There came the sharp reply of, "Come in!" and he pushed open the door. He then very nearly hit his head on a low deck beam.

"Yes, that one nearly gets me too," said Commodore Daniel Patterson from behind his cabin desk. "It's far too close to the door, terrible placement. One of my Lieutenants has bumped his head three times on that blasted thing."

Seeing that his new commander was in good humor put Patrick at ease. He tucked his cocked hat under his arm and saluted. "Lieutenant Sullivan reporting, Sir. I've only just arrived a few minutes ago."

"Sullivan?" repeated Patterson, wrinkling his brow. The Commodore was a young man, not much older than Patrick, with close cropped hair despite his receding hairline, and stylish side whiskers. He was full in the face, and his nose was a bit red on the end.

"I wasn't expecting any new officers," he went on, confused.

Patrick reached into his jacket and took out an envelope. "It's a special assignment, Sir. I'm here on the orders of Secretary Monroe."

"Monroe?" Patterson replied with a hint of dismay. "What business does the Army have ordering around naval officers?"

"I've been ordered to come here under his authority as Secretary of State, not Secretary of War, Sir. It's a matter of secrecy."

Patterson swiped the envelope from Patrick's hand. "I've no qualms about cooperating with the Army but they've no right infringing on the Navy." The Commodore then opened the envelope and began to read the letter within. His expression turned slightly bemused as his eyes scanned back and forth across the page.

"A spy, eh?" summarized Patterson. "We'll have to inform General Jackson. When are you to make contact?"

"She will contact me," Patrick replied.

"She?" repeated Patterson. "Well, haven't you pulled the lucky assignment? I hope you can trust the agent. Female spies are the most dangerous."

"I've worked with her before, Sir," responded Patrick. Patterson's eyebrows raised slightly as the senior officer detected a bit of nervousness in Patrick's voice. "I can't divulge anything more than that," he quickly added. *No sense in telling the whole world she's my bride*, he thought. *It'll just make them distrustful of both of us.*

"I see," said Patterson, replacing the letter in the envelope and handing it back to Patrick. "I best get you caught up on the situation."

Patterson gestured to a nearby chair against the side of the cabin, beckoning Patrick to take a seat. As Patrick moved the chair nearer to Patterson's desk, the Commodore opened up a cabinet along the wall and withdrew a rolled-up piece of parchment. Patterson unrolled the parchment across the desk, anchoring the corner of the parchment with his ink well.

"We've not much in the way of a squadron, here on the New Orleans station," Patterson began, tapping his finger on the center of the map where the grid marking New Orleans was drawn. "I have two ships. I have raised my flag here aboard the *Louisiana*, and Lieutenant Henley commands the *Carolina*. Lieutenant Jones commands a flotilla of gunboats out on Lake Borgne." Patterson swept his finger to the northeast, circling the body of water which looked more a bay rather than a lake.

"It's a damn pitiful force to defend the most important trading port on the continent. How long have you been in the Navy, Mister Sullivan?" asked Patterson. "Have you experience?"

"I served ten years before the mast, Sir," replied Patrick. "Signed on with Captain Decatur in 1803. I recall Mister Henley from Tripoli. I was promoted to Lieutenant when they disbanded the rank of Master's Mate and spent last year with the Lakes Squadron. I was then in the capital when the British attacked a few months ago. I've seen more than my fair share of battle, Sir."

"Splendid," said Patterson. "It'll be invaluable when the British arrive. And they *will* be coming, the only question is when. We'll need experienced officers, and we've seen little action down here. Would I be able to tempt you with command of the gunboat flotilla once your spy business is concluded?"

"Of course, Sir. I'm at your disposal."

"Good," said Patterson with a nod as he leaned back in his chair. "This is a bit of good fortune as I was hoping another officer would come on the station with enough seniority for command. You see, there's been a bit of friction with Jones of late. He doesn't get on well with the men and he's facing an inquiry soon over a quarrel with a subordinate. He caned a Midshipman, and the young man in return accused him of buggery."

"Is it true?" asked Patrick.

Patterson shifted in his seat. "Possibly," the Commodore grunted uncomfortably. "Regardless of the accusation, I can't have these sorts of squabbles hanging over the squadron, not when the British are breathing down our necks." Patterson then leaned forward again pointing to locations on the map.

"Our problem at the moment is that we still haven't the faintest idea where the British will land. We know they're not far off. We received a report they were recently in the vicinity of Mobile in Spanish Florida." The Commodore traced his finger along the route of the Mississippi to a point well below New Orleans. "It would be unlikely that they come up the river. It's a long slow journey for a warship, and Fort St. Phillip alone should be strong enough to see them off."

Patterson now stood up and stooped over the map. "Most of the other military leaders in the city believe the south shore of Lake Ponchartrain is the likeliest landing point as it is nearest to the city. Lake Borgne is a possibility as there are some inlets on the shore, but they'd have to cross through the swamp to get to the dry land near the river. The only other avenue is from the south, and it's the flank that most worries me. This spy you're meeting, does her mission have anything to do with those wretched Baratarians?"

Patrick was perplexed. "I'm not sure as of now, Sir. I know King George rules Hanover, but I can't imagine what Germans would be doing in Louisiana."

Patterson shook his head in frustration. "No, not Bavarians. Baratarians. This area down here, south of the city, is Barataria Island. It's a pirate lair. They're led a pair of brothers, the Lafittes. The two practically run this city. Gambling, brothels, black market saloons, every criminal enterprise you can think of, they own. Not two months ago I went in and cleared them out with my ships. Now the whole city is clamoring for Governor Claiborne to issue pardons so they can join the Army to fight the British!"

"What is General Jackson's opinion on the matter?"

Patterson shrugged. "He's keeping his cards close to his chest, but I suspect he agrees. He's the kind of man that is willing to do what needs to be done. If any sort of advantage is to be gained, he'll take it."

Patterson then stood up and motioned for Patrick to follow him. As he rose, Patrick asked, "Sir, what more can you tell me of General Jackson?"

Patterson stopped short as he was reaching for the handle of the door to his cabin. The Commodore grimaced and said, "He's difficult." He then opened the door and continued talking as they made their way back on deck.

"He's a forceful personality, but that is also his least endearing trait. He's gracious and well-mannered of course but does not share power easily. He's made an enemy of every politician in Louisiana, and I do reckon that's the way he wants it. He is particularly at odds with Governor Claiborne, though rightfully in that case as Claiborne believes he should be in command of the army. He does have a certain common touch. High society may despise him, but his men love him."

They soon reached the deck. Spencer immediately saluted, and Patrick briefly introduced the Commodore to the Midshipman. Across the large square, the bells of the cathedral rang out eleven times.

"What's the disposition of General Jackson's army, Sir?" Patrick asked Patterson, continuing their conversation from before.

"He has a few regulars, but most of his force is Tennessee militia. It's quite a rabble really, backwoodsmen, Choctaws. They've done plenty of battle against the Creek tribes but have never faced the British. More militia are expected to come downriver from Kentucky, but no one is confident it will be enough. Claiborne has been raising militia here in Louisiana as well." Patterson paused to chuckle. "You should see some of them, Creoles dressed in gaudy French uniforms. Spaniards too. They're even talking about freeing negro slaves and letting them fight."

The Commodore had barely finished his sentence when a hand called out from above. "Sir! I hear cannon fire off to the north!"

Everyone on deck fell quiet as they strained to listen. Sure enough, they could hear the booming of cannon fire coming from the direction of Lake Borgne.

"Can you see anything?" Patterson called up to the man on the mainmast.

The seaman shook his head. "No, Sir, the mast isn't tall enough."

Patrick touched Patterson's shoulder and pointed across the square. "Might one of those bell towers be tall enough, Sir?"

Patterson nodded. "Good thinking, Lieutenant." The Commodore then grabbed a spyglass offered to him by the Midshipman of the watch, and he and Patrick jogged across the square to the cathedral.

Bursting through the front doors, Patrick saw a priest at the altar with his hair cut in the old fashion of a monk startle at their entrance. The priest said something to them in the same indecipherable local dialect the longshoreman had. His tone fortunately did not suggest he was overly angered by their interruption of his midday prayers. Patrick instinctively made the sign of the cross and bent one knee ever so slightly to approximate genuflecting.

"Your pardon, padre," said Patterson. "Might you show us the way to scale your bell tower?"

The priest came off the altar and walked toward them, still speaking in the dialect they could not understand. Patrick then decided to give French a try, repeating Patterson's request to guide them to the bell tower.

The priest came to a halt before them. He looked at Patrick and said in English that he barely understood, "Your French is horrible."

The priest then gestured off to the side and they followed him to a door that led to the second-floor balcony, so hurriedly they were unable to admire the ornate baroque interior for even a moment. From the balcony level, another door led to the stairway up to the top of the northern bell tower.

Reaching one of the windows, Patterson opened the shutters and extended his spyglass and looked northeast along the horizon. After a few moments he pointed and handed the spyglass to Patrick. "There! Just a bit east-northeast."

Patrick looked through the spyglass in the direction Patterson had indicated. After a few seconds he spotted the tops of masts, distant enough that the hulls of the ships could not be seen over the horizon. He also thought he saw smoke, though it was hard to be certain with overcast skies as a backdrop.

The two men took turns passing the spyglass back and forth to each other, though they were unable to make out how the battle was progressing. Before long the sound of the cannons died away, leaving only the wind whistling through the shutters on the bell tower.

"I have a feeling that the outcome was not in our favor," Patterson intoned quietly.

"I can't see if any of the ships have struck their colors," Patrick replied, trying to remain hopeful.

Patterson simply shook his head. "You wouldn't from this distance." He paused, looked once more off into the distance and sighed. "We'll at least we know from where they're coming. I regret, Lieutenant, that you won't be taking command of the gunboats after all."

Chapter 2

December 14th, 1814, New Orleans

Patrick shivered as he closed the door to his hotel room. He was surprised by how cold the weather had been, as he had always heard New Orleans remained much warmer in the winter. *Granted, walking back from the bath with nothing but a towel isn't helping matters much either*, he thought.

He had sorely wanted a bath once he and Spencer had settled in to their new accommodations. He had been picking coal dust out of his hair and off his clothes ever since he had gotten off the steamship and could stomach it no longer.

Casting aside the towel on the back of a chair, he tugged on his undergarments, cursing himself for not having the foresight to bring long underwear. Spencer, meanwhile, was absent, having told Patrick he wanted to do a bit of sightseeing. In truth Patrick suspected that the Midshipman had gone out to chase girls. Despite being a in a relationship with two women at the same time, Patrick did not think Spencer had the wherewithal to restrain his urges.

Patrick shook his head in disbelief as he thought of the strange triad and looked out the window of his room. It was dark by now, and the oil street lamps had been lit. The Commodore had been able to secure them a room in a hotel overlooking the square, or Place D'arms as it was called locally. The city had been oddly quiet, aside from men carrying out drills and marching. It did give the impression that populace was experiencing the calm before the storm. With everyone able to hear the battle on Lake Borgne, it confirmed that the British would indeed be here in a matter of days. Furthermore, no word had been received from Lieutenant Jones, which served to confirm Commodore Patterson's fears that the entire gunboat flotilla had been destroyed. The northern approaches to the city lay wide open.

There came a knock on the door. "One moment," he answered as he stumbled around putting on his trousers. He then draped the towel around his neck in order to at least partially cover his chest.

Probably some chamber maid coming to complain that I hadn't told them I was finished with the bath.

He opened the door and stood staring wordlessly for a brief second. The woman on the other side never gave him a chance to speak as in an instant she threw her arms around him and was forcing him backwards into the room. She gave him a forceful kiss that she held so long he almost struggled for breath. When at last their lips parted, he whispered a single word,

"Anna," he smiled.

His wife smiled back at him. She swiftly shut the door behind her and kissed him again, once more keeping their lips fused until they could not go any longer without air.

As she pulled her head away, he smiled at her again and ran his fingers through her crimson locks. The candles in the room reflected off her smoky hazel eyes, and he peered into them longingly.

She smiled back at him again. She then touched the ring he was wearing around his neck, *her* ring that he had held in safekeeping while she was with the British.

"I told you I'd find you," she said softly, slipping into her native Irish accent. It was something she only did when they were alone together.

"Mo ghra thu," she said in Gaelic. *I love you.*

"Mo ghra thu," he repeated back to her.

He kissed her again, and for the first time in months held her in his arms. His fears and anxieties left him, and the thoughts of coming battle did not enter his mind.

After Anna's arrival, they immediately disrobed and made love with frantic passion. Hardly a word was said between them, and none were needed.

"I missed you so," she finally spoke, as she lay her head on his shoulder after having exhausted themselves.

"You can't imagine how much I feared for you," he said, giving her a soft kiss on the top of her head.

She tilted her head up to look at him. "I know how to keep myself out of trouble," she answered with a smirk. "I was afraid they wouldn't let you come."

Patrick sighed. "Well, Monroe did suspect us being involved right from the off, but gave me orders anyway." He took her left hand, and held it up, toying with the ring that was now where it rightfully belonged.

"I noticed you had it tightened," she commented. "It's a proper fit now."

He brought her hand to his lips and kissed the ring. "I hope you never need to take it off again." He then rested her hand on his chest, and they slowly began to become drowsy. Just as they were about to peacefully drift off, the door to the room was flung open.

"Sir, I must have drunk a barrel's worth of water, my tongue feels as though it's on fire!" Spencer said as he entered the room.

Patrick and Anna both jolted upright, now fully awake, and Anna quickly covered her chest with the bedsheet. They had earlier blown out almost all the candles and Spencer had not noticed her as he stumbled around the far side of the room looking for a wick to light the rest.

"I don't know what spices the people down here put in their food, but it leaves a shocking burning sensation afterwards," the Midshipman went on, his back turned to them as he lit some of the other candles. He turned around, his mouth open to continue rambling on and his eyebrows shot up in surprise.

"Miss Anna! You're alive!" he said, smiling broadly. "I'm so glad you're safe. Lieutenant Sullivan was very worried about you." Spencer then pulled over a chair and sat down leaning forward, seemingly oblivious to what he had interrupted.

"It's very good to see you as well, Phillip," Anna told him through gritted teeth.

"Thank you," he replied, still smiling. "I'll have to write Martha and Sarah and tell them you arrived. Sarah was very upset that she didn't have the chance to apologize to you—"

"Spencer!" Patrick barked at him. He then nodded a bit toward Anna.

The Midshipman's eyebrows went up again as he finally took the hint. "I'm very sorry, Sir, I'd quite forgotten. Shall I come back at half past the hour?"

Patrick sighed and rolled his eyes. "Give us about ten minutes."

Spencer stood up, replaced the chair against the wall, and walked out of the room, closing the door behind him. Patrick and Anna waited a few moments as they heard him walk down the hall.

"The boy has his head in the clouds all the time," said Patrick shaking his head.

"Oh, I think he isn't nearly the fool he pretends," answered Anna. "It's likely he was hoping he'd catch a glimpse of my breasts."

They quickly got out of bed and dressed. Once they were decent, Patrick opened the door to the room and left it open, waiting for Spencer to return. He poked his head sheepishly around the doorframe exactly ten minutes on the dot after he had left.

"It's safe to come in now," Anna joked at him.

Spencer reentered the room and retook his seat opposite them as they continued sitting on the bed.

"You were saying something about sampling the local cuisine?" Anna pressed him with a smirk to put him back at ease.

"Oh, yes!" Spencer said, his eyebrows perking up again. "I went to look around the city while the Lieutenant settled in, and found myself two streets over in a cozy little establishment. The French call the eateries restaurants instead of taverns, so I felt a bit confused when searching. The sign said, 'Bourbon Street', and I assumed they would surely have some if they went so far as to name a street that. I did not know it meant the Bourbon Monarchy until the owner of the restaurant corrected me. He did not have any bourbon but saw that I was newly arrived in the city and offered me some food. It would be impolite to refuse, so he brought me a shrimp dish covered in spices! It tasted very good but left my mouth burning. I drank quite a lot of water before the sensation finally went away."

"Congratulations on surviving your first encounter with Creole food," Anna laughed.

Patrick put his hand on Anna's leg. "How were you able to find us so quickly?"

Anna rested her hand on his and looked at him. "I conducted a search when I first entered the city. When it was clear you had not arrived, I simply told a few of the longshoremen that I was expecting my sweetheart to be traveling from upriver and asked them to keep watch for a red-haired naval officer."

Patrick squeezed her hand. "You were able to converse with the longshoremen? I couldn't understand a thing he said."

Anna sighed. "Yes, the dialect here is much harder to stomach than the food. I found myself lodging a few streets over and asked the man to send a note there if he saw a man matching your description. I knew that some other officers were being billeted here, and I asked the clerk downstairs if you had signed for a room. Very easy, all in all. Spying isn't nearly as hard as everyone thinks. Most people readily give away too much information because they never belive that anyone would spy on them."

Patrick nodded, telling himself he would have to be more mindful of that advice in the future. "We'll need to report to Commodore Patterson first thing in the morning. I had to inform him why I was here when I arrived. He asked me if any of this had to do with the Baratarians?"

Anna shook her head. "No, that wasn't my assignment. A British officer made contact with that Lafitte fellow some time ago, but from what I understand Lafitte rebuffed him. I was ordered to discover if there were any prominent French and Spanish citizens in the city that might aid the British."

"Are there?" asked Patrick.

Anna shook her head again. "No one of note. We can talk of this in the morning tomorrow." She paused and then looked at Spencer.

The Midshipman was still leaning forward, intently listening. Seeing Anna staring at him, his eyes darted back and forth between her and Patrick for a few moments before he realized what she was doing.

"Ah, yes," Spencer said standing up. "You said you had lodgings elsewhere? I'm sure of course you would prefer to stay with the Lieutenant tonight. I'd be happy to exchange with you."

Anna smiled and leaned over to picked up a small handbag she had dropped at the foot of the bed. She opened it and took out a key. "A boarding house on Royal Street. On the river side three houses past St. Phillip Street."

Spencer took the key from her outstretched hand. He smiled nervously, touched the brim of his hat which he had never bothered to remove in a sort of salute, and backed out of the door.

Anna sighed and gave a slight chuckle. "It's almost as if he's your younger brother or cousin that you've been tasked with watching after."

Patrick laughed. "You know he's a good sort. At least he understands when to make an exit."

Anna looked at him and smiled. "Yes," she agreed, kissing him.

The next day, following a short meeting with Commodore Patterson, Patrick and Anna were ushered into a conference with General Jackson at his headquarters in a house on Royal Street. It was a small reception, consisting of only Jackson, Patterson, and Governor Claiborne, who was also dressed in uniform.

"These are the only people you can say with certainty are sympathetic to British?" asked Jackson from behind a desk, looking at a piece of paper Anna had given him.

"Yes, General," she replied. "I had been tasked by the British to seek out potential turncoats, particularly prominent citizens among the Spanish population, but few proved receptive. Most are frightened that the British will sack the city as they did Washington."

Jackson's eyes looked up from the paper to Anna. "Men are always motivated more by property than ideology." His eyes remained fixed on her as he held out the paper sideways to Claiborne. The Governor, who had been standing off to the side with his arms crossed, swiped the paper from Jackson's hand.

"Not a single name I recognize," he said after examining it briefly, and handed it back to Jackson. The General took it from him, again without looking at him.

It was startling to Patrick how tense the atmosphere was in the room. Even the most casual observer could make out the obvious enmity between Jackson and Claiborne. Patterson had told him that two were at odds of matters of command, but it was concerning to see it so openly. State Governors had great powers over their militia, and no doubt Claiborne resented Jackson sweeping into town and challenging what he saw as his rightful position to command the defenders.

Jackson himself was a surprise as well. From his reputation, Patrick expected a boisterous and burly frontiersman, but the middle-aged General was quite the opposite. His manner of speech was calm and even, and he carried himself with an air of sophistication. In appearance, he was extremely thin and gaunt in the face with hollow cheeks, and short reddish hair that was beginning to turn white on the edges. Patterson had mentioned to Patrick that Jackson was still feeling the effects of dysentery, which might have explained some of his apparent weight loss, but Patrick still doubted he would have been thin enough to fit in the General's uniform. After seeing him in person for the first time, observing his hardened, creased, and weathered face, Patrick understood why Jackson's men referred to him as 'Old Hickory.'

"Nevertheless," began Jackson, "We must take care that even a person of the least significance does not fatally compromise our defenses. It is clear that I must declare martial law. Only such powers will allow me to do what is necessary for the security of the city."

Claiborne visibly bristled at Jackson usurping his authority. "The legislature will have a fit if you do that."

"Let them," answered Jackson tersely. "You said yourself that the whole of them are rotten. We likely have more to fear of being stabbed in the back by them than any of the persons presented on this parchment."

Claiborne tilted his head a bit and set his mouth askew as if to rebut the statement, then after considering Jackson's words for a moment, nodded slightly in agreement.

"I will draw up the formal order immediately," stated Jackson, finding a clean sheet of paper on which to write. "We will establish a nine o'clock curfew, and any person found on the street without a pass after that hour is to be arrested on the assumption that they are an enemy spy. No one is to enter or leave the city without a written pass by a senior military officer." Jackson dipped his pen into the inkwell on his desk and wrote out the order as he continued to speak.

"Commodore?" Patterson straightened up at the mention of his name. "The requirement for any persons travelling will of course apply to river traffic as well. Given both the strategic and tactical importance of the river we must be most vigilant against anyone seeking to use it to aid the enemy. All ships coming or going must receive a pass signed personally by only you or I."

Patterson nodded. "Understood, General."

Jackson turned in his chair to look at Claiborne for the first time during the entire meeting. "Governor, you will of course see to it that Fort St. Phillip is reinforced?"

Claiborne nodded. "Of course," he replied somewhat icily.

Jackson looked back to Anna. "Miss, before we conclude I must ask if there is any additional information that you may reveal to us that might be of use?"

"I was not made privy to the entirety of the British plans, but I would estimate that they will land an army of roughly three-thousand men. They will be commanded by General Edward Pakenham. He is the brother-in-law of the Duke of Wellington, and served under his command in Portugal and Spain during the Peninsula War against the French."

Jackson's eyebrows raised slightly at this statement, but Anna immediately continued with, "It would be unwise to assume he has attained his position through nepotism. He is a capable commander of whose performance I have observed firsthand in the Peninsula."

Anna took a breath and searched her memory for additional information. "Whether the British plan to force a passage up the river or march overland I cannot say. Many of the men are veterans of the Peninsula campaigns against Bonaparte. I know for certain the Eighty-Fifth regiment, which participated in burning Washington, will be a part of the expedition. A battalion of the Ninety-Fifth regiment has been included. They are rifle-equipped marksmen and have an elite reputation."

Jackson grinned at the last remark. "I've no doubt my Tennesseans will be able to match them shot for shot."

Anna gave a slight smile in return, though a bit nervously. *We all need a bit of the General's confidence*, Patrick thought, seeing her expression. *But I know Anna has likely seen those riflemen in action, and knows better than to underestimate them.*

"There are also at least two West Indies regiments that were added as reinforcements when the British fleet paused at Nassau to replenish their victuals."

Claiborne snorted. "West Indies regiments? Unless someone thought to bring along overcoats for the poor devils, they won't be much use in this dreadfully cold weather we've been suffering." He then looked to Jackson and sardonically added, "Which would of course be to our advantage."

Jackson allowed himself to let out of a small laugh. His face turned pale an instant afterward, and he closed his eyes, taking in a breath. "Eternal God in heaven," the General muttered under his breath. He quickly got to his feet and hurriedly said, "Thank you very much for your assistance, Miss O'Malley, I am grateful for your services to the nation. Governor, would you please see them out?" Jackson then left the room, walking swiftly, visibly trying to maintain his dignity by not breaking into a run.

"It would appear that the General still has a touch of illness," said Claiborne once Jackson was out of earshot. From his tone Patrick surmised that the Governor was hoping the General's bout of dysentery would be debilitating enough to warrant Claiborne taking command.

"I believe we have discussed all of the relevant matters, Commodore," Claiborne said to Patterson. "If you have no more questions for the lady, I believe we can conclude the meeting."

Patterson shook his head. "I have not."

Claiborne nodded. "Very well. We are adjourned. Miss, thank you for presenting us with your information." The Governor then exchanged pleasantries with Patterson and Patrick and left the room.

"Well, you survived your first encounter with Jackson," Patterson said to Patrick.

Patrick laughed. "Only by virtue of not being important enough to notice. He didn't say a word to me."

"You're probably better off that way," said Patterson. "There's a reception tonight at the house of Edward Livingston. He's a prominent lawyer, has the ear of both Jackson and Claiborne. Senior naval officers have been invited if you've an interest."

Patrick looked over his shoulder to Anna, who simply gave him a broad smile. "We'll be there, Sir," he answered.

Patterson chuckled. "You did indeed pick the lucky assignment, Lieutenant. Very well, I'll see you both there tonight."

Patrick titled his head as he watched Anna styling her hair in the mirror of their hotel room. "That's a new dress," he commented as she set a pin.

"I did have to purchase a complete set of new clothing after all. I trust Sam is looking after my trunk?"

"She is," he answered with a nod. "She left it in my room."

Anna paused and looked over her shoulder. "How is she?"

Patrick sighed. He felt immense guilt over leaving Tom's widowed wife in the state he did, as Sam was several months pregnant when Tom had been killed, but duty necessitated that. Sam, kind as ever, held no hard feelings over it.

"As well as can be, I suppose," he answered, sullen. "Spencer's girls are helping mind the children and the tavern."

"That's kind of them," she said, looking back to the mirror. "Do you know if she's had the child yet?"

Patrick shook his head. "I've sent a handful of letters upriver as we made our way here, but haven't received any from her. The child should come next month."

"I do hope there's no complications. I recall you saying they lost their last one." Anna stopped tending to her hair and set down her comb. She then affixed a pair of earrings, a pair of single pearls, and turned around to look at him.

"Do you like it?" she asked, doing a half-spin while running her hands along the satin fabric to smooth out the folds.

Patrick smiled. "Yes. Though you could make sailors' rags look fashionable. That shade of blue is very catching, I think it goes well with my uniform."

Anna nodded. "Yes, it is nice, though I prefer dark green. I've always heard green goes well with red." She patted the back of her done-up ginger tresses proudly.

Patrick stood up and wrapped his arms around her as they faced the mirror. "I can't deny that," he said as they looked at their reflections. "Although I do believe you're most beautiful when not wearing anything at all," he went on with a laugh, playfully running his hands along her body.

She gave him a sharp but equally playful jab in the ribs with her elbow in return, while trying to suppress a grin. "Come, we best be going."

Leaving the hotel, they proceeded through the streets of New Orleans, Anna on Patrick's arm like a well-mannered couple, though he had draped his overcoat on her shoulders to ward off the chill. There were still some citizens out and about, trying to take care of as much business as possible before the curfew was to take effect the following night. The city was the most cosmopolitan

Patrick had experienced, with English, Spanish, and French mingling into one dialect as they passed people conversing on the street.

Anna scowled as they walked by a young man speaking in French up to a woman above him leaning on the railing of a balcony. Patrick knew that Anna had seen and done enough in her life to not be bothered by a man soliciting a prostitute.

"Is something troubling you?"

Anna glanced at him, a flash of anger in her eyes, but shook her head. "I'd been away from Europe so long I'd forgotten how much I hate the French."

Anna's antipathy for anything French was something she had often spoken of in passing to Patrick, yet never explained. She would only say that her motivation to become a spy in the service of Britain was because of some personal grievance they had caused her, but she had never elaborated.

"Do remember that these frogs are on our side," he said in jest, patting the hand with which she held onto his arm.

Anna scowled again and quietly muttered, "I've heard that promise before."

They arrived shortly after at the Livingston house, a stately but not overly ostentatious building. Patrick gave his name to the enslaved manservant at the door, mentioning he had been extended an invitation by Patterson. It was not the first time he had dealt with an enslaved person, but had to remind himself it would be inevitable that a prominent family would have them in the south.

"Of course, Sir," answered the man, taking Patrick's overcoat and handing it off to another servant. "And the lady? How shall I announce you?"

Beside him Anna put a hand to her mouth to cover a slight chuckle.

"I don't think announcing us is necessary," Patrick told him. "We're hardly important enough."

"Very well, Sir," said the man emotionlessly, stepping aside and ushering them through the door.

Walking through the open door, the couple found themselves in a crowded foyer. Unlike on the streets outside, the language inside was exclusively English, albeit with some speaking in heavy accents. Most of the men were in uniform, but Patrick could tell by their bearing and posture they were civilians who, like Governor Claiborne, and taken positions with the militia. As they surveyed the guests Patrick also noticed most of the guests were older, likely making he and Anna the youngest attendees.

"Ah, Mister Sullivan!" called out Commodore Patterson from across the room. The senior officer raised his hand to further get Patrick's attention and then wormed his way through the crowd towards them.

"Very good of you both to come," he said, shaking Patrick's hand and nodding to Anna.

"Couldn't pass up an opportunity for a free supper," Patrick joked.

Patterson laughed. "Well, you should be in for a fine night. I hear they have a roast cooking. Now don't be afraid to mingle tonight. There's plenty of politicians here and if you come across favorably you may gain some benefactors. That never hurts a man's career."

Patrick nodded. "I understand, Sir."

Patterson smiled, then nodded upwards as something behind Patrick caught his eye. "Ah, here's Jackson now."

Patrick turned as there was a noise from the crowd, a small burst of cheering and clapping as the General entered the room. Jackson waved politely to them in response. He was looking much better, evidently having properly rested through the afternoon. One of the ladies walked up to him and curtsied, then extended her hand.

"General Jackson, thank you so kindly for agreeing to join us this evening," she said to him.

"Why of course, madam," Jackson responded, taking her hand and bowing. "I could hardly refuse your husband's invitation. My only regret is that my dearest Rachel remains in Tennessee. She would surely enjoy your hospitality. In her absence, may I have the honor of escorting the lady of the house to supper?"

Mrs. Livingston turned to a man next to her, whom Patrick assumed to be Mister Livingston and said, "This is your backwoodsman? He is a prince!"

Livingston threw back his head with a laugh. "General, it is a privilege to entertain you this evening," he addressed Jackson. He extended his arm in the direction of the dining room. "If you would follow me."

Jackson extended his arm, which Mrs. Livingston took, and they followed Mister Livingston down the hall to the dining room. The chattering crowd surged along in their wake, taking Patrick and Anna with them.

Upon being ushered into the dining room by the Livingston's servants, Jackson took up the place of honor at the head of the table, each of his hosts on either side. The remainder of the guests went about finding their own places.

Finding two seats near the far end of the table, Patrick pulled out one of the chairs for Anna, then took his own seat. Once he sat down, he felt a small measure of panic as he looked at the array of silverware laid out before him.

Patrick had almost never had occasion to mix with high society, and while he did his best to learn, his table manners were more suited to the bawdy confines of the wardroom. Early in the summer he had been invited to a ball for officers at the Executive Mansion, but fortunately there had been no dinner. His eyes began to nervously pan around the room at the other guests, wondering how he could disguise his ignorance.

"What's wrong?" Anna asked him, leaning close.

"I don't know etiquette," he replied under his breath.

She bit on her lip to hide a smile at his uneasiness. She placed her hand over his hand, and whispered into his ear, "Watch and do as I do."

Patrick let out a sigh of relief. Within a few moments more of the Livingston's servants appeared and began to serve the food.

The dinner proceeded slowly, with Patrick amazed at how organized the serving of each course was. He mostly ignored the conversation of the evening, as he was concentrating on mimicking Anna's movements, always careful to use the same utensil she was using and to hold it in the proper way. He noticed her often trying to suppress a smile, amused at his embarrassment, though she continued to guide his way. He was immensely relieved none of the others at the table took notice of him, as they were all captivated by the guest of honor.

Shortly after the conclusion of the final course, Mrs. Livingston announced that the ladies would be retiring to the drawing room. The men all stood, helping their wives or companions from their chairs. Anna let her hand brush over his as she walked by, giving him a subtle wink, as a way to reassure him. Once the ladies had left, Mister Livingston asked one of his servants to bring him a box of cigars and he gave one to each man in the room. Patrick did not smoke but was obliged to accept it.

The conversation between the gentlemen quickly turned to the business at hand, many of the men inquiring from Jackson what ramifications the impending declaration of martial law would have. There was some discussion of military matters, but all of them had sense enough not to divulge anything in detail.

Being the most junior officer in the room, Patrick had little to contribute. He merely observed the others speaking, nodding in agreement when it seemed appropriate, and occasionally drawing on his cigar to make it appear he was actually smoking. On either side of him had moved two politicians, members of the state legislature whose names he had not learned. When Governor Claiborne mentioned the possibility of freeing and recruiting slaves into the militia one of them spoke up.

"Governor, are we sure that is a wise course of action?" the man said. "After all, we had a large slave revolt here not three years ago."

Governor Claiborne, looked down the table at the man who had spoken with a bit of a frown. "I believe that the exigencies of the moment necessitate such action. We will need every man available."

"But to arm them, Sir?" replied the legislator. "I cannot imagine many of the plantation owners will support that, even with the British on their doorstep. Every last one in the parish is more than willing to lend labor to dig entrenchments, but arming freed slaves will assuredly cause an outcry."

Claiborne rolled his eyes at the comment. "One crisis at a time, if you please," he said eminently annoyed.

"Oh, come now," started the man on Patrick's other shoulder. "You really believe that there would be a slave uprising when we have a large army ensconced in the city with the sole purpose of defending it?"

"For now," countered the legislator. "And when the war is ended and the army leaves? We'll have a cadre of freed negroes that know how to use muskets ready to rise up and unleash their brethren. What then?"

Patrick leaned back in his chair to allow the two men to bicker, but made the mistake of muttering, "If they were free there wouldn't be any risk of revolt."

The legislator turned to look at him with an astonished expression. "I beg your pardon, Lieutenant? I did not quite hear that."

Patrick swallowed hard and drew on his cigar to give him a moment to think. "Merely a jest, Sir, that freeing the enslaved population would preempt an uprising."

"Do you take yourself to be an abolitionist, Lieutenant?" the man interrogated him.

Patrick hesitated another moment, feeling the eyes of everyone else in the room on him. "I fought the Barbary pirates to end slavery on foreign shores, I don't see how any civilized country can tolerate the practice."

"And what would you propose we do with them once we free them? To say nothing of the economic destruction that would entail."

Patrick shrugged. "I can't claim to know the answer to that. I'll let the politicians sort out such things."

There were guffaws around the room at this last statement. The other man on Patrick's left looked at him and said, "Spoken very much like a politician, Lieutenant." He then added in jest, "Have you considered seeking office?"

There was another round of laughter. Jackson at last stood up and said, "Gentlemen, I do believe that is enough politics for the evening. Let us now rejoin the ladies."

The men all rose from the table and filed out of the dining room. Stopping him on their way out, Patterson said, "That was quite an escape."

Patrick shrugged. "I got careless."

"You handled it well," answered Patterson. "Now you know better. These southerners are sensitive about their 'peculiar institution'."

Patrick looked down the hall and saw Anna emerging from the drawing room. Gliding over she rolled her eyes and wrapped her arm around his. "I do believe I've had enough of the inane talk in there," she said, nodding backwards over her shoulder. "I'd leave now if it wasn't impolite." She then deftly seized a glass of champaign off the tray of a passing servant and took a sip.

"Oh, you wouldn't want to leave just yet," said Patterson to Patrick with a grin. "General Humbert was promising earlier that he would regale everyone with a tale or two of his adventures in the service of France during the late wars."

Anna's head jerked up slightly. Her eyes went cold, and her face immediately hardened. "General Jean Humbert?" she asked.

Patterson's eyebrows went up at her question. "Yes. He immigrated here a few years ago. Do you know him?"

Anna's eyes widened slightly. "Yes," she hissed, barely moving her mouth. Patrick was startled by her expression as he could tell she was bottling up an intense rage he had never seen in her before. She released her grip on his arm and began to stalk back down the hallway, her steps forceful and determined.

"Anna?" he called after her, but she ignored him. He hurriedly followed her back to the drawing room.

The guests had begun to filter out around the house, so only half a dozen ladies were still within the room and a pair of men. Patrick recognized one as the politician who had questioned him regarding slavery, the other was a man in uniform speaking in French to one of the women. During dinner Patrick had taken no notice of the man, thinking him just another local who had donned an opulent militia uniform. He now saw Anna walking up behind the man.

"Pardon, Sir," Anna asked, still biting her tongue to conceal her emotions. "I was told your name was General Humbert?"

Humbert turned around from his conversation, a smile coming to his face seeing that Anna was young and attractive. "I am Humbert."

"General Jean Humbert, who commanded the French army at Castlebar?"

Humbert blinked, confused, but maintained his smile. "Why, yes. Do I know you?"

Anna feigned a smile back at him. "No, General. I do know you however. My name is Anna O'Malley, I come from Castlebar."

Humbert's face brightened. "How wonderful, mademoiselle! I was going to tell the guests the story of my victory over the British there. Surely you were there to witness it?"

"Yes. I was nine at the time."

"Indeed? My how time has passed. Do they still call it the Castlebar races?"

Anna nodded. "They did when last I lived there.

"Ah! What a glorious day it was," Humbert responded, clearly not detecting Anna's simmering anger. "I have always regretted that more could not come from the victory, but it was a glorious moment to behold nonetheless. Your people were very hospitable in the aftermath. I recall the victory celebration was quite merry."

This last remark finally broke Anna's composure. Her feigned smile turned to a snarl and she threw the champaign from her glass into Humbert's face, following it with a slap from her other hand. The ladies nearby all gasped at once, and Patrick could only blurt out a shocked, "Anna!" Humbert merely stood looking at her, stunned with his mouth agape.

"Merry!" Anna stammered, trying not to shriek. "It may have been for your men, but it wasn't for my sisters!"

Humbert merely blinked at her, still too stunned to speak, champaign dripping off his face.

Anna's expression now became tortured, her mouth twisting. "You don't even know, do you?" she said to him, though not expecting an answer. She closed her eyes and turned away from him, and pushed past Patrick back into the hall. Patrick followed her, only to see her slumped against the wall and sobbing.

He reached out to touch her and she swatted away his hand. She then seemed to realize who it was and instead massaged the fingers she had struck, softly saying, "I'm sorry, I did not mean that." Wiping the streaks off her face she then said, "I want to leave."

Patrick only nodded and put his arm around her, leading her to the door. Retrieving his hat and overcoat, he asked the servant there to extend his apologies to Mrs. Livingston for the commotion. He threw his overcoat once more over Anna's shoulders, and they walked back to their hotel room in silence.

Once they had entered the room, she angrily discarded his overcoat against a chair. "Get me out of this thing," she demanded, trying to reach the laces of her dress. Patrick untied them for her and she let the dress fall to the ground. She kicked it away from her, kicked off her shoes as well, and stood there in her petticoats looking back and forth, seemingly unable to decide what she wanted to do next. Eventually she sat down on the bed, holding her head in her hands for a few moments.

"I suppose I shall have to tell you now," she said to him in a low voice.

He put a hand on her shoulder and rubbed it gently. "You don't have to if you don't want to."

Anna shook her head. "No, you're my husband, you have a right to know these things." She then took his hand and pulled him down on the bed beside her. She looked up at him, her eyes red and still moist with tears.

"We've never talked at length about our families," she said.

Patrick held her hand with both of his and stroked it. "There wasn't much for me to speak of. My mother died in childbirth. It was me and my father then until he was killed by the British in 'Ninety-Eight."

She looked down at his hands. "We both had tragedy come from that damned rising. But my family suffered at the hands of the French, not the British." Anna then lay down on the bed and motioned for him to join her. Patrick took off his uniform jacket and boots and crawled across the bed to lay day next to her, and wrapped his arms around her.

"I had two sisters and a brother," she began, staring straight up at the pitch-dark ceiling, looking at the light the streetlamps gave off dancing through the windowpanes. "Jane and Maggie. And Michael, my brother." A smile tweaked her lips and she glanced at him. "If you think I'm beautiful you should have seen Jane. She was seventeen, hair brighter red than mine and blue eyes." Her words caught in her throat, and she began to tear up again. "When the French arrived to aid the rebellion, we were all ecstatic. 'Surely, we can defeat the English now,' we all thought. And when the French and the rebels fought off the British at Castlebar it was a dream come true."

She swallowed before going on, her mouth becoming dry. "After the battle some of the French came back into town, and some of the townsfolk began giving them ale and whiskey. We had won after all, everyone wanted to celebrate. My father and brother had gone off with the rebels and hadn't returned yet when it started. We had all been outside, cheering the soldiers, having a grand old party. My mother noticed some of them making eyes at Jane, so she herded us all back into our house and bolted the door. But those men wanted the spoils of victory, which to them meant my sister."

Anna rolled away from him and onto her side so he could not see her tears. "They started banging on the door. I was the youngest, and my mother hid me under the bed. There wasn't anywhere else to hide. About a dozen of them broke the door down, all drunk. My mother tried to stop them, but they beat her, savagely. Then they forced themselves on my sisters."

Patrick felt Anna's whole body convulse as she spoke, and he tried to hold her tighter.

"I relive it in my nightmares," she went on. "They all wanted Jane, but some of them got impatient and went for Maggie. I can still hear her screams. Good God, she was only fifteen!" She paused, sobbing harder than before. "Over and over, one after another. And then when they were done, they just walked away."

Anna rolled back toward Patrick, tears flowing across her face. "I hate them, Patrick," she said, then with a low guttural growl repeated, "I HATE them!" She buried her face in his chest and continued sobbing uncontrollably. "I want them to suffer for what they've done," she went on, her voice muffled from having her face pressed against his chest.

"Anna," he tried to say gently. "They did suffer. The war is over, Bonaparte has been defeated. France is in ruins. You helped defeat them."

She tilted her head up to look at him. "It cost me everything," she whispered. "My family no longer knows me. I had to debase myself to harm them." She threw her head back, her chest shuddering with her heaving breaths as she wept. "Let them use my body for their pleasure! Done foul things to satisfy them! I've lied so much, played so many parts, I feel I don't even know who I am!"

"Anna!" Patrick shouted, shaking her. She seized up for a moment and her eyes locked back on his. He cradled her head with his hand and kissed her. "Don't say that!" he told her. "I know who you are. You're still the girl from Castlebar, who wouldn't harm me because I was a fellow Irishman. The girl who wanted me because with me she could be herself." He kissed her again and looked into her bloodshot hazel eyes. "You're my wife, the woman I love. *Mo ghra thu.*"

Anna looked back at him for a few moments, regaining a bit of calm, and her breathing steadied. She pressed her face against his chest again and whispered, "Hold me, please."

Patrick tightened his arms around her body as she asked and held her close through the night.

Chapter 3

December 23rd, 1814, New Orleans, Louisiana

"With the addition of Coffee's and Carroll's brigades, we number roughly thirty-two hundred men," one of Jackson's aides reported, lowering a piece of paper on which were several lines of notes detailing the detachments under Jackson's command.

"Yes, but hundreds of those men are posted at the forts downriver," countered Governor Claiborne.

"Also, that number includes the two hundred men of the Navy and Marines currently aboard the *Louisiana* and *Carolina*," spoke up Patrick. He felt a small thrill at having the chance to have something to add to the conversation between the senior officers. With no open positions for officers aboard the ships, Commodore Patterson had made him an aide de camp. As such, he was attending the council of war at Jackson's headquarters in Patterson's stead while the Commodore attended to other matters.

"Subtracting men of the garrisons and the Navy, would give us something near to twenty-one hundred infantry," Jackson's aide concluded.

"That is not nearly enough," grumbled a militia officer with a French accent, dressed in one of the gaudy Napoleonic inspired creole uniforms.

"Patience, Colonel," said Claiborne. "Colonel Coffee reported that additional Kentuckians are making their way downriver as we speak. We could soon have ten thousand men under arms."

"But when?" the creole officer asked, rising from his chair. "We've heard nothing of the British for days. They could be here at any moment!"

The other officers around Patrick rolled their eyes, and he guessed from their reactions that the Colonel was prone to melodrama.

There came a knock at the door to the office. Jackson called out for the man to enter and another young Army Lieutenant stuck his head in. "General Jackson, Sir, a Major Villere has just arrived saying he has knowledge of the whereabouts of the British."

Everyone in the room immediately glared at the creole. "It would appear, Colonel that you have the gift of prophecy," Jackson quipped, giving voice to the thoughts of the others that the creole's statement had somehow conjured up the British army. The General then added to the Lieutenant, "See him in."

The officer backed away for a few moments, quickly returning with a man around the age of thirty dressed as a civilian. "General Jackson, yes?" asked the man, another French creole. Jackson merely nodded in reply. "I am Major Gabriel Villere, of the Third-Louisiana militia. You must forgive my lack of uniform, General, I was in haste and could not take the time to dress properly."

Jackson again nodded with an air of understanding, and waved his hand for Villere to continue. "I was breakfasting at my family's estate on the left bank of the river, where my company has established a guard post. The British have arrived General. An advanced party of their infantry surprised my men and captured them. We never saw them coming, General, they wore green jackets that blended in with the swamp. I was barely able to escape. I made my way straight here, though I passed Colonel De La Ronde on the way and alerted him. He is already rallying his militia detachments."

The room went silent with dread. The report by the Major meant that the British had indeed landed on the shores of Lake Borgne and somehow traversed the bayou to emerge on dry ground mere miles below the city. They were now advancing along the least defensible approach.

Jackson slammed his fist down on his desk with such violence it caused everyone in the room to jolt. "By the Eternal!" he shouted, bolting to his feet, and the officers present were taken aback by his sudden fury. "We must drive them back to their boats. The British shall not sleep upon our territory! I'll fight them tonight!"

Jackson turned to his aide an pointed a boney finger at him. "Lieutenant, send word for the gunners at Fort St. Charles to fire the alarm gun to assemble the militia on the Place d' Arms every ten minutes beginning at…" he looked over at the grandfather clock across the room, "two o'clock. I want the regulars in formation by the time they arrive, and send a party of dragoons to reconnoiter the enemy's bivouac." The aide saluted and immediately left the room to see to his task. "Once the militia has been assembled, we shall march at once," Jackson went on. "We shall take them by surprise in a night attack! I shall issue further instructions while we are on the march. We must move with all haste."

Jackson then turned to Claiborne. "Governor, I shall be leading the army personally. I will leave a small force behind under your command. If the battle should go ill, it will be your duty to hold until the last extremity, or bury your men nobly."

Claiborne nodded wordlessly, his expression a combination of annoyance that Jackson was issuing directives to him and an irritated display of wounded pride. Everyone knew that Claiborne had immediately jumped to the conclusion that Jackson was sidelining him to hog the glory.

Casting his gaze about the room, Jackson then said, "Gentlemen, to your commands." The room, which had moments before been stunned into silence by the awful news was now electrified by Jackson's decisive response. The senior officers immediately began to disperse out the door in a rush to get to their regiments.

"Lieutenant Sullivan, a moment if you please," Jackson said to Patrick as he had started for the door. He straightened his posture as Jackson walked over to him.

"I have instructions I wish to transmit to Commodore Patterson," he told Patrick. "The cooperation of the Navy will be vital for the success of my plan. Please have him bring his ships downriver. The British will be hemmed in along a narrow front between the river and the swamp. It is my intent that the *Louisiana* and *Carolina* bring flanking fire against them as we make our attack. Am I understood?"

"Yes, Sir, of course," replied Patrick.

"Very well. Off you go."

Patrick saluted Jackson and left the office. Stepping outside, he was nearly run over by a column of regulars hurrying down the street in the direction of the Place D'Arms. They passed him by so quickly he was not even able to make out the regiment number emblazoned on the metal plate on the front of their shakos.

Following the infantrymen, Patrick heard the warning gun boom out for the first time, and civilians now started to throw open their windows to see what the commotion was. By the time he reached the Place D'Arms, the regulars of the 7th and 44th regiments were in formation on the square, with militia detachments beginning to filter in from various directions. Along the balconies of the buildings surrounding the plaza, ladies cheered the men, waving handkerchiefs and calling out to loved ones in the militia.

"Patrick!" he heard Anna's voice calling out to him from above as he passed the hotel they were staying at. He looked up and waved to his wife, who was leaning out the window of their room.

"The British have landed downriver," he informed her succinctly. "I have orders, I must return to the Commodore. I can't say more."

Anna nodded, knowing full well the need for discretion on the subject of military matters. "I'll be volunteering with some of the other women as nurses. I don't want to have to be seeing you there, you hear me?"

Patrick smiled up at her. "I can take care of myself too, you know."

She blew him a kiss. "Be safe. I love you."

"I love you too," he answered, and gave her a wink. He then rushed down to the dock where the *Louisiana* and *Carolina* were sitting idle.

Storming up the gangplank of the *Louisiana*, he abbreviated the formalities with the officer of the watch, and immediately made his way over to Commodore Patterson who was standing over the hatchway supervising some men hoisting cargo below.

"Ah, Lieutenant," he said upon seeing Patrick. "What's going on? That's the alarm gun at Fort St. Charles I hear firing."

"The British have landed downriver, Sir," he reported to Patterson.

"Downriver?" he repeated with surprise. "Whereabouts?"

"The Villere plantation?" said Patrick with a raised eyebrow, hoping his commander would recognize the location.

Patterson's eyes bulged. "That close?" he asked with astonishment. "Damn. So, they did come through the bayou from Lake Borgne. There's hardly anything standing between them and the city!"

"Aye, Sir," said Patrick. "Once the infantry has mustered, General Jackson is planning an immediate counterattack. He believes if he strikes swiftly, he can drive the British back to their ships. He requests our cooperation and wants our ships to provide flanking fire on the British from the river."

Patterson raised his eyebrow again. "That's mighty bold of him." The Commodore then looked around his ship. "The *Louisiana* isn't ready for action. We're still loading stores of powder and shot. It'll have to just be the *Carolina*. Lieutenant, please report this back to General Jackson and inquire from him further instructions. After that, report aboard the *Carolina*. Lieutenant Henley will need a hand. His ship is fully stocked with ammunition but only just finished filling out the crew roll. Having another experienced officer wouldn't be amiss."

"Aye, aye, Sir," said Patrick, saluting again and making for the gangplank to leave the ship.

Patrick hurried back to Jackson, finding the General mounted on his horse and making his way to the Place D'Arms. The General had bristled when told that only one of Patterson's ships would be available for the night attack. "Additional scouts have reported that the British are not pressing to advance on the city but making camp for the night at the Villere plantation," the General told Patrick as he walked alongside the General's horse. "A more perfect situation could not be envisioned. I would have the *Carolina* take up station on the river opposite their encampment, and open fire upon it precisely at eight o'clock. Be sure to instruct the commander to float the ship downriver with the current so the enemy will not be able to make out the sails in the dark. We must ensure to keep the element of surprise." Jackson then handed him papers with further written instructions.

"Understood, Sir," Patrick saluted, and he ran ahead to get back the dock. Reaching the *Carolina* this time, he found a familiar face greeting him.

"Good to see you, Sir. Will you be joining us?" asked Spencer, holding his salute as Patrick came aboard. The Midshipman had been posted to the ship following their arrival and they had not seen much of each other in the intervening week.

Patrick hastily returned the salute. "I will, Phillip. Could you direct me to Lieutenant Henley?"

"Just there, Sir," Spencer answered, pointing to an officer standing near the capstan.

Patrick walked over to Henley, who noticed him approaching and the two saluted each other.

"You must be Sullivan," said Henley.

"Aye, Sir," replied Patrick. "Commodore Patterson said you could use an extra hand with the new crew."

Henley nodded. "Yes, I'll need someone steady. Have you seen battle before?"

"Aye, Sir. Several times. I can still recall the image in my mind of you holding up Lieutenant Trippe the day we fought the gunboats in Tripoli."

Henley's eyebrows went up in surprise. "You were there that day? Forgive me for not recalling you, I thought I knew all of the officers still with the Navy from those days."

"I was before-the-mast back then," answered Patrick. "I served with Decatur aboard the *Enterprise*."

Henley smiled. "Any man that's done battle alongside Decatur is someone I know I can count on. Welcome aboard, Lieutenant."

Preparations to get the ship underway continued, while on shore Jackson's army continued to assemble on the Place D'Arms. By the time dusk approached, both the soldiers on land as well as the sailors on the water were ready to head downriver to finally come to grips with the British.

"Give way!" shouted Henley to the longshoremen on the dock, and they tossed over the lines holding the ship in place. The *Carolina* began to warp away from the dock, with a few hands giving an extra push with oars from the ship's gig. The quartermaster spun the wheel over to starboard to put them on course for the center of the river, and from there they lazily drifted with the current.

Looking back, Patrick watched as the army departed as well, their dark uniforms blending into the growing darkness until soon they were a formless ripple shifting along in the night.

None of the lanterns on deck had been lit and the men took care moving about in the dark so as not to stumble. The sky was clear, and they had no trouble navigating as the moon was three nights from being full. For a moment Patrick wondered how the moonlight would affect Jackson's plan to take the enemy by surprise, as it bathed everything in a pale glow. There was also a chill in the air, and he shivered, cursing his absentmindedness for having forgotten his overcoat back in the hotel room.

At least Anna will be warm then, he thought, assuming she would use it instead. He then breathed into his hands and rubbed them together, and he began to pace alongside the larboard guns to keep moving. He kept his eyes forward on the black river, noticing how easily the quartermaster kept them in the center of the band of water as they rounded the large crescent bend. Once they were past the only navigation obstacle, he could see for miles downriver, even detecting pinpricks of light in the distance on the left bank.

One of the other officers aboard began to pass the word for the men to load the guns. It was clear some of the men on deck were among the new landsmen that Patrick had been warned were only recruited that day, as they loitered aimlessly near the cannons.

"You the new men?" he asked them, and a few of them nodded.

"We've naught to do, Sir," said one, a local creole by his accent.

"Every one of you will need to haul these lines," Patrick told them, backing out of the way as another hand brushed by him, the links in the chain shot he was carrying rattling with every step. "Spread yourselves out, and if you see a gun shorthanded, join them. Follow the orders of the gunlayers, they'll tell you what to do."

"Thank you, Sir," responded the man.

"And keep your heads down," Patrick added, as he moved on to the next group to repeat his brief words of advice. It was the sort of task he had done often in his over ten years of service. He knew his role aboard the *Carolina* was superfluous, there were plenty of officers and ratings to give the actual orders. It was his presence that was important, a battle-hardened figure to keep the men steady when the fire became hot.

I just have to keep them from seeing my hand shaking, he thought, as he felt the familiar tremor that came when battle was imminent. He clasped his hands behind his back to keep them from view. It was a sensation that had surfaced after his first battle over a decade prior during a short period where he had been pressed into the Royal Navy, a vicious frigate duel that had been decided by boarding action. In the time between the Barbary War and the current hostilities he thought it had gone away, but to his disappointment it returned. It only seemed to go away when he was angry or too preoccupied to think.

Lieutenant Henley came back alongside him as Patrick continued to watch the lights on the riverbank growing nearer. "Campfires," said Henley, stating the obvious. "They're either awfully confident or awfully foolish to be making their camp so close to the river."

Patrick nodded. "Yes, they do make fine targets."

"It gives me a chill to think what our guns will do if we catch them huddled around those fires." Henley then shivered, though whether it was from the cold or his revulsion at eviscerating men, Patrick could not be sure. The senior Lieutenant then took a watch from out of his pocket and read it by the moonlight.

"The order to open fire was to be for eight o'clock, yes?"

"Aye, Sir," replied Patrick.

Henley chewed on his lip. "Seven-thirty," he commented, replacing his watch in his pocket. "Almost there. Old Hickory had better have his men in position."

The *Carolina* continued its silent cruise down the Mississippi toward the British encampment. The campfires gradually grew larger, and as they came closer Patrick noticed not only the smell of smoke, but the scent of cooked meat wafting out over the river. Still there were no shouts of alarm, warning shots, or even calls to identify themselves from the riverbank. *Surely, they have pickets posted?* Patrick thought.

Now they were so close that Patrick could make out the silhouettes of redcoats moving around the camp, as well as rows of tents. He also noticed the levee alongside the river, only a few feet higher than the earth behind it. While the *Carolina* was riding high enough that her shots would be able to clear the embankment, Patrick knew that those British regiments closest to the river would be able to use it as cover. *The first volley will have the most impact. We have to make it count.*

The ship drifted into position opposite the British encampment with almost no sign of the enemy noticing their presence. Before they went too far, Henley whispered to one of the Boatswain's Mates to go forward and drop anchor. The line played out across the deck quietly enough, but there was no muffling the splash once the anchor touched the water.

"Schooner ahoy!" a lone English voice called out, and Patrick spotted the outline of a figure atop the levee waving to them. "What have you got to sell?"

Patrick turned to Henley. "Sell?" he whispered. "They must take us for a merchantman."

Henley, who was looking down again at his watch again, replied, "Well, let's see how they feel about buying grapeshot, free of charge." He snapped shut the lid on his watch, and looking up shouted, "Now! Damn their eyes, give it to them!"

The *Carolina's* gunners yanked on their lanyards simultaneously. The guns boomed out a staggering explosion and sent their deadly projectiles slicing through the encampment. From his vantage point on deck, Patrick could see the devasting effects even in the dark. Whole groups of men sitting by their campfires wilted and crumpled to the ground as grapeshot tore into them. Tents collapsed, with men who only seconds before had peacefully slumbered now ripping them apart and tossing them aside as they struggled to their feet. The chain shot he had seen a hand loading earlier went twirling through the air, decapitating an officer before snapping a trio of stacked muskets in half.

"Reload!" sounded Henley, but many of the men had already begun the task, eager to repeat the results. Looking around him, Patrick noticed how the men were almost enjoying themselves, laughing at the gruesome spectacle they had delivered to the enemy. It was an unmistakable sign of a fresh crew that had never seen battle before, and never had misery inflicted on them. *They'll stop laughing when the Redcoats begin shooting back*, Patrick confidently surmised.

Already the British seemed to be recovering from the shock. There was a rush of men scrambling to the riverbank, taking advantage of the little cover provided by the levee. Elsewhere some Redcoats began to douse their campfires, tossing water on them or kicking them out with their feet. Officers could be heard bellowing orders, and at least one told his men, "Remember, you are Britons!"

Patrick rolled his eyes and sighed. "British," he muttered.

The *Carolina* now let loose a second volley, but it was less clear what casualties they could have caused. Henley now paced the deck back and forth. "Keep it hot, men!" he shouted. The gunners took the encouragement to heart and started to reload faster, and before long the guns began to fire at will. There was so much activity that Patrick almost did not notice the beginning of Jackson's attack.

To their left, back up along the riverbank, a ripple of musketry flashed out of the darkness. Nearby to it came another, and another as regiments opened fire one at a time. Smoke now swirled and hung close to the ground, unable to drift away on a windless night.

Outlined by the bursts of musketry shattering the dark, Patrick could see the British reacting to the new threat. British soldiers formed into ragged lined and returned fire. The response was sporadic, a lone musket here and there, pairs of men firing in skirmish order, at least one platoon letting loose a coordinated volley. The scene descended into chaos as American and British formations closed on each other and began to engage in hand-to-hand combat. The clash of cold steel echoed out to the *Carolina*, and it was impossible to see more as both sides were enveloped in smoke and fog. Only intermittent orange flashes from discharged muskets penetrated the cloud.

"Keep your fire trained on their camp," Henley ordered his gunners. "We don't want to risk hitting our own men."

The *Carolina* fired off another broadside, this time each gun firing in sequence down the length of the ship rather than all at once. This change of tactics would allow them to keep a constant fire on the British, allowing each gun time to reload before the rolling barrage required them to fire again.

Just then, the whole area was illuminated with a red-tinted glow from above, and Patrick heard a familiar shriek rip through the sky. "Not rockets again!" he heard Spencer call out further down the gundeck, matching Patrick's own thoughts, as they had both encountered the weapons when the British attacked the capital. He looked up and saw the rocket was vaguely aimed at the *Carolina* but fired much too high and went sailing clear over. Another rocket went screaming into the air from beyond the British camp, just as poorly aimed as the first, and in its light Patrick saw a dizzying spectacle.

The light of the rockets was able to pierce the smoke and fog, Patrick could see the masses of men ashore locked in combat. Men fired their muskets at point blank range, skewering each other with bayonets, wildly swinging their weapons like clubs. The two armies were hopelessly intermingled, though the lighter color of the British Redcoats at least made it easier to tell who was whom. The sight only lasted a few seconds before the battlefield was again plunged into darkness.

"I wonder why they've brought no cannon to bear against us?" Henley wondered aloud.

"Perhaps they've not brought them ashore yet?" offered Patrick. "It could be that in order to fire on us they would have to expose themselves on the levee."

Another of the red rockets arced high into the air, its trajectory giving Patrick the impression that the British were not attempting to adjust their aim. As the swirling melee was once again brought on full display, Patrick noticed movement along the levee to their right, beyond where the ship's cannons could be pivoted to fire. He spotted the outline of several figures, definitely not wearing Redcoats, but darker uniforms. Before he could get a better look, the light of the rocket had faded, and it was again dark.

"Did you see that?" Henley asked him.

Patrick nodded, "Aye, Sir." The two men then stepped closer to the rail to get a better look.

"Do you think they could have been our men from the forts downriver?"

Patrick shrugged. "General Jackson's written orders did state he had sent riders to the nearest garrison, and to have them take the British from the rear," he told Henley. "I'm not sure if they could have arrived here by now. They would have needed to cross the river first.

Another rocket came flashing out of the British camp. This time it had a blue tint and flew on a flatter trajectory than the previous ones, much nearer to the *Carolina*. As the rocket flashed past them, he spotted the dark figures atop the levee, about half a dozen, all down on one knee. In the split second before it faded, the brighter blue tinted light of the rocket showed him the figures were wearing green jackets.

"Down!" Patrick screamed, and he pulled Henley below the rail. He heard the crack of musketry as he did, and barely moments later, bullets zipped through the hammock netting atop the rail where the pair had been standing.

"Riflemen," Patrick coughed out, catching his breath, and being thankful for having paid attention when Anna had told Jackson of the feared 95th. Looking to his left he spotted Spencer holding his tall hat in his hands, poking a finger through a hole in it. The Midshipman looked up with a nervous smile on his face.

"A little close for comfort," he joked with an uneasy laugh.

Henley pointed out a trio of nearby men, then over to the ship's capstan. "Winch the capstan a few turns to pivot us."

The men he had given the task to nodded and gave the knuckled salute, then went to the capstan, crouching low the whole way. They began to turn the capstan, and the bow of the ship rotated as the line on the anchor became taught. Taking brief glance through a gunport, Henley was satisfied that the ship had turned enough and ordered, "Now! Fire on those riflemen!"

The guns began their rippling barrage down the length of the ship once again. Patrick similarly took a look out a gunport, and no longer saw the offending green jackets atop the levee. Nevertheless, a few shots stabbed at the *Carolina* out of the darkness, showing that the men had gone to ground behind the levee rather than be cut down.

Henley looked at Patrick with a grin. "I read of Macdonough's maneuver with his anchors at Plattsburg," he said, referring to the commander of the American squadron on Lake Champlain who had recently defeated an attacking British force. "I had a feeling learning that would prove useful."

"I'm grateful you did, or else we'd be dodging rifle fire all night," replied Patrick.

The ship's cannons fired off a few more volleys at the green jacketed interlopers, to keep them under cover. Risking a quick look over the rails, Patrick looked out and saw that the land battle appeared to be petering out, the flashes of musketry becoming ever more sporadic.

"It would seem that Jackson's gambit has failed," Patrick surmised, returning to Henley's side.

The senior Lieutenant nodded grimly. "Aye. He certainly hasn't overrun their camp. Regardless, we'll lay at anchor here until morning at the least to see what damage we've done."

The sailors of the *Carolina* spent a chilly night at quarters, though they did not fire their guns for the remainder of the night. Around five in the morning, they heard the call for reveille echoing out of the dark from the British camp. Eventually the sky brightened enough despite the murky overcast for them to finally observe the results of the night's engagement.

Climbing up the mainmast in order to get an unobstructed view over the levee, Patrick, Henley, and a few of the other officers looked down over the floodplain. The ground was strewn with detritus, mostly in the form of shredded tents and wrecked equipment. Red coated bodies lay scattered throughout the camp and farther west along the riverbank, the latter mixed in with a smattering of blue and grey uniforms of Americans that had fallen. Wandering British soldiers roamed the battlefield, picking up the odd fallen article or looking for wounded to be carried back to the surgeons. Some men, including the riflemen along the levee were still sleeping, resting their heads on their haversacks.

"Shall we wake them?" Henley asked Patrick with a malicious grin.

Patrick smirked and nodded. "Load grape and resume firing!" he called down to the gun crews. The cannons boomed out once more, sending another deadly hail of metal across the floodplain. Below them, Patrick saw the riflemen behind the levee startle, while other British farther afield dove for cover. One dozing Redcoat had his haversack swiped out from under his head yet remained miraculously unscathed.

As the smoke from the volley cleared, a green jacket poked his head up over the levee and shouted at them, "Would you bloody Yankees bugger off!"

"No!" shouted back Spencer, Patrick detecting from his tone that he was perhaps enjoying himself a little too much, though the men on deck all shared in a laugh. The Midshipman then patted the barrel of the cannon he was standing next to and the gunlayer fired off another round.

Later that afternoon, the *Louisiana* finally arrived, dropping anchor a few cable lengths behind them upstream. Patrick took one of the ship's boats and had a few hands row him over to make his report on the night action to Patterson, braving the occasional pot hot from the riflemen. The two American ships then continued a sporadic barrage for the next two days, the men eating their Christmas dinners at their guns.

Returning to the flagship at least proved helpful in letting Patrick know what had transpired during the land battle. Jackson may not have been able to drive the British into the sea as he had hoped, but he had certainly given them pause. It was obvious that they had managed to inflict serious casualties, and British prisoners informed them of how shocked they were to be attacked, having landed with the expectation of an easy victory.

In the meantime, Jackson was preparing a new defensive line upriver. Digging in along a dried-up canal, the General was erecting earthworks anchored by the river on the right, and the dense swamps to its left. Such a position would leave the British no choice but a frontal assault over open ground.

"He's gathering every damn cannon in the city," said Patterson, as he and Patrick stood together on the *Louisiana's* deck, eyeing the shoreline. Ahead of them the crew of the *Carolina* were attempting to warp their ship back up the river by having a boat carry the anchor, then drop it overboard to allow the crew to winch the ship backwards. Thus far the results proved dismal as the strong current combined with still winds to hold them in place, and the ship was nearly stranded on the west bank.

"Did those pirates deliver as promised?" asked Patrick.

"The Lefittes? Yes, couldn't believe it until I heard it. They brought several guns and enough powder to account for themselves. The sad thing is, I know I won't be able to confiscate it as soon as the battle is ended. Once they have their pardon they'll scurry out of here like rats and find some other hideaway to plunder from."

Patrick sighed, understanding the Commodore's frustration. "I suppose this is an example of one battle at a time."

Patterson in turn rolled his eyes. "I hate the thought of fighting the same battle twice."

Patrick looked back at the river bank the British were encamped behind. Redcoats stilled milled about, less apprehensive of attracting fire from the American ships now that they were conserving ammunition. Taking his spyglass from his belt, he extended it and ran his gaze along the levee. He noticed several officers mostly hidden from view, though exposed enough that he could make out their uniforms. A blue coated artillery officer seemed to be gesturing about in an animated way.

"Sir?" Patrick said to Patterson a bit discretely as to not let any of the crew overhear. He put forward his spyglass to the Commodore and pointed to the cluster of British officers. "I'm fairly certain they're readying embrasures in the levee for artillery," he continued as Patterson took the spyglass. "Either my eyesight may be failing, or they've cut into the levee. Do you see the divots in the ground?"

Patterson looked through the spyglass and nodded. "Aye. One of the Bosun's Mates said he heard them working with picks and shovels during the night. We've got to get these ships back upriver to Jackson's new line. We're sitting ducks for hot shot at this range."

Not needing to be reminded of the dangers heated shot posed to wooden ships, Patrick asked, "Shall I give the order for us to begin returning upriver now, Sir?"

Patterson shook his head. "No, I'm not going to leave until we can bring the *Carolina* out first. We'll stay here to provide cover until Henley can move her."

"Aye, aye, Sir," Patrick responded with a salute. Retrieving his spyglass from the Commodore, he retired below deck for the evening, only making a brief appearance in the wardroom for supper. Serving as an adjutant came with its benefits, as he was not required to take a watch, and hoped to get some well needed rest.

Around an hour before sunrise, he was startled awake by the sound of cannon fire. Rolling out of his hammock and throwing on his jacket, he bounded up the hatchway onto the deck. He was greeted by a Midshipman giving the order to fire, and the flash of one of *Louisiana's* cannons.

"Report!" Patrick barked at the younger man.

The Midshipman saw him and saluted. "We're returning fire on the riverbank, Sir," he told Patrick. "They're pouring most of their fire into—" He was cut off by a rocket streaking into the sky, illuminating the river. Round shot also appeared to be arcing through the air as well, exploding overhead of the *Carolina*.

"They're firing mostly on the *Carolina*," the Midshipman stated, turning back around. "It looks like with howitzers too, judging from those bursts."

"Have they taken us under fire?" Patrick asked.

"A few wayward shots, Sir, but they're aiming high."

Patterson now appeared on deck in his nightshirt but did not ask for a further explanation as he had heard most of the conversation coming up the hatchway.

"Get men aloft now!" he ordered, turning to the Boatswain. The man then piped a command on his whistle, and men started moving up the ratlines.

"We've got to take advantage of the wind and get clear of those guns," said Patterson grimly, noticing the wind had picked up during the night. "Get men on the capstan to pivot us on the anchor so we can make our way upstream under sail."

"Sir!" a hand forward shouted. "The *Carolina's* on fire!"

Both Patrick and Patterson scrambled forward to the bow. Looking over the rail, they could see fire beginning to lick the sides of their fellow warship. Frantic screaming could be heard in between the booming of cannon, and men started to jump over the starboard side and swim for shore.

"Damned hot shot!" growled Patterson. Patrick had been on both the delivering and receiving end of heated shot, and no matter which end of the exchange he felt a terror instinctive to all sailors at the thought of ships on fire.

"As I had feared," Patterson went on. Turning back to his crew he barked, "Get this ship turned round now! Set all sail the moment we're pointed upriver!"

The *Louisiana* began to turn ever so slowly as the crew weighed the anchor. Patrick's attention was still focused on the *Carolina*, which was now rapidly being consumed by flames. *Blast it Spencer, get out of there!* he thought.

More men were clambering over the side, easing into the water or trying to jump clear to the shore, though none managed to get ashore dry. Soon only one man was left on deck, certainly Henley, who quickly departed before the whole ship was consumed. The crew of the *Carolina* then staggered ashore and over the levee, before running along the riverbank to escape before the ship's powder magazine exploded.

Patrick could only shake his head sullenly as the *Louisiana* completed its pivot and faced upriver. Turning around he could detect the same emotion in the faces of the men. They had put up a good fight over the last several days, some even thought they had given the British a drubbing. *But running off with your tail between your legs ever instills confidence*, he thought, knowing what a development like this could do to morale.

"Don't worry, boys," he said, "We'll get back at them for it soon."

There were grim nods and a few murmurs of agreement, but for the most part the words rang hollow.

Patrick made is way aft along the deck back to the quarterdeck where Patterson had taken up position near the wheel.

"Two weeks ago, I had a squadron," he said, folding his arms. "At least I've not lost my flagship."

"I believe we'll be safer under the protection of our own guns at the new line," Patrick replied, trying to reassure him.

"We better be," said Patterson, chewing on his lip. "I hope Jackson knows what he's doing."

Chapter 4

December 28th, 1814, Chalmette Plantation, Louisiana

"I lost my hat," said Spencer dejectedly as he sat on a bench inside the canopy of one of the surgeon's tents.

Patrick chuckled and Anna tousled his hair as if he was a boy. She then handed the Midshipman a porcelain mug of hot coffee to warm him.

"Do you have more of that?" Patrick asked her, pointing to the mug.

"It's for the wounded," she chastised. "You didn't fall in the river."

"I haven't had my overcoat either," he replied, tugging on the sleeve of the very same coat which she was now wearing.

"You're not getting it back yet," she answered. "You've at least gotten to sleep inside the last few nights. I've been freezing out in this tent with some of the other women."

"Hopefully it won't be much longer," Patrick told her. "You should go back into town with Spencer for the evening at least." Turning to the younger man he smiled and said, "You can replace your hat. Otherwise, you'll get a reprimand for being out of uniform."

Spencer gave a small laugh and sipped the coffee he had been given while tugging a blanket around his shoulders. Patrick gave him one last thumping on the arm before he and Anna started walking away.

"How bad was it in here the other night?" he asked, noticing a blood stain on the side of the tent.

"Not as bad as I had feared," she answered. "Still not pleasant, it never is. I've seen worse, far worse. You would have been aghast after the siege of Badajoz." She stopped and turned to him as they neared the entrance to the tent. "I saw my brother that night. It was the first time in years. He was with the 88th and had carried a friend back to us. Between seeing so many of his friends slaughtered and seeing what the survivors did to the women in that town, it left him in tears." She put her hand on his chest and closed her eyes for a few moments before looking back up at him. "I was frightened when Spencer came in here without you. I hadn't known you had changed ships. I now fear seeing one of you dragging in the other like my brother carried in his friend."

Patrick put his arms around her and kissed her forehead. "Don't fear, I'm better at keeping my head down than he is," he said, thinking of the riflemen that had put a round through Spencer's missing hat. "Your brother. He's not on the other side of that field, is he?"

Anna shook her head. "The 88th isn't one of the regiments here, praise God. I know he'd have no stomach for fighting Americans. He's likely back in Mayo now, taking up carpentry after my father."

"That's a good living," Patrick commented.

Anna nodded. "It is. Kept us better fed than most folk."

"And your sisters?"

Anna looked away from him for moment, the pain of the memory of what had happened to her sisters returning to her eyes. "Jane entered a convent and joined an order. She thought no man would ever want her after being defiled like that. Maggie…" Her voice caught in her throat, and she blinked away a tear. "Maggie tried to slash her wrists when she was nineteen." She paused again, putting a hand on his shoulder as if to steady herself. He rubbed her shoulder gently to calm her.

"No, it's alright," she said, patting his hand and wiping away another tear. "She lived. It's just hard to speak of. Happy things came from it actually. While she was healing, my mother asked Father Murphy to speak with her and console her. He was young, fresh out of the seminary. He fell in love with her and left the priesthood to marry her. They have a family now, and he still serves as a Deacon. Maggie became very devout, saw her surviving and meeting Murphy as Providence."

She frowned and furrowed her brow, looking off to the side. "Perhaps not just for her either. I might not have met you if she hadn't married Johnny. Father Murphy that is, we call him Johnny now," she corrected. "He told me about Father Curtis, whom he'd been a student of at the university in Salamanca. Curtis was Wellington's spymaster in the Peninsula. I traveled to Spain to meet him, and he taught me how to become a spy."

Patrick raised an eyebrow. "An Irish priest was the Duke of Wellington's spymaster?"

Anna chuckled. "Yes, the last person the French would expect."

Patrick looked outside the tent into the gray and cold day outside. "I best be off. I'll come by as often as I can."

She smiled up at him and squeezed his arm. "I'll be waiting."

The couple parted and Patrick exited the tent. Walking away, he headed in the direction of the new defensive line Jackson had ordered constructed. Curious to inspect the position for himself, he ambled through the camp of a militia regiment behind the center of the line until reaching the earthworks.

'Line Jackson' as it was dubbed, was little more than a simple earthen breastwork thrown up behind the bank of a dried-up canal. It was a far cry from what all the Americans would have wished, but it was the best that could be done given the circumstances. *At least we've a clear field of fire*, he noted, seeing the flat floodplain before him.

Looking to his left he spotted some men hauling an artillery piece into position. None of them were clad in anything like a uniform, and he realized these were the infamous Baratarian pirates. Off to the side, a man was overseeing their work, his arms crossed, and head tilted slightly. Patrick realized he may have been looking at none other than Jean Lafitte. From everything he had heard, he expected a swarthy, mustachioed, swashbuckling adventurer. In reality, while he was finely dressed, the dreaded pirate had more of the appearance of a mild-mannered businessman. He was even disappointingly clean shaven.

"I can't believe we're actually going to fight alongside them," Patrick heard a man say from behind him. An Army Lieutenant walked up beside him shaking his head.

"Agreed," Patrick replied with several nods of his own. "I have a feeling as soon as this engagement's over, I'll be hunting those men all across the Gulf of Mexico."

The other man snorted. "Lieutenant Houston, regulars," he introduced himself, holding out his hand.

Patrick shook it. "Lieutenant Sullivan, Navy." Turning their attention back to the pirates, Patrick further commented. "At least they were kind enough to bring their own gunpowder."

Houston nearly laughed. "Every ounce of it plundered." He then shrugged. "But we're not in a position to care one bit where they got it, so long as they're going to use it on redcoats." They watched the pirates working for another moment until Houston asked, "Have you seen action?"

Patrick sighed. "More than I'd care to remember."

"Where at?"

"I arrived recently from Baltimore, saw plenty of action there. Lake Erie before that. Further back I was in the Barbary War."

Houston's eyebrows went up and he nodded respectfully. "You've been just about everywhere. Can't say I've seen that much, but at least I've been in battle. I was with Old Hickory at Horseshoe Bend against the Creeks. Damn Indians nearly shot my balls off," he said crassly, gesturing to a spot on the edge of his groin.

Before Houston could continue his story, a soldier came running up to them.

"Sir, I need you to come quick," he said, out of breath. "It's Private Horton, Sir."

"What's he done this time, Corporal?"

"He's captured himself an alligator and is wandering the camp looking for gunpowder. He thinks he can use the alligator to shoot the British."

Houston blinked at the man. "He wants to load the alligator into a cannon and fire it at the British?"

The soldier shook his head. "No, Sir, he wants to use the alligator *as* the cannon."

Houston chuckled. "And how much has Private Horton been drinking, Corporal?"

"Quite a bit, Sir," the soldier reported.

"As I suspected," answered Houston with a smile. "Forgive me, Lieutenant, but I have to go chase down a drunken Private who wants to turn an alligator into a cannon. Perhaps we'll continue our conversation another time? Gooday."

Later that morning, the British arrived on the field. There was intense skirmishing, but the enemy never seriously pressed the American defensive line. Their withdrawal left the men under Jackson's command confused as to whether that had succeeded in repulsing an attack, or merely driven off a reconnaissance-in-force.

Desultory exchanges of artillery fire continued for the next several days.

On New Year's Day, the British let loose with a spectacular cannonade to ring in 1815. The British infantry had formed behind their batteries, seemingly intent on making an assault, yet none came. For all the expenditure of powder and shot, the results only confirmed that American artillery actually outgunned their opponents, in no small part thanks to Lafitte and his marauders.

In the meantime, the Americans sat and waited. While some subordinates were itching for another chance to attack the British, most understood that Jackson knew better than to engage British regulars on open ground. He would make the enemy come to him and use the intervening time to bolster the American defenses. Taking advantage of the Navy's control of the river, new artillery batteries were constructed on the opposite bank, able to fire across the river and into the British flank if they dared make a frontal attack.

They wouldn't dare, thought Patrick as he paced the deck of the *Louisiana* in the dark as it lay at anchor where Jackson's earthworks met the riverbank. *It would be madness to attack over flat open ground! And with enfilade fire? It would be a slaughter.* He looked over the railing at the new batteries on the far bank, manned by sailors and Marines, feeling confident they would cause havoc among enemy formations. Commodore Patterson had gone ashore to command the batteries in person, leaving Patrick as the senior officer on the *Louisiana*.

He paced the deck once more, almost stomping his feet to get his blood circulating. *Damned chill*, he thought, breathing into his hands and rubbing them together. He still could not fathom how unseasonably cold it had been of late.

The skies were gloomy again, murky grey and overcast. It was near sunrise he estimated, and the dark grey of night was turning into the slightly brighter grey of dawn. Thinking of the new day, he realized he was unsure what day it was. *What date is it? The seventh? No, no, the eighth, now. They all blur together now it seems.*

He heard a hissing noise and saw single rocket leap into the air from the direction of the British lines. The projectile drifted lazily until falling harmlessly into the river. Patrick waited a few more moments, expecting more rockets to begin streaking haphazardly across the sky as the prelude to another day of artillery skirmishing, but none came. He thought he heard noise coming from the shoreline, but he could not see anything as heavy fog covered the ground.

"Beat to quarters," he ordered instinctively to a nearby Boatswain's Mate. The man hurried to the hatchway and called below for the Marine drummer to stand to. Others below had heard the order and started swinging out of their hammocks and coming on deck before the drummer was in position to begin his roll. From the shore could be heard similar sounds of drummers and fifes rousing men in Jackson's camp.

Scarcely a dozen men had clambered above decks when Patrick heard the first booms of artillery fire. They were unmistakably coming from the British lines. Soon cannon fire was sounding rapidly, matched in short order by American counter-fire, though how anyone could see targets through the fog he could not know.

"What's going on, Sir?" asked a bewildered Midshipman as he bounded up from below, dressed in little more than his long underwear.

"I'm not certain yet," he answered. "They may be making a general attack."

A few moments later, the wind picked up and the fog began to drift away. Through the remaining mist the men aboard the *Louisiana* were stunned by the sight before them. Arrayed on the field in front of Jackson's line were thousands of British redcoats.

The British bandsmen now began playing their own fifes and drums, the tunes of different regiments intermingled, though Patrick did distinctly make out at least one rendition of 'The British Grenadiers.' Taking out his spyglass, he scanned the enemy columns, noting the regimental colours, and the different trim of each units' uniforms. In particular, he saw once again the Ninety-Fifth in their green jackets, and Scottish Highlanders wearing bonnets with a plaid band. At this point he could look through his spyglass no further as his left hand was shaking too violently. Patrick hurried shut the telescope and clenched his fist to disguise the tremor before anyone noticed.

The British now started forward. Nearest to the river came a regiment at the double-quick along the road behind the levee. An officer stood at their head, dressed in a grey overcoat, and waving his saber over his head calling for his men to follow him. They were heading straight for the bastion that anchored Jackson's breastwork on the river, likely the key to the entire position.

They had barely started out when the Marines' cannons across the river began firing at them. Solid shot went hurling through the air over their heads, plowing into the muddy field. Jackson's militia to their front opened fire with a pair of their own cannons loaded with grape shot, and their muskets at one hundred yards.

Standing there watching from the comparative safety of the *Louisiana*, Patrick felt a certain admiration for their courage, an odd feeling given that he had spent most of his life hating the British for the things they had done to him. The horrifying sight that the gallant charge quickly transformed into nearly turned his stomach.

Redcoats were bowled over like ninepins. Huge gaps in their line appeared, wiping out half a dozen men at a time. The iron grapeshot tore men apart, severing limbs, leaving men spinning into the ground disemboweled. Another formation immediately behind them, one of the all-black West Indian regiments carrying ladders to scale the ditch and rampart, flung themselves on the ground to avoid the hail of shot.

Yet somehow the British staggered on. The officer again held aloft his sword, crying out for his men to follow him, and hobbled wounded toward the bastion. Incredibly, he not only reached the ditch but then climbed the breastwork as Americans fired their muskets at him. He drew a pair of pistols, firing one after the other into the American defenders and leaped down into the bastion. For a moment it looked as if the headlong assault would carry the day, but as the officer then charged over the palisade at the rear of the bastion, an American shot him through the head and he tumbled backward, dead. Behind the fallen officer, the redcoats that had followed him scampered back over the rampart of the bastion as the Americans retook the battery.

"Shall we open fire, Sir?"

Patrick shook his head, snapping himself out of the stupor he had slumped into watching the carnage inflicted on the first British charge.

"Yes. Of course. Open fire," he absentmindedly said to the gunner that had asked. The men of the *Louisiana* promptly fired their cannons. The American sailors were using solid round shot, aiming it high to send it well over the rampart instead of grapeshot to avoid the risk of friendly casualties.

With the immediate threat to the right flank dealt with, Patrick turned his attention back to the other British columns still waiting to begin their attack. He noticed his hand had stopped shaking, and he put his spyglass back up to his eye. Through it he saw the green jackets of the Ninety-Fifth deploying forward in skirmish order, spread out far enough so that they would not attract cannon fire. Several hundred yards distant, a new regiment of redcoats started forward at the double-quick, aiming at the Americans' left flank.

The response of the defenders in that quarter was as vigorous as those on the right flank. With every step the British were met with a hail of grapeshot. Huge gaps in their lines were ripped open as men were eviscerated by iron balls. Yet each time men were scythed down, their ranks closed up, either by men moving forward from the rear, or the men simply moving over shoulder to shoulder.

The British continued on with dogged determination. As they neared the American breastwork, the Tennesseans and Kentuckians opened up with a murderous fusillade, which sent more men flopping face-first into the sodden ground. The Americans had held fire until such close range that there had not even been a need to aim, an effect Patrick knew was magnified by the fact that the militiamen had been ordered to load buck-and-ball ammunition, turning rifles into shotguns. The whole length of the American line was enveloped in billowing smoke as the shooting became increasingly chaotic with men not waiting for orderly volleys but simply firing at will.

A cluster of redcoats were able to reach the ditch in front of the breastwork. Ladders to scale the ditch and gain the parapet were brought forward, but few of their bearers were able to get close. British infantry either tried to hug the ground or the walls of the ditch, but neither provided any security from the lead being poured into them from the muskets of the militia. Soon, the smoke at the point where the British had entered the ditch became too thick for Patrick to see much more.

A further regiment of redcoats was dashing forward in support of the first, similarly being shredded by grapeshot and musketry. The attack seemed to be completely impotent, with the Americans standing four deep behind the line in some places, constantly rotating amongst themselves to fire and reload.

An odd sound then rose above the cacophony of battle. Straining his ears, Patrick heard the distinct whine of bagpipes, and swung his spyglass around to look at the highland regiment. The Scotsmen had started forward, only to abruptly stop in the center of the field, well within range of artillery fire. He could only assume that some grave miscommunication had taken place, as no commander in his right mind would senselessly leave his men standing on open ground while under fire. Despite the galling fire felling soldiers all along their line, the Scotsmen never wavered. Eventually a group of mounted officers arrived, waving their hats in the air, obviously encouraging them forward. To Patrick's horror, the highlanders began moving diagonally across the field, making for the same position the other British regiments were stubbornly trying to break through.

The result was slaughter. Walking across the front of so many artillery pieces left them more exposed than the other columns that had charged the American line head on. Seeing so many men being struck down began to churn his stomach, and he turned away from the ugly scene.

With his back to the fighting, he continued to give orders to the men manning the *Louisiana's* guns, though they were redundant as the men knew what they were doing. The seamen were mostly silent, going about their work methodically. Patrick was not sure if this silence was brought on by similar feelings of disgust, or simply men engrossed in their jobs. One or two enthusiastic individuals nevertheless whooped and cheered their fellows ashore, but any feeling of jubilation did not spread throughout the crew.

Eventually the firing began to die down, and Patrick turned to look back at the battlefield. The empty field was carpeted with dots of red, some writhing in agony, others motionless. Scores of men were staggering to the rear, limping, supporting wounded fellows, or just wearily stumbling across the field. Nearer to the American line, survivors from the assault who could not retreat threw down their muskets and put up their hands in surrender. A few Americans went over the earthworks with bayonets fixed to prod them into captivity.

"Good God," someone on deck breathed as everything slowly quieted.

Patrick hung his head, almost feeling ashamed at what had transpired. *That wasn't a battle, it was a massacre*, he thought, shaking his head.

"Sir!" a hand shouted out. "There's another British column on the far side of the river!"

The eyes of all those on deck turned downriver. The fog had clung to the water longer than it had over the battlefield, and the Americans could only just make out a line of red moving along the distant riverbank. Some of Jackson's artillerymen did not wait for orders and pivoted their cannons to lob shot across the river. Likewise, the crew of the *Louisiana* shifted to man the guns on the opposite side of the ship.

Once again extending his spyglass, Patrick scanned the far bank. The Americans had erected a pair of defensive lines on the opposite side of the Mississippi similar to Line Jackson, with the enfilading artillery emplacements between them. The lines had been little more than a precaution against a flanking attack and were not as thickly manned as Jackson's primary earthworks. Most of the men posted to the west bank were militia, with a smattering of Navy and Marine personnel, mostly drawn from the former crew of the *Carolina*. He could not help feeling apprehensive knowing that Spencer was among them.

The first shot from the *Louisiana* screeched through the air, only to land short of its target and plunk into the river. The Midshipman barked out the order for the next gun to correct the range, and the next round was fired. Where it went could not be determined, though they could see that Commodore Patterson had already turned some of his guns around to face the immediate threat.

However, before they could even get a shot off, the militia holding the first line fired a disorganized volley and fled, crossing in front of Patterson's guns and preventing them from firing. With several hundred redcoats bearing down on them, Patrick observed the sailors and Marines hurriedly spiking their guns and throwing their gunpowder in the river before falling back on the second line.

Undercut by the militia again, Patrick thought seeing the militiamen streaming back toward the next defensive line. He openly growled, remembering how the militia had deserted the sailors and Marines in a similar fashion on the field of Bladensburg several months before. *At least it appears we haven't taken many casualties. Spencer best be safe. I don't want to face the wrath of two women should he be harmed.*

"Keep the fire on those fellows hot," Patrick told the gunners, pointing at the advancing British. "We need to keep them away from seizing those cannons and allow our men a chance to fall back." The men of the *Louisiana* nodded, and opened fire, keeping up a brisk pace, hoping to frustrate the British attempts to turn the American's guns on Jackson's line. Aside from the occasional lucky long shot, most of the rounds did little more than send redcoats diving for cover.

Even with British soldiers now seizing the river batteries, it became very quiet once more. There was the sound of some scattered firing on the far left, which Patrick presumed was a tardy attempt by the British to send men through the cypress swamp to flank the Americans. However, the defenses extended so far along the canal that it would have been impractical for any force to reach the flank trudging through freezing knee-deep water. Meanwhile, the main field of battle was virtually silent, aside from the moaning of the wounded crying out for relief.

Returning his attention to the opposite shore, Patrick noticed that the British were clearly unable to get the captured guns into action. *They needn't bother at this point*, he thought, casting his eyes on the carpet of red covering the field in front of Line Jackson. He looked then at the men manning the guns of the *Louisiana*. Even though they continued to serve their pieces, he could tell they were becoming annoyed with the futility of trying to do any damage against the redcoats on the opposite bank.

"Cease fire," he finally ordered, and then men fired off the last of their shots to clear their guns. There were a few jeers audible from the British on the far side of the river as they realized the Americans had stopped shooting. Giving up on returning fire, they dispersed to pillage the nearby militia encampments.

Patrick exhaled, his breath no longer freezing in the cold due to the heat from the nearby cannons. He looked down at his hand, now calm, and flexed it. *Remarkable how it comes and goes*, he thought. Looking up, he saw the men leaning on the rails or gun carriages, most wearing either a weary or confused expression.

"How long did that last?" Patrick asked, turning to the Midshipman on deck. The younger man went over to the ship's bell, checking the hourglass on its hooks and then asking the Quartermaster to show him the log.

"I would estimate roughly one half-hour, Sir," the young man said.

Patrick sighed and shook his head. *So much carnage in such a short time.*

"Pardon me, Sir," the Midshipman piped up again. "What will happen now?

Patrick looked back over the battlefield. "Nothing," he said quietly. "If all those bodies are any indication, I believe we've won. It's over."

Chapter 5

April 1815, New Orleans, Louisiana

    The battle was indeed over. The British force that had overrun the river batteries on the west bank realized that, despite their success, continuing the fight was pointless, and retreated late in the day. The next night the men of Jackson's command heard a distant thundering of cannon fire, and the flashes of a barrage downriver. Messengers soon came galloping into New Orleans with news that the British fleet had tried to force a passage passed Fort St. Phillip, to no avail.

    The aftermath of the battle was decidedly unpleasant. There were hundreds of British slain, including the commanding general, Pakenham. Most would be buried in a mass grave, while the wounded were brought into the city and tended to by compassionate civilians. Likewise, hundreds of British soldiers had been captured, many of them veterans of campaigns against France and claimed the battle was the worst they had ever seen. American casualties were shockingly light, about only a dozen killed.

    New Orleans celebrated, the church bells ringing out before the clock had even struck noon. The defenders were greeted by cheering civilians as they reentered the city and lavished with food and drink. Though the British remained in the area for another two weeks, their army had been shattered, and their navy blunted. They departed toward the end of the month, with later reports saying that the British were striking fortifications in the vicinity of Mobile Bay. No further action was taken, as news soon arrived from Europe that the belligerents had signed a peace treaty in Ghent, Belgium.

    "It was all for nothing," Patrick lamented to Anna as they strolled arm in arm through the Place d'Arms. He had finished his duties for the day and wanted to take advantage of the sunny and mild spring weather to enjoy a quiet afternoon with his wife. "The treaty was signed on December 26th. We didn't fight the main engagement until January 8th!" He stopped and shook his head. "I never thought I'd feel sorry for the British, but good God, all those men! They all died for nothing. We killed them all, for a war that was already over."

"Patrick, you can't think that way," she replied, placing her hand on his chest. "Whether they had signed the treaty or not, it hadn't ended here. Until they had received word, the British would continue their attack. For all we know, if they had won, they might have abrogated the treaty."

Patrick shook his head again. "You know the British wanted an end to the war as much as we did."

Anna sighed, having become accustomed to Patrick's maudlin thoughts ever since the battle had ended. She patted his arm gently. "There's no sense in dwelling on it, love. It's in the past and can't be changed. The only thing you can do is move on."

He opened his mouth to speak but she held her hand up to silence him. "Yes, I do know what it's like. I may not have dealt as much death as you have, but you know the awful things I've done. You move on and look to what's ahead." She paused to sigh again. "Now, have you heard any news about your next assignment?" she asked, wisely changing the subject.

"No, I'm rather surprised," Patrick said, with a hint of disappointment. "A pair of new ships for the squadron arrived in port this morning, but I've not heard anything." There had been little to do since the news of peace had reached the city. The militia had disbanded and gone back to their homes, with only a handful of regulars remaining. Jackson had departed as well, feted as a hero all across the country, leaving Governor Claiborne to brood over being robbed of a chance for glory.

With the vessels of Commodore Patterson's squadron depleted, most of the sailors and Marines were ashore drilling incessantly and drinking the moment they went off duty. Patrick for the most part spent his mornings seeing to the squadron's paperwork, after which he enjoyed the remainder of his days with Anna. Deprived the chance upon their marriage of anything more than the briefest intimacy, they now made love constantly, using their time together as something of a proper honeymoon.

"Word has come down that a squadron is being readied to sail to the Mediterranean," he explained. "Seems the Barbary pirates are at it again, Algiers this time. Decatur is rumored to be in command,

and I would expect he'd want me along seeing as I served under him the first time. You know, having an experienced hand and all that." Anna nodded in return, fully understanding. "I'm also probably the only officer in the Navy who can speak a word of Greek or Arabic, which would be useful."

Anna tilted her head at him and gave a slight smile. "I know you're eager to be off doing something new, but I'm quite enjoying finally spending some time with you. I for one hope you stay in home waters."

Patrick frowned for a moment as he considered it. "Yes, you're right. I don't need to be charging off to the other side of the world right now. We have each other to think about. I make a fair amount on an officer's salary, but where would we live?"

"I did enjoy our time in Washington City," she answered. "And I know you'll want to help support Sam and her little ones."

Patrick nodded. "It's the least I can do. Tom and Sam were the only family I've ever had. I'm obligated to them. I did tell you I'd been leaving her my wages?"

"You did," she answered. "I do believe I may be able to help financially. You see, the King's ministers owe me a substantial sum for my services."

"How substantial?" asked Patrick.

Anna made a frown and raised an eyebrow as she contemplated. "After the exchange rate, I would estimate it to be a little over three thousand dollars."

"Three thousand!" he blurted out, quickly looking over his shoulder to see if anyone in the plaza had noticed.

Anna only shrugged and sheepishly grinned at him. "I'm a talented negotiator."

Patrick chuckled. "I wonder what Lord Liverpool's reaction would be to finding out a defector made off with thousands of pounds from the Royal Exchequer?"

"Oh, between a mad King, a fat Prince, and Bonaparte escaping from Elba, I'd say he has more important matters at hand." She then stopped and turned to face him. "You won't like this, but I'll have to sail for Kingston in Jamaica to obtain it. There's a ship leaving tomorrow, it's the first to Jamaica since the peace. They would expect I'd make a report at the earliest opportunity."

Patrick took in a breath and sighed with annoyance. "You should have told me sooner."

"I'm sorry," she said, placing her hand on his chest. "I only saw the posting this morning. It won't be long. I can be back in less than a month."

Patrick squeezed her hand. "Well, if it's only that, and you'll return with three thousand dollars, I'll abide," he said with a slight smile.

Continuing their walk, as they neared the waterfront, they spied the steamboat that had first brought him downriver to New Orleans chugging along, puffing smoke, and preparing to dock. They watched the technological marvel with curiosity as the crew maneuvered the unwieldy craft next to the dock and proceeded to tie her up. Several passengers then began to disembark.

Anna tapped Patrick's arm. "Is that…?" she began to ask, pointing to a woman who had stepped off the steamboat and onto the dock.

Patrick squinted. "I believe it is," he answered with astonishment. He then made a gesture to suggest they make for the dock, and they quickened their pace. As they neared, the tall, brown haired, and dark eyed woman they had recognized spotted them and gave a broad smile.

"Lieutenant Sullivan! Miss Anna!" she called out cheerfully, waving to them. It was Martha, the elder of the two sisters Spencer had been romantically entangled with. Neither Patrick nor Anna knew either of the girls well, indeed they had not even learned the girls' surname.

As the young woman walked toward them, Patrick realized that she was accompanied by a darker skinned girl who was a few years younger. The girl was clearly of mixed heritage and knowing that Martha's father was a congressman from Maryland, he immediately assumed her to be an enslaved maid.

"I'm so glad to see you both safe!" she said, still beaming, while the other girl with the dark complexion smiled gently as well. "Especially you, Miss Anna. Sarah has been beside herself knowing all the grief she caused you," she went on, referring to how her younger sister had given away Anna's identity to a Spanish agent the previous summer in Washington City.

Anna cordially waved off the young woman's concerns. "She has nothing to feel guilty about, I know she was coerced."

Martha let out a sigh of relief. "She'll be most happy to hear that. Unfortunately, she could not come with me, she wished to apologize in person."

"Please write her that her apology is accepted," Anna responded. She then held up her left hand and showed off her plain wedding band. "It's Mrs. Anna now," she joked with a laugh.

Martha's eyes widened and her smile broadened. "How wonderful! Congratulations to you both!" She then leaned forward and embraced Anna. Stepping back, she gestured to the younger girl beside her. "Oh, do forgive me. This is Rebecca, she's my —"

Martha stopped midsentence, very obviously catching herself from saying what she had originally intended. "She's my lady's maid," she finished, unconvincingly, whilst Rebecca giggled. Patrick and Anna glanced at each other but said nothing.

Martha then reached into her handbag and pulled out an envelope. "Oh, Lieutenant, I'm glad I found you so quickly. Mrs. Jones has been receiving your letters but from what you had written it seemed you weren't receiving hers."

"I reckon the mail sees me as a hard man to find," he joked, taking the offered envelope. "I trust she and the newborn are well?"

Martha nodded with a smile. "A gorgeous little girl that looks just like her. She named her Mary after her mother."

"I'm relieved to hear. I want to thank you and your sister for what you've done for her the last few months. Now, I can only assume you've come all this way to see Phillip?" asked Patrick.

"Oh yes, I could not bear going without seeing him any longer. I also bring some rather sad news for him. You see my sister Sarah is now betrothed, and I thought it only right he should find out from me."

"Betrothed?" asked Anna. "So quickly?"

Martha rolled her eyes. "Yes, it was my father's idea. The young man is nice enough, and wealthy of course. He's the son of a plantation owner in the Shenandoah valley. My father hopes to build political connections. My sister is rather disappointed."

"Understandable," said Patrick. "Spencer will be delighted to see you at last though. He's pined ceaselessly every day. He's lodging at a boarding house on Royal Street, near the corner with St. Phillip."

Martha smiled again. "St. Phillip. Should be easy to remember." As she started to walk away, Patrick and Anna overheard her say to the other girl, "I think you'll like him, Becky."

Once the two young women were out of earshot, Anna commented, "That girl was not a lady's maid."

"Certainly not," agreed Patrick. "I wonder what all that is about?"

Before Anna could answer, he heard someone calling out, "Lieutenant Sullivan!" and saw a naval rating come running down the dock from where the *Louisiana* was moored.

"Commodore Patterson's compliments, Sir," the man began. "You are ordered to report to his cabin aboard the *Louisiana* immediately."

"Understood," he responded. "Tell the Commodore I'll be along presently." He then turned to Anna. "I'm sorry, dearest, but duty calls."

Anna kissed his cheek. "You know where to find me," she said with a wink, and headed off across the plaza toward the hotel.

Patrick briskly walked along the dock to the *Louisiana*. He had not paid much attention to the two new ships that had arrived, but now saw that they were a pair of two masted brigs. The first was named *Firefly*, a name he did not recognize. The other was a name he could not forget.

"The *Enterprise*?" he said to himself, passing by the ship's stern as he continued on his way to the *Louisiana*. She looked different than the last time he had seen her. Originally a schooner, she had been refitted as a brig before the war. He smiled with fond memories, as the *Enterprise* was the first American ship he had served aboard. Stephen Decatur had been her commanding officer then, when he had rescued Patrick, Tom, and Sam from impressment aboard a British frigate during the Barbary War.

Hurrying aboard the *Louisiana*, he was ushered below deck to Commodore Patterson's cabin. After being announced to Patterson by the ship's steward, he entered the cabin and immediately saluted the two senior officers present within.

"Captain Porter, Sir," he began with a grin. "It's good to see you again."

The curly haired Porter returned the salute and then shook Patrick's hand. "Likewise, Lieutenant," he answered. Porter was to have been the captain of Patrick's previous ship, the USS *Columbia*. Sadly, the unfinished frigate had to be destroyed before the British could capture it when they attacked the District of Columbia.

"I'd not even been informed you had arrived," said Patrick, trying not to be too inquisitive.

"No," said Porter succinctly. "I'm sure you're puzzled to see the *Enterprise* as well?"

"Yes, Sir," answered Patrick. "Last I heard she was in Wilmington preparing to join Captain Decatur's squadron bound for Algiers."

Porter chuckled. "That's what we told the papers. Damned press can never be relied upon to keep a secret. Which is why I'm here, a matter of some secrecy, Lieutenant." Porter and Patrick took a seat while Commodore Patterson stretched out a chart on his desk before them.

"We have received word that one of our ships is continuing to attack British merchantmen in the eastern Caribbean," spoke Porter, gravely.

"Is it possible they've not gotten word of the end of the war?" asked Patrick.

Patterson shook his head. "No. The isles heard about the peace before we did. Any ship still attacking merchantmen or man-of-war in those waters would have been informed by their opponent. Furthermore, there are only four ships that could not have received word of the peace by this point. Three of them, *Hornet*, *Tom Bowline*, and *Peacock* were sailing together for the South Atlantic, and could even be in the Indian Ocean by now. Even if they had returned to the Caribbean they would have been informed by now. That just leaves us with one option remaining."

"The USS *Wasp*," Porter concluded. "She was last sighted in September returning from European waters. The prizes she had taken all reached our harbors by December, but we've had no word from the *Wasp* herself since. However, what accounts we have received from British and Spanish witnesses speak of a ship matching her description."

"Given this turn of events, we can only guess at a few assumptions," said Patterson. "Master Commandant Blakely could have taken too much a liking for capturing prizes and has chosen the path of piracy. We can all but dismiss this option as Blakely has been far too honorable an officer to realistically believe this. A more unsavory scenario would have his crew mutinying and becoming pirates. This is more plausible, but also unlikely. Blakely never had a reputation for mistreating his men. A last option could be that the *Wasp* was at some point taken in battle by a pirate or privateer, and her captors now use her to sow confusion among her victims."

"Is there any chance it could be one of our privateers, Sir?" asked Patrick.

Patterson shook his head. "If it is, they're pirates now, regardless of circumstances. All Letters of Marque expired at the end of hostilities. Any ship captain that continues action after receiving word of the peace makes himself an outlaw."

"Either way, we must find this ship, and quickly," Porter commented. "This has the potential to become a diplomatic disaster. We absolutely cannot risk a resumption of the war with Britain. Our economy is in tatters, and national unity has been threatened by the New England Federalists. Furthermore, this could quite quickly draw other nations into conflict with us. The Spanish have made complaints that some of their ships have been attacked at well."

Porter stood up and moved over to Patterson's desk. "The Caribbean will soon be in a state of chaos. The British occupied most French possessions and other minor powers during the late war, but now are relinquishing them without those countries being able to properly secure them." The Captain stabbed at the map with his index finger, running it over the line of islands making up the Lesser Antilles. "The French are slowing moving back into their colonies, but with the recent news that Bonaparte has returned to power, the British could invade them again. Then we have Spanish colonies breaking off from Spanish rule. A power vacuum is about to develop here."

Looking up at Patrick he said, "European powers will be eager to pick the corpse of the Spanish Empire clean like a pack of vultures. We cannot invite any excuse for them to return to the western hemisphere to interfere with our matters."

Porter reached within his uniform jacket and retrieved a thick envelope. "Lieutenant, you are being tasked with a mission of considerable secrecy. Secretary Monroe has been in contact with Spanish and British authorities in the Caribbean. They have agreed that despite our antipathy for each other, we shall work together to search for the interloper before permanent damage can be done."

Captain Porter handed the envelope to Patrick. "As I said Lieutenant, this is a mission of the strictest secrecy. Among our government officers, only the President and Secretary Monroe are aware of it as we cannot risk word of it becoming public. Likewise, the Spanish Governor of Havana and the Admiral of the British West Indies Squadron are suppressing news of these attacks. You were personally recommended by Secretary Monroe of this assignment as he said you had prior experience with clandestine matters?"

Patrick nodded slowly. "Yes, Sir," he said simply, cautious to not elaborate.

"Very well," answered Porter. "Your orders are to take immediate command of the USS *Enterprise* and sail for San Juan, on the island of Porto Rico. There you will meet with the commander of the Spanish garrison, as well as the commander of a British ship with whom you will be operating in consort with."

Porter circled a portion of the map to the east of Porto Rico with his finger. "From what information we have obtained, majority of the attacks are taking place in the Leeward Islands."

Patrick nodded examining the map. "That would be an ideal place for a pirate to operate. I've been to the islands before, and I recall there were numerous bays and inlets that would offer shelter. The chain itself is almost a maze."

"In addition to being sparsely populated," said Porter. "A lone vessel could move from inlet to inlet at night, strike a passing victim during the day, and use the multitude of islands to screen their escape to their next anchorage. It's a perfect hunting ground, particularly with no navy from any country in a position to chase them."

He tapped the envelope in Patrick's hand. "I'm giving you the skeleton crew that brought the *Enterprise* here from Wilmington, as well as a few extra hands from the *Firefly*. I have a Bosun's Mate from the *Wasp* that returned on one of her prizes. He'll be along to help identify the ship should you come across her. You'll have to fill out the remainder of the ranks yourself. I've no spare officers to give you either."

"I can see to that," spoke up Patterson. "I can give you Lieutenant Forester. He was taken prisoner at Lake Borgne with Catesby Jones. He's a quiet man, religious too from what I've heard. I know you're a Papist, so I thought I'd warn you in case there's any friction."

"Thank you, Sir," answered Patrick. "I'd like Midshipman Spencer along as well. He's been with me for almost a year, and I'd like to finally give him a chance to see some sea duty."

"Very well," replied Patterson with a nod. "The victualing yard will be open to you. We've plenty of leftover powder and shot, so take as much as you like. I'll cover your expenses for the wardroom so you don't have to pay out of your own pocket. Charts, instruments, and everything else should already be aboard."

"Thank you, Sir," Patrick repeated, grateful for his commander's generosity.

Porter thrust forward his hand, which Patrick shook. "Good luck, Sullivan. I've left more detailed information in your orders. I recall you speak several languages, correct?"

"Yes, Sir," he answered with a nod.

"Good, you may have need of it. You wouldn't be amiss flattering the Spanish in their own tongue. You'll want to steer clear of Jamaica so as not to give the British reason to think we're poking around their naval facilities now that the war is over. They'll be on the alert for a lone American ship, so best not give them a reason to start shooting. You may have as much to worry about restarting the war yourself as you do of this mystery ship."

"I understand, Sir," Patrick replied, trying to project an air of confidence to reassure his superiors.

"Very well," concluded Porter. "Provision and recruit tomorrow and you can be on your way the day after. Good hunting, Lieutenant."

"And that was all he told you?" asked Anna as they walked down Bourbon Street later that evening.

"It was about all he could tell me," Patrick answered with a shrug. "I have sealed orders, but I'm not permitted to open them until we're underway. I don't think there will be much to add until I get to San Juan."

A few moments later they arrived at the restaurant Spencer had previously told them about, finding Martha waiting outside.

"Good evening, Lieutenant, Mrs. Sullivan," she hailed them. "Phillip is just inside speaking to the owner. He wanted to inquire if we could obtain a private room. Thank you kindly for your invitation to dine with you."

"You're most welcome," answered Patrick. "You didn't think we would have shoved off without having a night out do you? Have you seen another officer hereabouts? I invited my new first officer to join us as well." He then leaned over to Anna and added in an aside, "I'll have words with that gunner's mate I entrusted with the invitation if he never received it."

Martha pointed within the door. "Oh, I saw another naval officer enter just a minute or two before you arrived. Dark haired fellow."

"Ah, this must be him," said Patrick as the man Martha had spoken of came back through the door.

"Lieutenant Commandant Sullivan?" the officer asked meekly, saluting. He was a short man, slightly built, with sad looking eyes. He appeared quite harmless, not fighting material at all.

"Aye," said Patrick. "You must be Lieutenant Forester."

"Yes, Sir," he nervously replied, dropping his salute and hurriedly shaking Patrick's offered hand.

"I'm glad you could join us this evening," Patrick told him in a tone that he hoped would calm the man. "May I present my wife." Anna gave a slight curtsy in response. "And this is Mister Spencer's lady, Miss Martha…"

"Sir! Up here!" called out Spencer from the balcony above them. The Midshipman smiled down cheerfully and waved. "The proprietor has furnished a private room for us!"

Patrick waved back, silently thankful that he had been saved from embarrassment of his ignorance of Martha's surname. "We'll be up presently." He then turned to Lieutenant Forester. "Lieutenant, since it appears that Mister Spencer will be waiting upstairs, would you kindly escort my wife while I see to the young lady?"

"Yes, Sir, of course," he stammered. Anna blushed and covered her mouth to keep from laughing at his discomfort. She put his arm around his, whispered a kind word to him that Patrick did not hear, and entered the restaurant.

Patrick held his arm at an angle and Martha likewise hooked hers through his. "Thank you, Lieutenant," she said. As they entered through the doorway, she leaned closer to speak. "I feel I must explain events from last summer, Lieutenant," she said in hushed tones. "I know that Mrs. Sullivan has said she forgives my sister for the trouble she caused, but I would feel more at ease if you understood fully."

"By all means, continue," said Patrick.

Martha took a breath before answering. "That Spanish spy who was hunting your wife, he discovered a secret about my family, and used it to ensure my sister's cooperation."

"Yes, my wife told me as much."

Stopping at the back of the restaurant at the foot of the stairs, Martha turned to him. "I saw that you were suspicious of Rebecca this morning when we arrived. You see, Becky is my half-sister."

Patrick said nothing but nodded. He and Anna had surmised that something was amiss and was not entirely surprised by the revelation. It was common knowledge many plantation owners carried on dalliances with their slaves.

"You see," Martha continued, "near on twenty years ago, my father left on business to Europe for over a year. In that time, my mother had an affair with one of the slaves on our plantation, and Becky resulted from it. My father of course has no knowledge, and heaven knows what would happen if he ever did. He is not a kind man Lieutenant, as you might have guessed when I told you of how Sarah was now betrothed. It was the threat of ruination to my family that the Spaniard used against my sister. I cannot risk that happening again. I have always protected Becky, and convinced my father to make her my lady's maid. When I am wed, he will bequeath her to me, and the very second after that she will be free."

Patrick motioned for them to continue walking up the stairs. "Is that why you have come so far to see Phillip? To speed him along with his intentions?"

Martha looked at Patrick. "I will not lie, Lieutenant, that it has been a motive. I hope you will not think less of me for it, as my feeling for Phillip are genuine. And now my father has spared him the pain of choosing between myself and Sarah."

"No, I will not fault you for such a thing," Patrick said, and her face brightened. "I do hope you've told him all of this."

She hesitated before answering. "Not yet. But I shall."

Finally arriving upstairs, Patrick handed Martha off to Spencer, and pulled out Anna's seat for her to sit down. "What delayed you?" she whispered.

"I'll explain later."

They sat down to the table, the windows nearby overlooking the street. The owner had already laid out glasses of madeira, and in short order servants arrived with the sample of local cuisine Spencer had previously spoken highly of, something called 'gumbo'. The ladies steered conversation for most of the evening, something Patrick was grateful for as he had little to contribute on the subjects of fashion and Martha's family's plantation.

Relief arrived when the talk turned to music. Following a compliment from Anna on Spencer's singing abilities, he inquired, "Sir, have they allotted us a fifer for the ship?"

Patrick looked up from his gumbo and shook his head. "I would consider myself fortunate if we had been given even so much as a Marine drummer. Perhaps one of the seamen will bring his own, otherwise you'll be out of luck."

"Strange that Captain Porter could find so few men for the crew," he wondered aloud.

"I believe he had little choice in the matter, given how hastily this assignment has been handed down," answered Patrick. "We sail in two days, and I've been barely able to find us more than two-thirds the *Enterprise's* standard compliment. We've no Sailing Master, no Marine officer, no Purser, no Chaplain, no Bosun, no Surgeon, the list goes on." He let out an exasperated sigh at the end of the list.

"I may be able to help in some regard," said Spencer. "I recently met a young medical student several weeks ago. We had an encounter over a game of whist and struck up a friendship. His name is Pierre Chartrand. I'm certain he would join on as ship's surgeon if I were to ask him."

Patrick nodded in the affirmative. "Very enterprising of you to think of him, Phillip."

Spencer covered his mouth, and even the stoic Forester let out a smirk at Patrick's accidental pun about their ship's name.

"Sir, should we be discussing military matters in front of the ladies?" asked the junior Lieutenant, the first words he had spoken since they had arrived.

"Oh, don't trouble yourself on my account," Anna said to him. "I'm well acquainted with military matters. I find them fascinating."

"I may not understand everything, but I have no qualms either," said Martha. She touched her hand to the side of her head. "I do unfortunately feel a headache coming on, perhaps this food is a pinch too spicy for my constitution." She looked at Spencer and joked, "Your doctor friend, does he make house calls?"

Everyone at the table chuckled. "I do regret that I believe I must retire for the evening," she went on, though Patrick noticed a furtive glance between her and Spencer hinted that she was merely making an excuse to leave the table early so they could go back to Spencer's boarding house. "I think Becky knows of a swift-acting tonic I can take for it. Lieutenant, Mrs. Sullivan, thank you for the invitation, it was a pleasure dining with you this evening."

Everyone stood up as Spencer and Martha left the table. One they had departed the room, Patrick, Anna, and Lieutenant Forester returned to their seats.

"So, Lieutenant," began Anna, evidently hoping having fewer people would convince the quiet officer to speak more. "Where are you from?"

The look he gave in response reminded Patrick of a cornered animal. "Philadelphia, ma'am," he replied simply.

"Ah, Captain Decatur and Captain Stewart are both from Philadelphia," said Patrick. "Do you know them?"

Forester shook his head, looking more nervous than before. He appeared exceedingly uncomfortable, and Patrick wondered how such a man could have sought to join the Navy in the first place.

"I've served with both of them," Patrick went on, hoping like Anna, that the conversation would help to put him at ease. "They're fine officers. I consider Decatur our very best. I'm sure you would have preferred more active service with him than chasing down lost ships in the Caribbean."

Forester seemed unable to answer at first. "Sir, I'd not seen battle before Lake Borgne," he managed to get out. "After that, and being taken by the British, I'm happy to have a quieter posting." He swallowed hard, immediately regretting how he had phrased his statement. "I hope you won't think me a coward, Sir. I never shirked my duty."

Patrick held his hand up to calm the younger man. "I understand the feeling. Truly, I do. It's not the easiest thing to speak of, as everyone expects naval officers to swagger around boasting tales of glorious deeds."

Forester relaxed a little and leaned back. *He'll come to understand*, Patrick thought. *We have to keep up appearances for civilians. They'd be horrified to see what war is really like.*

Patrick then pointed to Forester's glass. "Drink up now. I've noticed you've not touched your madeira. Mister Spencer wouldn't want you to put it to waste after he paid a pretty penny on this dinner."

Forester waved his hand hurriedly, looking a bit embarrassed. "Forgive me, Sir. I should have spared Mister Spencer the trouble. I'm a teetotaler, my father's a minister you see."

Patrick nodded. "Ah, I understand." He then downed the rest of his own madeira as Anna pointed across the table. "The silly boy's gone and lost his hat again," she said, and Patrick saw that in his haste to leave, Spencer had left his hat hanging on the knob of his chair.

Patrick chuckled. "I suppose we best return it. His boarding house isn't too far. Come along with us, Lieutenant, we have more to discuss."

Quickly gathering themselves, along with Spencer's forgotten hat, Patrick first left a large gratuity with the owner for the exemplary service that evening, and then the three of them departed, walking in the direction of Spencer's boarding house.

"Tell me, Lieutenant," said Patrick, "How are your skills at navigation?"

Forester hesitated in what Patrick noticed was quickly becoming a pattern. *That'll do no good. Can't have a man constantly pausing before giving orders. I'll have to shape him up a bit. Gently of course, I can't berate the man too much or it would have the opposite effect.*

85

"Fairly good, Sir," he spoke, making it sound as if competency were a bad thing.

"That is well," answered Patrick. "I was never the best at it myself. If we're not able to find a Sailing Master before we leave, would you be capable of handling those duties?"

For once Forester immediately responded with a firm, "Aye, Sir," and a nod. *Hmmm, I suppose he reacts better to an order*, Patrick thought as they continued walking.

It had only been a stroll of less than two blocks from the restaurant to Spencer's boarding house, and the three of them had been setting a brisk pace. As they neared, Patrick saw the windows of Spencer's room were wide open, and the moans of a woman in the throes of pleasure were emanating for the entire street to hear.

"He's at it again," said Anna with a giggle, while Forester had gone pale, clearly embarrassed. Patrick then made out the distinct moans of a second woman.

"Oh, good God! He's got them both up there at the same time!"

Having likely heard his outburst from the street below, Martha flopped into view, her hair disheveled and breathing heavily, while dangling an arm over the windowsill. She waved merrily at them and smiled

Patrick was prepared to make a quip about her headache being miraculously cured but did not get the chance as Rebecca now slunk against the edge of the window as well, giggling. Spencer at last made his appearance, popping up between the two women.

"Oh, hello, Sir," he said with a jaunty wave.

At Patrick's side, Anna snorted and covered her mouth to prevent her from dissolving into unrestrained laughter, while Forester squeaked, "Good heavens!"

Patrick looked up at the younger man and waved his tall Midshipman's hat. Spencer's eyebrows went up, and he said, "I knew I'd forgotten something. Thank you for retrieving it, Sir."

Patrick then flung the hat sideways up to the second-floor window, and Spencer deftly caught it. "As you were, Mister Spencer," he said.

Spencer smiled. "Aye, aye, Sir," he answered, jokingly putting the hat back on his head, then beckoning his companions away from the window.

"If you'll forgive me, Sir, I believe I shall retire for the evening," said Forester, who had more than his quota of excitement for the night.

Patrick nodded. "Very well, Mister Forester. Report aboard the *Enterprise* tomorrow morning at six bells." The two officers saluted each other and then Forester scampered off as if he were escaping the scene of a crime.

"Saints preserve us," Patrick muttered as he turned back to Anna. She had by now stopped giggling, but a broad smile remained on her face. "He's too decent a fellow for the Navy." She then nodded up to Spencer's window, from where further moans were echoing into the street. "The French call it 'menage a trois'."

Patrick's head whipped around to look at her. "Have you ever…"

Anna's eyes went wide. "No! Never, I swear!" She then made the sign of the cross for extra emphasis. "Propositioned on more than one occasion, but never partook."

Patrick stared at his wife in disbelief. "Really?" he asked bluntly.

Anna nodded. "I told you that the French engage in any sort of lovemaking."

Patrick chuckled. "You also said you would share some lurid stories from the Peninsula."

Anna playfully raised an eyebrow. She stepped forward, grasped the lapels on his jacket and forcefully kissed him. "Well, seeing as starting tomorrow we're going to be spending a few more weeks apart, I suppose tonight might make for a good start."

Patrick smiled back and kissed her. He then put his arm around her, and they swiftly made their way back to their room.

Chapter 6

April 1815, USS *Enterprise* in the Gulf of Mexico

After seeing Anna off at the dock the next morning, Patrick and the other officers spent the remainder of the day scrambling to ready the ship for sea. As he had feared, they were unable to find a warrant officer suitable to take on the duties of the Sailing Master, leaving Forester in charge of navigation. They also had no Purser, though none of them considered it any great loss as this was expected to be a short cruise and the crew were paid two months wages in advance. The problem of finding a Boatswain was solved after Patrick had interviewed the Boatswain's Mate from the *Wasp*, a man named Barnes. He had served as the Boatswain on one of the *Wasp's* prizes that had made it safely back to port and was eager to be of use rather than merely being along as an observer.

They made sail that evening in order to take advantage of the outgoing tide in the morning once they reached the Gulf of Mexico. While they had been able to scrounge enough men in their final day ashore to bump the crew compliment as high as three-quarters of full strength, the situation was less than optimal. Their hurried departure meant that the officers had not even the time to properly set the watches, nor had Patrick the opportunity to speak with Spencer's new friend, Chartrand the doctor.

"I assure you, Captain, the battle at New Orleans afforded me a rude introduction to the medicine of war," Chartrand said to Patrick as they and the other officers sat in the Captain's Cabin aboard the *Enterprise*. The doctor was young of course, with wavy light brown hair and a narrow face which matched his thin frame, very much giving the appearance of an intellectual. Despite his Creole roots, he did not speak with a French accent, evidence that he had received his schooling elsewhere in the country.

Patrick's eyebrows went up and he nodded in agreement. "That battle would have been a rude introduction to anyone." He then paused and added, "Not Captain, by the way, I'm merely a Lieutenant Commandant."

"As you wish," Chartrand replied a bit curtly, also omitting to address Patrick as 'Sir'.

"I'm only clarifying," explained Patrick with a wave of his hand, not wanting the man to believe he was being rude. "As the ship's surgeon, you lie outside the normal standards of military discipline, so you may address me however you wish."

"Very well," Chartrand responded. "As I was saying, I have experience of warlike wounds. Although the subject was not something I encountered in my studies, I made sure to purchase a copy of Sir Gilbert Blane's *'Observations on the Diseases of Seamen'* yesterday. I will begin to familiarize myself with it at once."

"Splendid, thank you, doctor," said Patrick. "You may be dismissed."

The doctor nodded and stood up to exit the cabin. As he neared the door, Patrick spoke again. "One last item I think you may find helpful, doctor. I would not presume to tell you how to do your job, but at the Battle of Lake Erie I learned from our surgeon there that he noticed a marked decrease in the incidence of infection if he boiled his instruments in water before using them."

Chartrand looked off to the side for a moment as he considered it, nodding, and giving a slight shrug as he judged the advice sound enough. "I shall keep that in mind, Lieutenant Commandant." He then departed the cabin.

Looking to Spencer, Patrick said, "He seems a bit stiff."

"I'm sure he's just getting accustomed to military formality, Sir," answered Spencer. "He's quite an intelligent fellow."

"I should hope so if he's a doctor," said Latimer, the other Midshipman, eliciting laughter from the others.

"At the very least, gentlemen," said Patrick, "we have enough officers to crew the ship, even if it is the bare minimum. Mister Spencer, you had best get on deck as you're the current officer of the watch. You as well, Mister Latimer, I want you observing Mister Spencer."

"Aye, aye, Sir," they both answered, and left the cabin.

Turning his attention to Forester, he then said, "I so badly wish we could have gotten one more officer. The pair of them have barely had any sea duty."

Forester looked concerned at Patrick's words but did not say anything. Getting no immediate response from the man, he went on, "Porter gave me Latimer's papers. He only gained a warrant in February right before we received word the war had ended. Since then, he's only served aboard the *Firefly*. I fear he'll be a wastrel having joined the Navy only to serve in peacetime."

Forester nodded, again saying nothing. Patrick could not be sure if the man was timid or thoughtful. *Tom always used to call me quiet and bookish, but I was never this bad!* Patrick then shifted his chart of the Caribbean around and held up the envelope Porter had given him containing their sealed orders.

"These are Captain Porter's written orders," he said, handing them over to the Lieutenant. "I want you to look them over for yourself. In addition, he gave me some documents that provided some insight into what we might be dealing with."

Forester took the envelope and pulled out the papers. He started reading through them as Patrick continued to talk. "The British have seen roughly a dozen merchant ships disappear in the area surrounding the leeward islands. At least three of these captures took place within sight of land, one at Anguilla, a second near Saint Kitts, and the third near Virgin Gorda." He circled the corner where the island chain curved from east to south. "The Spanish also report three ships lost, with one capture sighted near Culebra." He tapped the island sitting between Spanish Porto Rico and the Danish West Indies. "In every instance, the witnesses ashore described a ship resembling the *Wasp*, and flying the American flag."

Forester leaned forward and rubbed his chin, looking over the map, and then looking back to the documents Patrick had given him. Still, he said nothing.

"We have our orders to meet with a Spanish naval officer, Captain Luis Alvarez, in San Juan. We'll also be meeting the captain of a British vessel, the sloop HMS *Athena*. I've not been told his identity, but we'll be operating in conjunction with them. As we cannot be certain of whom exactly is capturing these ships, we are instructed to treat any suspicious ships as hostile, and to engage any and all pirates wherever we may find them."

Forester again nodded, with more determination, showing that he had absorbed the information. He stubbornly remained silent.

"Any questions?" asked Patrick.

Forester shook his head. "No, Sir," he finally spoke.

"Very well, dismissed."

Forester started for the door, then stopped. "Sir, what time shall I assemble the hands?"

Patrick looked up at him and furrowed his eyebrows. "Assemble them for what?"

"Sunday service, Sir," he said plainly.

Patrick's eyebrows shot up. "Oh, that is right, it's a Sunday, isn't it?" he said, rhetorically. "I do hate to impose upon you, Mister Forester, given that you've taken on so many other roles, but would you see to this as well? I don't believe most of the men would care for my religious beliefs."

"Yes, Sir, of course," Forester answered. He started for the door again and paused once more, slowly turning with a grave look on his face. "Pardon for the intrusion, Sir, but... are you not a believer?"

"What?" asked Patrick, jerking his head up from the charts on the table. "Oh, far worse than that I'm afraid. I'm a Catholic."

Forester stared at him blankly for a moment, until he finally processed the comment. He then gave an uncharacteristic smile. "Oh, very cheeky, Sir."

Patrick smiled back in good humor. "They told me you were of a religious bent. I wasn't sure how you'd take the notion of serving under a 'Bloody Papist'."

Forester shrugged. "We're all brothers in Christ, Sir. We just have different opinions as to how best to go about it."

"That's a very enlightened view, Lieutenant."

Forester smiled again. "My father would disagree of course, preaching fire and brimstone. We don't see eye to eye on many things though."

Patrick stood. "I wish I could say I understand, but I lost my father at a young age. You go on deck and sound the call for 'all hands.' I'll be above shortly."

Forester departed the cabin, allowing Patrick time to tidy up his charts and papers. He soon heard the Boatswain's whistle calling all hands to assemble. Picking up his cocked hat, he straightened his uniform jacket and then exited the cabin and walked up to the quarterdeck.

The crew was assembled in the space before the ship's wheel. It was not a large crew, barely one hundred men, which was of course still not full strength. Taking up a position next to the ship's wheel, he scanned their faces. It was the first time he had been given to see all of them at once and wanted to quickly get a look at them. They were almost all invariably young, and a fairly homogenous mix of white New Englanders, despite the odd black sailor or creole signed on in New Orleans. He soon began to feel all of their eyes on him in turn. *So, this is what command feels like*, he thought. *Everyone watching you, looking for you to lead, ready to either follow you into hell if you're good, or stab you in the back if you're poor.*

Patrick cleared his throat and said, "Good morning, gentlemen." There were a few snickers and looks between the hands at being called 'gentlemen'. "I am Lieutenant Commandant Sullivan. In a few moments, I will be informing you of our orders for this cruise. Before we begin, our First Lieutenant, Mister Forester, will be acting as chaplain and conducting our Sunday service."

The crew promptly doffed their hats, as Forester opened his personal Bible. He read a short passage from the Letter of Saint Paul to the Romans about being subject to the laws of the government. Despite his apparent unease at speaking in front of a crowd, Forester then gave a thought-provoking sermon on the men's duty to uphold the laws of the sea, to defend the helpless from lawbreakers and restore order in the aftermath of war. Once finished, he tucked his Bible under his arm and took a step back, a look of relief washing over him now that it was over.

Returning his hat to his head along with everyone else, Patrick stepped forward again. "Thank you, Mister Forester." *He did manage to set the tone by speaking of restoring order and bringing justice to the lawless*, he thought. "Now that we are underway, I am able to disclose the nature of our mission. As you might have guessed from rumors, as well as Mister Forester's sermon, we are tasked with hunting down pirates in Caribbean waters."

Judging from the looks the crew gave in return, most had already come to this assumption. He then continued, "However, we do have orders to seek out one ship in particular. There are fears that the USS *Wasp*, which has gone missing, is now a pirate vessel, hunting prey in the leeward islands. Whether her crew has chosen this, or she was taken in battle is not known. What is known is that a ship reported to be her has been seen attacking and seizing both British and Spanish ships. With the peace between ourselves and Britain so fresh, our government is concerned that if these attacks continue, it will lead to a resumption of hostilities."

The men's expressions now turned graver, no doubt many of them uneasy at the thought of having to hunt down fellow Americans. Others seemed more perturbed that their easy cruise of home waters could be interrupted by combat with pirates.

"Our orders also state that we will be working in consort with a British vessel to find this renegade." There were now a few murmurs, and more than a few scowls, but a quick bark from Barnes to remain silent put them in their place. "I know that many of you will not be enthused by working with our late foe, and I share your sentiments. I have no love of the English, but we have our orders nonetheless."

Patrick then turned to Barnes, the Boatswain. "There is one last article I wish to address before you are all dismissed. Mister Barnes, may I have the cat o' nine tails?"

Barnes tilted his head and raised an eyebrow that disappeared into the mop of unruly thick black hair on his head. "Sir?"

"If you please, Mister Barnes."

"Aye, aye, Sir," replied, both eyebrows going up in resignation. The Boatswain flicked his wrist at one of his mates, who ran below decks, returning a short time later with the dreaded instrument. Taking it in his hand, Barnes handed it off to Patrick, still confused as to why he would already be wanting to mete out punishment before they had even been at sea for a day. Beyond Barnes, he could see some apprehension in the faces of other men, fear that their new commander was a petty tyrant.

Patrick held up the whip. Grabbing the nine strands of knotted cord, he twisted them with one hand. He gritted his teeth, remembering the pain of having those cords slapped into his back. *1803. Has it been twelve years already?*

It had been an unforgettable beginning to life in the navy, albeit at the time the Royal Navy. A vicious Lieutenant, a man named Carlyle, had ordered him flogged after Patrick had struck a Royal Marine while he and Tom were being pressed off an American merchant ship when they were only seventeen. He had later gained other reasons for hating Carlyle, but that was the start of it, a cycle of revenge between the two that had lasted until two years ago when Carlyle finally broke under the strain of his wife's death.

Patrick took a breath. He then pitched the whip sideways over the rail into the water, resulting in a number of surprised gasps from those assembled. Looking over his men, he said, "I served before the mast. I'm not telling you this because I wish to gain favor with you, only to say I know how life is for you men. I also have a dozen scars on my back from one of those damn things. I may have a commission, but I've never had a man flogged, and I'll not stand for any other officer having you flogged. I'll halve your rations, I'll clap you in irons down in the hold, I'll lash you to the rigging. I might even keel haul you. But no man will receive a single lash aboard my ship."

Many of the men were astonished at his words. Most sailors had come to expect foul treatment, even serving under a lenient officer, so the promise of never a single flogging was unheard of. Barnes in particular looked rather glad, because as Boatswain it would be his duty to administer the punishment. The officers meanwhile only looked mildly confused, something Patrick attributed to none of them having substantial sea duty. Anyone who had been at sea as long as he had would have been shocked to see a captain throw the cat o' nine tails overboard.

After giving the crew a moment to contemplate what had happened, he simply said, "Hands dismissed."

Patrick stayed on deck through most of the day, silently observing as Forester put them through their paces. Despite his timid and soft-spoken behavior, the Lieutenant surprisingly had a booming, and growling voice when issuing commands. After every time he did though, he seemed to shrink back a bit and nervously glance around. He was proving capable, but not at all comfortable with his position.

As long as he's up to the task is what matters, Patrick thought as he looked over the charts on the desk in his cabin. Picking up his protractor compass, he averaged out the distance that the ship's speed would take over the course of a day and began plotting how long it would take to cross the Gulf of Mexico. Forester had already plotted the course, so Patrick was only interested in checking the Lieutenant's arithmetic. *He's a fine mathematician at any rate*, he concluded after seeing that Forester's figures were more accurate than his own.

There was a knock on the door to the cabin. "Come in," Patrick called out, and the ship's cook, a man named Henderson poked his head through. Normally the ship's steward was allowed to enter the captain's cabin without knocking, but they were short a steward as well, so the cook was filling in that role.

"Would you be liking anything special from the galley this evening, Sir?" Henderson asked.

Patrick looked up from his charts. "Special? Oh, I wouldn't think so." It was customary for the captain to have a better choice of food available than even the officers, with the steward preparing the rations into fine meals. Though he certainly enjoyed fine dining, Patrick hardly felt the need to bother with such a frivolity.

"What are the officers being served in the wardroom?" he asked.

"Roast chicken tonight, Sir," Henderson answered.

Patrick nodded appreciatively. "I believe I'll join them. Thank you, Henderson."

The cook gave the enlisted men's knuckled salute and backed up closing the door behind him. Patrick took a last look at his charts, set his instruments aside, and got up from his desk. He exited the cabin and proceeded forward through the officer's berth to the wardroom. He could hear some light conversation within and decided to enter without knocking.

Slowly opening the door, he saw Spencer with his feet up on the table, playing cards with Doctor Chartrand who was opposite him. Barnes the Boatswain, who despite not even being a Warrant Officer with privileges to the wardroom was also at the table, puffing on a pipe with a few cards in his hand as well. Forester sat off to the side, watching while nibbling on a chicken leg. Latimer, the other Midshipman, was absent on watch.

Barnes saw Patrick coming through the door and immediately jumped to his feet. Forester did the same, while Spencer had only managed to take his feet off the table.

Patrick held up his hand to stop them. "Don't trouble yourselves on my account gentlemen. The cook told me you were having roast chicken this evening and I rather detest eating alone." He then looked to Barnes. "Mister Barnes, Bosuns are not senior enough to enter the wardroom."

"Mister Forester and Mister Spencer invited me, Sir," he said hurriedly. "They had felt I had right to it as I was standing as officer of the watch for both dog watches."

Patrick looked briefly at Forester and Spencer. "Very well, gentlemen, I'll allow you to make your own company in the ward room as you see fit."

The other officers began returning to their seats. As Patrick moved to take a chair near Forester, Spencer asked, "Would you like us to deal you in, Sir?" He then waved his hand of cards recklessly, giving Chartrand a view of them. The doctor gave only the slightest hint in his face that he had seen the cards, and discretely readied his chips to bet more heavily.

"Not at the moment," Patrick answered. "Perhaps in a few more hands. What's the game?"

"Four card stud, Sir," said Spencer.

Patrick had played more than his fair share of card games back in his days serving before the mast. He already saw that Chartrand had all the hallmarks of a card shark. *Yes, best stay out of it for the time being*, he thought. *I'll need to watch him for a bit, then come rescue Spencer before the doctor fleeces him out of every penny.*

"Perhaps Mister Forester would care to join you?" he suggested with a glance at his First Officer.

Forester looked up, surprised he had been mentioned. "Oh, not me, Sir. Wouldn't dream of gambling."

The steward arrived, delivering more roast chicken, which Patrick now tore into, with Spencer likewise picking up a spare leg as he continued his bout with the other two men.

"Your navigation calculations were quite accurate, Mister Forester," Patrick said quietly so as not to disturb the players.

"Thank you, Sir," he answered. "It always was my strong suit when I was in school. My father thought I should teach mathematics at the seminary. He even arranged a job for me, but the war began."

"I take it he was disappointed?" asked Patrick.

Forester nodded. "He was, Sir. We're Quakers you see. He was furious when I told him I wished to join the Navy. He could not understand how a Quaker sworn to pacifism could serve in the military."

"I believe Nathaniel Greene was a Quaker," said Patrick, in reference to George Washington's most trusted General.

"I reminded him as much," continued Forester. "But it was of no use. My father had great plans for me, hoped I would pursue a career in his ministry. If not that, become a professor at a university. Something intellectual, where I could be of aid in shaping young minds and building the generations of the future."

Across from Patrick the card game was now turning heated. Spencer had lost two hands in a row to Chartrand, who was now allowing himself to look a bit smug. He casually flung an extra chip on the pot to convince Spencer to reveal his cards. Spencer, no longer his jovial self, gritted his teeth and gave the doctor an irritated look. He revealed his hand, a pair of jacks being the only cards of use. Chartrand raised an eyebrow, then placed his cards on the table, revealing he had a flush with diamonds.

Spencer slammed his fist down on the table, then downed the rest of his drink, which Patrick guessed was brandy. Chartrand smirked and reached forward to collect the chips.

"Not so fast, doctor," said Barnes, who was still holding his cards. He slapped them down to reveal four 3's. Chartrand looked down at the cards, his mouth agape. The unassuming Boatswain had folded the last two hands, and made little fuss during this round, successfully luring Chartrand into a false sense of security.

Patrick openly laughed, and even Forester cracked a smile at the doctor's comeuppance. Chartrand in turn took the defeat with grace, merely shaking his head and putting on a smile.

"Are you sure you wouldn't care to join us, Lieutenant Commandant?"

Patrick shook his head. "The competition is too cutthroat for me," he replied with a laugh. "Please, doctor, don't feel you need to address me by my full rank."

"Would abbreviating to Commandant be more amenable?" the doctor asked.

Patrick rocked his head back and forth as he considered it. "It would. I wish the Navy didn't insist on using the term Commandant. It makes it sound as if I'm running a prison."

This got a chuckled from Barnes, who, as an enlisted man, likely thought the comparison appropriate. Spencer then turned to look at Patrick and said, "I would prefer the British system in this regard.

Master and Commander sounds much better than Master Commandant. Likewise, simply shortening it to Commander."

Patrick shrugged. "Since we'll be working with them, perhaps I should style myself 'Lieutenant Commander' to impress them?"

"I believe that would be beneficial," said Chartrand. "Lieutenant Commander rolls off the tongue and has a certain 'je ne sais quoi' about it. Also, the British love that sort of self-aggrandizement."

There was another round of laughter before the players went back to their game. Patrick continued to watch alongside Forester for another hour. Spencer proved an easy mark for Chartrand, but Barnes was able to keep him in check enough that the Midshipman did not lose all his money. Nevertheless, by the end of the evening the doctor had acquired quite a sum.

"What do you plan on doing with your winnings, doctor?" asked Forester, blissfully unaware of card playing etiquette. Spencer shot him a dirty look, which Forester did not notice, but otherwise the Midshipman kept silent. Even in the friendly confines of the wardroom, becoming confrontational with a superior officer was out of the question.

"I had considered acquiring some Jesuit's Bark when we arrived in San Juan," answered Chartrand.

"Your pardon, doctor, but what is Jesuit's Bark?" Forester then queried.

"It's a particular tree bark native to South America," Chartrand explained. "When ground into a powder it is useful in treating all manner of fevers, especially of the kind found in the tropics. The Spanish have had a near monopoly on its sale. I plan on mixing the powder into the ship's grog as a precaution for the crew while we are in West Indian waters."

"That was very forward thinking of you, doctor," said Patrick. "You needn't gamble for funds though. I can arrange it to be billed to the ship's expenses."

"Very kind of you, Commander," answered Chartrand with a slight bow of the head in Patrick's direction.

From the deck above came the sound of the ship's bell striking eight times. "Is it that late already?" Patrick wondered aloud.

"I fear Mister Latimer may be flogging the glass, Sir," said Barnes, implying that the Midshipman was tapping the hourglass to make the sand run faster.

"Check at noon to see how far off our timekeeping is, if you please, Mister Forester?" ordered Patrick.

"Aye, aye, Sir," the Lieutenant answered as he got up to head on deck to take the next watch. Turning to Spencer, Patrick then added, "Best get to sleep, you're on the next watch."

"Aye, aye, Sir," Spencer also answered. As he neared the door he paused and tapped his finger on a small piece of paper nailed to the wall. "Have you seen this yet, Sir?"

Patrick stepped over to take a closer look. The paper was a cartoon, ripped out of a newspaper, now faded, and wrinkled, indicating it was a few years old. The scene illustrated the national caricatures, the British 'John Bull' and the American 'Brother Jonathan' engaged in fisticuffs, with John Bull battered and bloody. Brother Jonathan was captioned as gloating, "Ha ah, Johnny! You thought yourself a _Boxer_ did you? I'll let you know we are an _Enterprising_ nation!" The underlining of boxer and enterprising was of course a reference to the *Enterprise's* capture of the HMS *Boxer* during the hostilities. Evidently, a prior member of the *Enterprise's* crew had found it humorous and pinned it to the wall as a mark of pride.

Patrick chuckled. "That is the worst pun I've ever seen," he commented, and Spencer laughed in return. The two officers then went their separate ways, with Patrick returning to his cabin. Sitting down again behind his desk, he dragged his sea bag across the floor and opened it, finally getting a chance to unpack. Taking out his spare uniforms and undergarments, he placed them in a drawer above the map case in the wall. Fishing through the bag again, he pulled out his worn copy of Herodotus, but saw a new book he had not packed himself. Looking at the cover, he saw it was the first volume of *'Fall of the Roman Empire'* by Edward Gibbon.

He took out a note that protruded from the top. It read, "*I know how you love your books, dearest. Love, Anna.*"

Patrick smiled at the short note. He kicked off his boots and rolled into his hammock, hanging a lantern behind his head so he could see. He started reading, but only got a few pages before falling asleep.

Chapter 7

April 1815, USS *Enterprise* near San Juan, Porto Rico

"Farewell and adieu to you Spanish Ladies, farewell and adieu to you ladies of Spain," sang Spencer from the quarterdeck as the *Enterprise* approached the entrance to San Juan harbor. "For we've received orders to sail for old England—"

"Mister Spencer!" Patrick called out. Spencer stopped singing and stood up straight, though Patrick did not turn to face him. "This is an American ship, not a British one. Adjust your lyrics accordingly."

"Aye, aye, Sir," he answered. He then started again from the top, substituting Boston for England, then 'US sailors' for 'British sailors', and Cape Cod and Newport for Ushant and Scilly in the chorus of the famed sea shanty.

The last few days of sailing had been rather uneventful. They had paused on their journey for a brief stop at the islands of the Dry Tortugas. Porter had wished them to make a survey of the islands to ascertain if they would make a suitable anchorage. The diversion proved disappointing, as they had only found small barren strips of sand inhabited only by desert scrub and sea turtles, unsuitable for a true navy yard of any kind. Proceeding eastwards, they traversed the straits of Florida, then along the northern coast of Santo Domingo to the island of Porto Rico.

"It sounds as if you're hoping to encounter a few of those Spanish ladies," said Latimer with a laugh.

"Mister Latimer!" Patrick then snapped at the younger Midshipman. "Officers of the watch do not socialize when on duty."

"Aye, Sir," he answered with a disgruntled growl. Forester had indeed proved that the ship's timekeeping was off thanks to Latimer tampering with the hourglass. After catching him doing it again despite an earlier warning, Patrick had put him on continuous watch for twenty-four hours as punishment. Thus far he was only about 9 hours in.

Patrick walked over to the larboard rail and leaned on it next to Forester, who was eyeing up the city. "Your first time, here?" he asked the Lieutenant.

"Yes, Sir. That's quite an imposing fort," he said, nodding to the massive fortification on the tip of the peninsula that guarded the harbor's entrance.

"The Spanish do love their forts," Patrick commented. "They built up ones just like that all over their Caribbean possessions. To protect the gold fleets that would sail from South America, you know. The El Morro in Havana is prettier I think, but this one is more formidable. I don't believe the Spanish ever fortified another city in the New World like they did San Juan."

The city was a bit of an anomaly, entirely walled as it was, reminding him somewhat of Quebec. San Juan had a fine harbor, sheltered behind a thin peninsula that blocked the winds coming from the northeast. Another small peninsula jutted out into the water on the west side of the harbor, making a narrow channel for ships to pass through that was easily defensible. A small rectangular fort on the western peninsula was simply for insurance, as the grand fortress on the tip of the eastern peninsula was more than enough to defend the entrance. From the El Morro, the fortifications continued along the shore around the northern side of the city until joining Fort San Cristobal, an even more massive fort that closed off the landward side of the peninsula.

As a sailor, Patrick had never been one to trouble himself with military architecture. The rule for navies was for ships to never fight a fort, and the seaward forts of San Juan was a perfect example of why not to. The El Morro of San was roughly triangular in shape, if it were possible to view it from the air, with the walls following the contours of the peninsula's shores. The rounded point which faced the harbor had several tiers, bristling with cannon. *The British couldn't even bombard Fort McHenry into submission*, thought Patrick, remembering vividly the British attempt to take Baltimore. *That fort was nowhere near as large as this. Any man that would think of attacking this would have to be insane!*

As the *Enterprise* rounded the point under the fort's guns, a hand aloft shouted out, "Pilot boat coming, Sir!"

Patrick waved to the man in acknowledgement and turned to Forester. "Shorten sail so the pilot can come alongside."

"Aye, aye, Sir," he answered. He then shouted in his incongruously rugged voice for the hands to shorten sail and for the Boatswain mates to prepare to bring aboard the pilot. A small dinghy under a single sail approached and came along on their larboard side. Patrick exchanged a few words with the man in Spanish and then the crew got out of the way to allow the man to do his job. Dock space at the harbor appeared to be at a premium, so once they were clear of the channel, they were forced to anchor some distance away from shore. The pilot returned ashore in his dinghy, and Patrick ordered Barnes to swing out his own gig.

"Mister Spencer, you will come ashore with me. Mister Forester, the ship is yours until we return," Patrick ordered.

"Aye, aye, Sir," they both replied, and Spencer moved to the rail to climb over the side into the gig. Patrick then took Forester a few paces away from everyone else on deck and spoke quietly to him. Patrick looked over his shoulder and saw along the dock a sloop flying British colors. "That's likely the *Athena*," he said, nodding in the direction of the ship. "We might be working with them, but I'm certain their men are as disgusted over the matter as ours are. I don't want any wigs on the green, so we best keep the crews separated. The last thing we need is men brawling in the streets. I'm not certain how long we'll be in San Juan, but while we are I don't want anyone going ashore except for explicit business, understood?" Forester nodded back. "Also, in the case that any British deserters try coming out to us and begging for asylum, you are to flatly refuse and cooperate with the British."

The last sentence was particularly galling for Patrick to utter, and he felt intense revulsion at it. Twelve years before, he had been one of those deserters, fleeing after a mutiny against the reviled officer that had flogged him. It was by Captain Decatur's determination to rescue them that he and his friends had escaped. However, times had changed, and he with them. No matter his own personal feelings, he had his orders, and that meant avoiding a diplomatic incident at all costs.

Taking his leave of Forester, Patrick descended into his gig. The Boatswain's mates and the Coxswain shoved off and rowed the two officers ashore. Reaching the dock, Patrick and Spencer left the boat, Patrick giving the Coxswain orders that none of the men were to go anywhere. Walking to the end of the dock, Patrick waved down a man holding a board with papers nailed to it who was writing down information as he spoke to civilian mariners who had come into port.

"Please direct me to the harbor master," Patrick requested in Spanish. The clerk gave him a single glance, then jerked his thumb behind him to a small office at the corner of what looked to be a warehouse.

Patrick nodded, touched the tip of his cocked hat, and said, "Gracias," then led Spencer over to the warehouse. Patrick knocked on the door, but not hearing an answer from within, opened the door anyway. There was a small room, with a counter, beyond which was the warehouse.

"Hello?" he called out in English. He then heard some hurried footsteps and a man stepped into view behind the counter. "Hello, señor," he answered, mixing the two languages.

"I am an American naval officer," Patrick told the man in Spanish. "I have come to meet with Capitano Alvarez of the Spanish navy."

The man's eyebrows went up with recognition. "Ah, Si, señor. You may speak English, I am fluent. Yes, Capitano Alvarez…" the man leaned down to reach under the counter. He rose back up and placed an envelope on the counter. "This must be for you, then, señor. A British officer came in this morning and received a similar envelope. Are you here for further peace talks now that the war is over?"

"Something of that nature," Patrick responded, taking the envelope, and avoiding the question. The matter was secret after all, and there was no point in spreading unnecessary information. "Gracias, señor," he added with a nod, after breaking the seal and looking at the note within. The harbor master nodded back, and Patrick went back outside. Spencer was waiting, leaning against the wall with his arms folded across his chest. He immediately straightened up and followed as Patrick started walking into town.

"We're to proceed to Fort San Cristobal," Patrick told him in a hushed tone as they walked. "There will be guards waiting for us when we arrive. No delays, understood?" He then thumped Spencer on the arm to regain his attention as the younger man was naturally eyeing up a pretty girl they were passing by.

"Aye, Sir," he answered. "A shame though. I've always heard Spanish women were the most passionate of them all."

Patrick rolled his eyes. "You're spoken for now."

"Oh, I don't think Martha would mind. She enjoys hearing about my other conquests."

Patrick shot Spencer an incredulous sideways glance. *What is it with the women in that family?* He saw the Midshipman was now distracted by another girl who was leaning on the rail of a second-floor balcony in a way that pushed up her breasts to make them more prominent. She twirled her shiny black hair with her fingers, smiled and winked at them. Spencer smiled back and waved jovially, causing Patrick to smack him on the back of the head and grab the back of his jacket to drag him along.

Finding Fort San Cristobal was an easy task. San Juan was not large, and Patrick knew that one simply needed to head east through the city until running into it. Coming to the rear of the massive fort, Patrick took the envelope with the Spanish pass out from under his uniform jacket. Reaching the lower gate, two sentries were on duty and crossed their muskets in front of them, one calling for them to halt.

"We are American naval officers. We have been directed to come here to meet with Captain Alvarez of His Most Catholic Majesty's Navy," Patrick told them in Spanish.

One of the sentries turned around and shouted for an officer to come down. An artillery officer came hurrying down a set of stairs, jogging the remaining distance to where they waited. The sentry handed the officer the pass Patrick had given them. "Come with me, please," the officer said to them in Spanish. He then led the two men north along the length of the fort until reaching a curving ramp, at the top of which was a more impressive gate, adorned with decorative features in the typical colonial Spanish style. Passing by more guards, they followed the officer onto a courtyard. The Spaniard then immediately turned to his right, taking them into a barracks building adjacent to the gate. They passed through several rooms before finally reaching an office.

"The Americans have arrived, Captain," the artillery officer spoke in Spanish as he entered the office, ushering Patrick and Spencer in behind him. "They mistakenly went to the civilian gate."

"Come in, Señors," said a man in a blue Spanish naval uniform, evidently Captain Alvarez. The captain then dismissed the artillery officer. Alvarez was outwardly diminutive, being fairly short and a bit stocky. He was clean shaven, and his hair was cut short, completely straight and pressed against his scalp.

"Lieutenant Commander Sullivan, and Midshipman Spencer of the USS *Enterprise*," Patrick introduced himself to Alvarez in Spanish. He withdrew a second envelope from his inside jacket pocket and handed it over to the Spanish officer. "My orders, and correspondence from my government concerning our mutual concerns."

"Gracias, Teniente," said Alvarez, taking the documents. "I commend your courtesy. Your command of my language is very good." He then switched to English. "Your British counterpart has already arrived," he said, gesturing to another man sitting in a chair off to the side.

Patrick's eyes went wide when he recognized the officer. "Mister Harvey!" he said with a smile.

"Well, my, my," said the blonde-haired Englishman sitting in the chair. The bull-necked man stood up, also smiling. "Commander Harvey, now," he answered, pivoting one shoulder forward to show off his single epaulette. "This is quite a twist of fate. I see you gained a promotion as well."

"You are already acquainted?" interjected Alvarez.

Patrick hesitated before answering. "Yes, Capitano Alvarez. It's a bit of a long story, however." Commander Harvey had been a Midshipman aboard the HMS *Valiant*, the British frigate Patrick had been forced to serve aboard. Unlike Lieutenant Carlyle, Harvey had been a decent officer, putting his career at risk when he had Carlyle arrested after he had summarily executed a friend of Patrick's during a hostage negotiation. They had subsequently met again in 1812, when the USS *United States* had captured the HMS *Macedonian*. Though Harvey had been a prisoner, the two had gotten on well during the return voyage to Newport.

"How is your navy taking care of my ship?" Harvey asked.

Patrick had to suppress a laugh. "The USS *Macedonian*," he emphasized in order to rub salt in the wound, "has been assigned to the Mediterranean squadron to deal with the Barbary pirates."

"Do take good care of her, the Prince Regent wants her back in one piece when you're done with her," Harvey joked.

Patrick allowed himself to laugh. Alvarez, however, was beginning to look annoyed at the two officers' reunion, and so he chose not to continue the banter.

"Señors, I am grateful to both your respective commanders that they have agreed to cooperate on this matter," he told them gravely once they comported themselves.

"Of course, Capitano Alvarez," answered Harvey. "We have no wish to resume hostilities." He then turned to Patrick. "The Admiral is new to the West Indies station and I daresay he feels badly for the spot this has put you poor chaps in."

Patrick nodded, appreciating the sentiment, though he did not know who the Admiral was that Harvey was referring to.

"I'm glad you were chosen for the assignment," Patrick told Harvey. "I've not had the best history with the English, and I admit I was less than enthused at the prospect of working with them."

"The war was damned unfortunate business. I suppose we can blame the politicians for that," responded Harvey.

"As you both have been informed of the situation, I shall make clear some further details," said Alvarez, drawing the conversation back to him. Like any good naval officer, he had a chart of the leeward islands already laid out on his desk facing Patrick and Harvey.

"Señors, three days ago while you were on your way here, another merchant under our flag was attacked east of Culebrita. Another ship nearby witnessed it but was not able to go to their aid in time. They did, however, give chase! The renegade, with its prize, proceeded further east. They escaped their pursuer once darkness fell but had been followed along the north shore of the Danish East Indies and through the channel between the islands of Santo Tomas and San Juan."

"Saint Thomas and Saint John, you mean," Harvey corrected.

"Ah, yes, force of habit," Alvarez explained. "The ship in question was reportedly handled by an experienced seaman. He was able to shake off his pursuit when he made a sudden course correction and took his ships through one of the narrow channels between the islands blocking the north side of Pillsbury Sound." Alvarez pointed to the straight between Saint Thomas and Saint

John on the map. "He then headed through the sound and was last seen tacking round the south side of Saint John."

Harvey rubbed his chin while Patrick and Spencer leaned over the map to take a better look. "I told Captain Porter this island chain was an ideal hiding place," Patrick said to Spencer in an aside.

"Indeed, Commander Sullivan," said Alvarez. "It is my contention that this pirate is sortieing from somewhere in the Islas Virgenes."

"I might have been inclined to disagree," began Harvey. "I would have doubted he would have been able to use any of them as a base as we have garrisons on all the islands. However, the Little Sisters have almost no population and have bays that could provide sheltered anchorages." He then pointed out the small islands on the southwestern edge of the British controlled territory.

"What about these Danish islands?" Spencer wondered aloud as he looked at the map.

"They have numerous favorable bays as well, though we have substantial garrisons on those islands," answered Harvey. "We moved to secure them against the French several years ago. They're due to be recalled and the islands handed back to Denmark later this month. The islands also have larger populations. I don't believe anyone could be using the islands as a base without us knowing."

"Nevertheless, Señors," said Alvarez, "we cannot keep word of these captures from getting out much longer."

"Was the ship flying an American flag?" Patrick asked.

"Yes, it was," answered Alvarez. "A sloop of at least twenty guns. It was painted black with a single white stripe along her gunports."

"That would match the description of the *Wasp*," replied Patrick, recognizing the ship's specifications and livery. "Sir, I must apologize that this has happened."

"No apology is needed, Commander," answered Alvarez. "It would seem that we are all in agreement that your government has had nothing to do with this, and it is only a single rogue hoping to cause more trouble than he already is."

"The politicians won't see it that way if he's not brought to heel soon," said Harvey. "Worse if the press gets wind of it. The Times will have all of London in an uproar demanding we burn every city on the American coast for breaking the treaty!"

"I fear Madrid would be in a similar state," concurred Alvarez. "Unfortunately, most of my navy lies at the bottom of the Atlantic off Cape Trafalgar," he continued, giving Harvey a look that had his eyes been hot shot, would have set the young officer's ship aflame. "There is little Spain can provide to help you. I only have a few gunboats to patrol the eastern islands and defend San Juan." Harvey only sighed and nodded, averting his eyes, letting Alvarez's bitter comment about the British victory at Trafalgar pass without a word.

"We understand, Capitano," said Patrick. He leaned over the map again. "Commander Harvey, about how wide across are these islands?"

Harvey leaned forward. "The Virgins? I believe Saint Thomas is the widest, only a couple of miles across. I think I know what you're playing at. You think we should sweep the chain from west to east with one ship on the north side of the islands and another on the south?"

"I do, Sir," answered Patrick. "I believe we could stay just within sight of each other, perhaps less than ten miles distant, except of course when we pass behind one of the islands. However, with one of us on each side of the island chain, we could flush him out of whatever his hiding place is and work together to chase him down."

"A sound plan given the limited resources at hand," said Harvey. "It will be risky to separate ourselves to operate in that fashion. We would be unable to support each other if he is inclined to fight us. Given what we know, we would be on roughly equal footing in an engagement."

"A risk then that we'll have to take," answered Patrick. "If one or the other should clear an island without sight of the other, we'll be able to assume the other is in distress and come to their aid."

"It will take a long time to beat around an island," warned Harvey.

Patrick shrugged. "I can't think of any alternative. Even if one of us were to fall in with him and the other could not come to our aid in time, at least we'd be able to damage him enough in battle where he wouldn't be able to escape before the other arrived."

"Fair enough," said Harvey. "Though I wouldn't relish being the one who had to wait for help." He then tilted his head to look down at the map again. "The Admiral was due to leave Kingston yesterday for an inspection of the Windward Islands, then on to Nassau. If we run into a spot of trouble we can send for additional aid. He'll have a frigate with him at the least."

"Understood," said Patrick. "We can leave in concert tomorrow morning."

"You will both have access to whatever stores you may require while you are here," spoke up Alvarez.

The two commanders offered thanks in reply. Alvarez then adjourned the meeting, and the officers were escorted back to the fort's entrance.

"I'll have one of my Midshipman confer with one of your officers to settle on a set of signals for us to use," said Harvey, putting on his hat as they exited the gate and started walking back down the curving ramp.

"Mister Spencer, you will see to that," Patrick told the younger man. "Head back to the boat immediately and return to the ship. Inform Lieutenant Forester that we'll be staying in port for the night. Have Bosun Barnes organize a small shore party to requisition victuals from the Spanish and return with them to meet with Commander Harvey's subordinate."

"Aye, aye, Sir," Spencer answered smartly with a salute, and he hurried down the ramp back into the city.

"He seems an eager fellow," observed Harvey as Spencer receded into the distance.

"He is," replied Patrick. "His first sea duty, which is about the same as the rest of my officers. We had to make do with whatever I could scrounge."

"I see," said Harvey. "My situation is not quite so dire, but less than ideal as you could imagine. Most of the men are fairly bitter about working with you chaps so soon after the war has ended."

"The feeling is mutual," answered Patrick.

Harvey shook his head. "It was a bloody foolish thing. We never held any ill will against you. The last thing we wanted was another fight while we had our hands full with 'Old Bony'."

"Foolish or not, we had cause," Patrick responded with a glare, though he tried to keep his voice from becoming too accusatory.

Harvey seemed to nod in agreement. "I can understand you feeling that way, given your past," he answered. "I'm glad we ended impressment of Americans. If only you had gotten the word of it sooner, we could have avoided everything."

Now it was Patrick's turn to nod in agreement. The British Parliament had rescinded the practice of forcibly pressing Americans into the Royal Navy the very day before Congress had declared war. *We had no way of knowing*, he thought. *Just as we had no way of knowing at New Orleans that the war was already over.*

"I see losing your ship didn't hurt your prospects," Patrick said, changing the subject whilst nodding at Harvey's epaulette.

Harvey chuckled. "Fortunately, the captain is court martialed for losing the ship, not a junior lieutenant. I do seem to be failing up the chain of command at any rate. Look at yourself though! Last I saw you, you were a Master's Mate. Now you're a Commander! I'll always marvel at how you Yankees elevate men up the ranks."

"Lieutenant Commander, actually," Patrick corrected, in a way that would give deference to Harvey as the senior officer.

"You must have had an exciting time to rise so quickly. Did you ever find Carlyle?" the Commander asked.

"I did," Patrick answered succinctly.

"And?" Harvey prompted. Despite being English, Harvey had despised Carlyle as much as any of the common seamen aboard the HMS *Valiant*. During their last meeting he had even wished Patrick luck in his quest for vengeance against him.

"I didn't kill him," said Patrick, and Harvey lurched to a stop.

"I was certain you would," he said. "I can still see, clear as day, him shooting that poor friend of yours on the quarterdeck."

"I know," Patrick replied quietly. "I had him at my mercy, and even then, I knew letting him live was a mistake, but I said no. He had begged for death, you see. It's a long story to tell, but when I found him, he was cradling his wife's body in his arms. She had thrown herself in front of a bullet to save him. He was utterly broken. I wanted the bastard to suffer, and I realized that any pain I inflicted on him would be nothing compared to what he was already feeling. Shooting him wouldn't have been justice, or revenge. It would have been putting him out of his misery."

Patrick looked up and saw Harvey looking back, a troubled expression on his face. "That must seem an awfully cruel thing," Patrick offered.

Harvey contemplated for a moment. "Yes. It's strange though, how a mercy can be cruel in some ways. Did you find out what became of him?"

Patrick shrugged. "I heard he sold his commission after being returned in a prisoner exchange, then he left for England."

"A sad thing that so many have had to suffer for one man's foolishness," lamented Harvey. "Still, one can hope he's learned the error of his ways. At least it appears he'll not trouble anyone any longer."

"I'll not be convinced of that until I know he's six feet under," responded Patrick.

Harvey's eyebrows raised up, but he said nothing. "I'll draw up some additional parameters for our search. I think we should refrain from gunnery practice when actively hunting so that we do not confuse it for an actual fight."

Patrick felt a little uneasy about the prospect but understood Harvey's reasoning. "That's alright, we made sure to run gunnery drills on our way here," he countered.

"Very good," said Harvey. "We did as well. I believe we should cast off early tomorrow, eight bells in the night watch. Forgive me if I don't extend an invitation to dine with us tonight. As I said, most of my officers would not be amenable to your presence."

"I understand, Sir," said Patrick. He gave Harvey a salute, then extended his hand, which Harvey shook. "Till tomorrow then, Commander."

Chapter 8

April 1815, USS *Enterprise* southeast of the island of Culebra

The first day of their joint sail had been uneventful. Setting out from San Juan in the pre-dawn darkness, the two ships made slow progress due to light winds. By the time they had finally cleared the northern coast of Porto Rico it was already past noon. Knowing they would be unable to clear the distance between Culebra and the Danish West Indies before nightfall, the two commanders opted to anchor at the Spanish island for the night and resume their cruise in the morning. Patrick had volunteered to take the *Enterprise* along the southern flank of the island chain, and duly tacked to the south while Harvey beat northward.

"Doctor, is there nothing you can do for the taste?" asked Thompson, the ship's carpenter, who was standing in the doorway of the ward room. The men had been complaining the entire previous day about the taste of the grog after Chartrand had added the powder from the Jesuit's Bark to it.

Doctor Chartrand shrugged. "Unfortunately, no," he told the man. "You could add more lemon juice to the mixture, that may help."

Thompson let out a weary sigh. "Alright doctor, but if we add much more there will be more lemon than rum in it!"

The doctor smirked a bit. "I understand the men's frustration, but do remind them that it's for their health."

"As you wish, doctor," he answered. Thompson then straightened, gave Patrick and Forester a knuckled salute, and went on his way.

"I have to agree with him about the taste, doctor," said Patrick, grimacing as he took a swig of brandy. The doctor had been thorough in adding the medicine to all the spirits to ensure both officers and men were taking them.

Chartrand frowned as he took a sip from his own glass. "I may have been a bit overzealous in the amount of powder I added. Perhaps I shall shrink the dosage for the next time."

Through the skylight Patrick saw Spencer pacing the deck, and could hear him humming, preparing the sing more of his sea shanties.

"I see Spencer is warming up for another performance," he commented to the other two men.

"Yes," Chartrand mused. "He's recruited a chorus and had some of the hands practicing on deck during the night watch."

"I'm grateful I sleep heavily then," Patrick laughed. "I think I'll go on deck and see what he's singing this time."

Patrick exited the wardroom, almost bumping into Henderson along the way. "Would you be liking something for the mid-day meal, Sir?" asked the cook.

"I'll be on deck for this watch, Henderson," he said. "Just cut me off a slice of beef and put it between some bread. You know, in the way that British nobleman would have them."

Henderson nodded. "Ah, Lord Sandwich. I'll have it right along, Sir."

Patrick headed up the hatchway and emerged on deck. The weather was perfect, mostly clear skies and a warm temperature. They were sailing a bit close-hauled to the wind but seemed to be making good speed. To the northwest, Culebra and its smaller companion island Culebrita were outlined on the horizon. To the east, the peaks of Saint Thomas could just be seen.

Near the ship's wheel, Spencer was pacing back and forth. The Midshipman cleared his throat a final time and raised one hand with a finger extended. He then began to swing his arm as if he were a symphony conductor. All around him, the Quartermaster, Boatswain Barnes, a Quarter Gunner, the Marine guarding the hourglass, and two Able Seamen, all began to hum a tune or mimic various musical instruments. Spencer himself then began to sing.

> *"Come on the sloop John B.*
> *My grandfather and me*
> *Round Nassau town ve did roam*
> *Drinking all night, ve got into a fight*
> *Ve feel so break-up, Ve want to go home."*

The hands who were singing along now began to mouth other new beats and rhythms. Spencer raised his hand again with a flourish and shouted out, "Altogether now!" The men now picked up the lyrics in unison.

> *"So hoist up the John B. sails*
> *See how the main sail set,*
> *Call for the Captain ashore-Let me go home,*
> *Let me go home, let me go home,*
> *I feel so break-up, I vant to go home."*

Patrick covered his mouth as he began to giggle but could not help dissolving into laughter at the sight of his men, normally stoic and serious, bursting out into song at Spencer's direction. The Midshipman heard him laughing and turned around, the impromptu concert coming to a screeching halt.

"Good afternoon, Sir. I hadn't noticed you."

Patrick shook his head while still smiling. "Mister Spencer, what *are* you singing? Is that supposed to be a Dutch accent?"

"A new song. Heard it from some Bahamian stevedores in San Juan, Sir," he reported proudly.

"Are you already tired of our expedition?" he asked, referring to the phrases about wanting to return home.

"Oh, no, Sir," Spencer answered, shaking his head. "I just thought it would help the men pass the time while on watch."

"I see," Patrick replied. He then walked across the deck, and leaned on the post holding the hourglass, craning his neck to look at the podium on which the logbook rested. "That may be all well and good, but do be sure not to let it drown out the hands above making reports on ship sightings."

Spencer straightened himself up, a bit embarrassed. "Aye, Sir."

Patrick disliked having to chastise Spencer for a bit of mostly harmless merriment. He did consider the younger man his friend, but the duties of command took precedence.

"Anything to report?" Patrick then asked.

"Two sails spotted about an hour ago, Sir," answered Spencer. "Due south of us. It appears they're making for Porto Rico from Saint Croix. The lookouts have been watching them, but they've not reported anything amiss."

Patrick nodded satisfactorily. "And the *Athena*?"

"Still in sight, due north, Sir," replied Spencer, pointing in that direction off the ship's larboard rail. "We've signaled back and forth a few times, but nothing out of the ordinary."

"Understood," said Patrick. "As you were."

Spencer gave a smile and turned back to the men. He told them to take the song from the top, and they started again, quieter though this time. Patrick headed forward to walk the deck and inspect the guns. Henderson appeared, bringing Patrick the sandwich he had requested.

"I'm sorry, Sir," the cook apologized. "The best I could do for bread was some hard tack."

"It's quite alright, Henderson," Patrick told him, accepting the sandwich with a smile. He dismissed the cook and started eating as he paced, only regretting that the meal was rather bland. He leaned back and sat against one of the starboard long guns, his eyes ahead on the island in the distance. As he chewed, he tuned out the crew's singing and let his mind wander. His charts ran through his mind as he pictured the layout of the Leeward Islands. He then thought of the islands themselves, covered in impenetrable foliage, verdant green. He remembered visiting some of the islands when he was younger, swimming in the surf of pristine beaches alongside Tom, marveling at the crystal-clear water. The thought of beaches caused his mind to wander farther still, as he recalled a sunset walk on a beach in the Azores. He smiled, thinking of the Portuguese girl he had held hands with as he walked, and his first kiss with her. She had barely known a word of English, but it had not mattered. His boyish flirtation with her had been so brief and distant he had never even bothered to tell Anna of it.

Patrick was broken out of his reverie by a hand calling out from above. "Sir! To leeward! One of the ships is firing on the other!"

Patrick immediately straightened up and looked out over the starboard rail. Shading his eyes and squinting through the glaring sunshine, he saw the masts of the two ships Spencer had mentioned earlier. Smoke was drifting away from one, and there came the distant rumble of cannon fire.

"Beat to quarters!" Patrick shouted at the men loitering around the quarterdeck. Spencer jolted in surprise as he was still distracted with his singing, but likewise jumped to his task of calling the Boatswain's Mate to pipe the call for all hand on deck. The ship's

Marine drummer stumbled up from below and started beating the tattoo. The hands soon began spilling onto deck, running to the guns and preparing them to cast loose.

"Helm, come about to starboard," Patrick ordered, and the Quartermaster began turning the ship's wheel hard over. "Make your heading due south. Mister Latimer!" He pointed to the younger Midshipman who had just come up the hatchway, rubbing his eyes to shake his grogginess. "Go forward to the flag locker and signal the *Athena* that we are going to the assistance of a ship that is under attack."

"Aye, aye, Sir," he answered and dashed down the deck. Forester had also come on deck, spyglass in hand. "Doctor Chartrand has gone below and taken up his position in the cockpit," he reported to Patrick.

"Hopefully the good doctor will not be busy today," answered Patrick. "Glass," he requested laconically, and held out his hand. Forester handed over the spyglass, which Patrick extended and trained it south on the two ships approaching.

"No colors on the trailing ship," he noted, and passed the spyglass back to Forester. "The other has a Spanish flag."

"Could it be the *Wasp*, Sir?" asked the Lieutenant.

Patrick shook his head. "No. The *Wasp* was a sloop, that's a schooner. Nevertheless, that Spanish ship is in distress. We must help them."

"Aye, Sir," responded Forester with a nod. The Lieutenant understood that no matter what the mission, a higher duty required that they help anyone in distress. *We are here to hunt pirates after all,* Patrick thought.

Forester extended the spyglass to take a look for himself. After a few moments he stated, "The attacker has now raised colors, Sir. I don't recognize them." The Lieutenant then handed the spyglass back to Patrick again. Taking a second look on the schooner, he saw what looked to be a yellow, red, and blue flag with a device in one corner.

Patrick closed the spyglass slowly and began to chew on his lip a bit. "I think we may have stumbled on an internal Spanish matter," he said, returning the spyglass to Forester. The Lieutenant's eyebrows furrowed in confusion. "I believe that ship is declaring itself to be Venezuelan," Patrick elaborated.

"Venezuelan?" repeated Forester.

"Yes," said Patrick as he looked out over the bow and mused on the situation. "The Spanish obviously would never recognize their sovereignty. They're probably betting that an American ship wouldn't side with a colonial master against a nation fighting for its own independence."

"Do you believe it to be a ruse then, Sir?" asked Forester.

Patrick nodded. "I do. Even if it's not though, our current arrangement with the Spanish would necessitate we intervene. I doubt Capitano Alvarez would be pleased if he were to find out that we ignored one of his ships coming under attack."

The wind had shifted and brought the *Enterprise* sweeping down on the two ships. The Venezuelan interloper was caught in irons with the wind blowing south, bringing them practically to a dead stop. Realizing the American ship was now quickly bearing down on them, the ship swung about to larboard to catch some wind in its sails and make good its escape.

"Signal from the *Athena*, Sir," said Latimer, walking up to Patrick. "They have acknowledged and are changing course."

Patrick nodded and took another look ahead. The Spanish ship, which he could see was a helpless merchant, was crippled from a shot that had torn away her jibs, leaving it difficult for her to maneuver.

"Mister Latimer," Patrick addressed the Midshipman, "Summon Mister Thompson. Gather a party of six men. Take one of the ship's boats and as we pass, row over to that Spanish merchant. They'll need help with repairs."

"Aye, aye, Sir," he responded, and flagged down some of the men who were working on putting the ship's boats over the side to clear the deck once the beat to quarters had sounded.

With the wind now at their backs, the *Enterprise* gained speed and bore down on the Venezuelan. Passing the stricken Spanish merchant, the civilian crew waived to them and called out a greeting. The Americans waved back, and Latimer's boat cast off, rocking in the heavy seas. The Midshipman foolishly stood in the boat, waving and calling out, "Ahoy!", until a wave knocked him backwards onto his backside, much to the amusement of the hands who were rowing.

As soon as they were in range, the gunlayer for the chase guns turned to Patrick. "Shall I put one across their bows, Sir?" he asked.

Patrick nodded in the affirmative. "Make it so," he said, thinking the phrase gave him an air of authority. The gunlayer lined up a perfect shot and sent the ball roughly one hundred yards off their starboard bow. The crew of the schooner knew they could not escape, yet unusually for a pirate, or even a privateer, they appeared determined to go down swinging. Taking the spyglass back from Forester, he saw men scrambling on the deck, one of them loading a swivel gun that was on the aft rail. Panning his glass along the side of the schooner, he noticed no gunports, which would have been unlikely for a ship that rode so lowly in the water. He could see that they had four guns on their deck, all small, long guns. *Only four guns total?* Patrick assessed. *We have eleven to a side. A totally uneven fight. They must really not want to be captured to fight against such long odds. Still, small number of guns or not, they can still be dangerous.*

As if to prove his point, one of the long guns returned fire. The round shot came arcing in and plunked into the water about thirty yards in front of the *Enterprise's* bow. *A miss*, thought Patrick, *but definitely not a warning shot*. Turning around, he barked to the Quartermaster, "Close with him amidships!" He then handed the spyglass back to Forester and ordered, "Run out the larboard battery. Wait for the up-roll, and fire as you bear."

"Aye, aye, Sir," the Lieutenant responded coolly, with a nod. Forester then went down the line, one by one, giving instructions to the gunners. When he reached the quarterdeck, he stood up straight to look over the rail to get a clear view of the target. Waiting for just the right moment, when the Quartermaster had completed his turn and for the ocean swell to roll the larboard side to its highest point, he then roared out, "Fire!"

The ship's cannons blasted out round shot in a rolling barrage down the length of the ship. The gunnery practice Patrick had given the crew during their transit to Porto Rico paid off, as half the shots struck home, which at three-hundred yards was impeccable shooting.

"Lay alongside at pistol shot!" Patrick then shouted back to the Quartermaster.

The *Enterprise* began to turn to larboard and the distance between the two ships continued to narrow. Although Patrick could not tell how much damage they had dealt, the Venezuelan's were clearly in disarray, trying to maneuver a bit wildly while attempting to bring their guns into action. He saw their cannons fire, and he ducked below the rail out of instinct. One shot ripped through the hammock netting and hit the backside of the starboard rail with a thud. The shot bounced off the wood and then rolled along the deck.

Patrick walked over and picked up the iron round shot, which was barely larger than a grapeshot ball. "A three pounder," he said to Forester, holding up the shot to show him. "This is fit for field artillery, not ships' guns." It was more evidence that the ship they faced was more than likely a brigand, as even a privateer would not be so poorly equipped.

"Keep your heads down!" Patrick reminded the men, even though he was feeling ever more confident of their situation. "Sergeant Bowyer!" he shouted, and the Sergeant of the Marines straightened up and touched his musket across his chest in a salute. "I want your men at the ready to take that ship. Bring them down from the tops and line the quarterdeck rail. Sweep their deck and be prepared to board if necessary."

"Aye, aye, Sir," he answered, and called up to his men who had gone above to the mainmast's fighting top to return below.

The gap between the two ships had closed considerably. The *Enterprise* had now closed to within musket shot range, and Forester gave the order for another volley. The cannons belched flame and smoke, and at only one hundred yards they could not miss. Iron shot tore into the schooner, punching gaping holes through her sides. The smoke cleared, and they continued to drift closer, yet the crew of the smaller ship still stubbornly refused to strike their colors.

As they came within fifty yards of each other, a seaman on the Venezuelan's deck staggered to the rail and made for a swivel gun. Before he could make it, one of the Marines, who had chosen to stay elevated by hooking an arm and a leg through the ratlines, took aim and fired. The dogged seaman briefly clutched his chest, and then fell to the deck. Patrick looked up and saw the Marine raise his musket, a satisfied smirk on his face.

"Shall we throw across grappling hooks and pull her in, Sir?" asked Spencer.

Patrick shook his head. "No. We'll take one of the boats. If these fools were mad enough to fight us, who knows what they're capable of. I don't want them deciding to set off their powder magazine."

After giving Barnes the order to recall the other two boats they had trailing in their wake, he turned again to Sergeant Bowyer. "Sergeant, you and two men in one boat, the remainder in the other. Mister Forester, can you make out Mister Latimer's progress?"

Forester went to the aft rail to look out with his spyglass. After a few moments he turned back and reported, "It appears that Mister Latimer has secured the merchantman, Sir."

"Very well. Mister Forester, the ship is yours. I will be joining the boarding party."

Forester swiftly walked across the deck over to Patrick, in a hurry, but not so fast as to alarm anyone. Leaning close, he said quietly, "Sir, is that wise given the concerns you have?"

"Perhaps not," Patrick admitted. "But I want to see these men for myself. I am in command. I should be willing to risk myself at a minimum." Turning back to Spencer, he then said, "Mister Spencer, you will take the second boat and command the prize."

"Aye, aye, Sir," Spencer replied with a broad smile and a salute, eager to get a chance to exercise a command of his own.

Once Barnes had the boats alongside, he chose some of the hands to row, and then the Marines lowered themselves in as well. Spencer practically leapt into his boat and had the men in the first boat rowing hard before Patrick had even reached the gangway. Patrick was the last to descend into the second boat, and once he was seated, they shoved off. As they rowed over, Forester keenly put some distance between the *Enterprise* and the Venezuelan. In the boats, they were alert for anything nefarious afoot, with the Marines at the bows with their muskets cocked and ready to fire.

Spencer's boat was the first to reach the schooner. Patrick was relieved to see that Spencer did not recklessly hurry forward to be the first up the gangway in a bid to capture glory, a lesson he had impressed upon him the previous summer. Instead, Sergeant Bowyer went first, the tip of his musket with bayonet fixed preceding him. The other two Marines went up next, then Spencer climbed up the schooner's side.

The process was repeated when Patrick's boat came alongside. The three Marines went first, muskets still at the ready. Patrick then clambered aboard. The sight on deck was not a pretty one. About a dozen men were backed up against the aft rail, all looking haggard and filthy, wearing clothes that were tattered and soiled. The man who had tried to turn the swivel cannon on them was writhing on the deck, clutching his chest, a pool of blood forming under his body. Another man lay dead beside one of the six pounders, the front of his body sporting so many splinters poking out of it that the corpse resembled a porcupine. Two more men lay propped against the far rail, bleeding from cuts and gashes to their legs.

"Mister Spencer, strike those colors," Patrick said, while pointing to the Venezuelan standard flying aloft. Spencer saluted and began pulling on the line to bring them down. "Sergeant Bowyer, take two men. Go below and secure the powder magazine and make sure there aren't any others hiding down there."

The Sergeant responded with an, "Aye, aye, Sir," and proceeded down the hatchway with two of his Marines. Patrick looked over the assembled prisoners and then asked in Spanish, "Who is in command here."

All of the men looked around at each other for a moment then wordlessly pointed at the wounded man on the deck. Patrick sighed and knelt down next to the wounded man. "Are you the Capitano?" he continued on in Spanish.

"Si! Si!" the man managed to groan through his pain, though Patrick could tell there would be little more he would be able to say. Turning around, he leaned back over the rail and said to the hands in his boat, "Row back and bring Doctor Chartrand, immediately." The Boatswain's Mate at the tiller nodded and gave the knuckled salute, and the men shoved off away from the schooner.

One of the schooner's crew now stepped forward. "Why did you attack us?" he demanded in Spanish, his fists clenched. One of the Marines ever so slightly pointed his bayonet at him, and the man halted before shifting back a pace.

"We were coming to the aid of the Spanish merchant," Patrick replied.

"We are at war with Spain!" the man roared, pointing the flag balled up in Spencer's hands. "Why would you defend a Spanish ship?"

Patrick frowned, beginning to wonder if he had indeed made a blunder by wading into the situation. "We have orders to bring an end to piracy in these waters. At the current time, the United States does not recognize Venezuela as a legitimate nation. However, if you can provide documentation from a Venezuelan government, I may be willing to allow you to go on your way."

Spencer now came walking slowly over to him and delivered the Venezuelan flag into his hands. It was as tattered and threadbare as the men's clothing, and Patrick now made out the design in the flag's corner was an image of a native sitting on a rock. "Sir," whispered Spencer, "I'm not an expert on South American relations, but wasn't the revolutionary government in Venezuela toppled months ago?"

Patrick only moved his eyes to look at him and nodded slowly. Spencer then took a deep breath and moved out of the way to stand beside him, evidently taking the hint that Patrick was baiting the crew into getting caught in a lie.

"I believe the Capitano has such papers in his cabin," the sailor said, his teeth gritted. It was a lie, and Patrick knew it. However, Sergeant Bowyer returning on deck made that point moot.

"Sir," the Sergeant addressed as he came back up the hatchway. "The ship's powder stores are secured. We found these women below though." One of the other Marines came through the hatchway, followed by a pair of women to whom he was leading by the hand. Both women were dark haired with a dark complexion, clearly of Latin origin. It was also evident that they had been beaten, with bruises and even a few cuts on their faces. They were barely clothed, wearing nothing more than dirty rags. "We found them chained below," reported Bowyer with disgust.

Patrick then heard a growl and out of the corner of his eye saw the Marine nearest the captured crew slam the butt of his musket into the stomach of the man who had been speaking to Patrick. "Private, belay that!" he shouted, and the Marine reluctantly backed away, still seething with anger.

Patrick stepped toward the two women. "We are Americans," he said to them in Spanish. One woman nodded and replied, "Thank you for rescuing us."

Wishing to be sensitive to the ordeal the women had certainly been put through, he wanted to keep his questions as brief and to the point as possible. "Who are these men? How long have they held you captive?"

The woman averted her eyes at first, massaging one arm. After a few deep breaths to gather herself, she said, "They are escaped convicts from Santiago de Cuba. We are from a village on the coast of Santo Domingo. We were taken three weeks ago."

Patrick told them, "Thank you," and turned to Sergeant Bowyer. "Sergeant, clap those scum in irons!"

"Aye, aye, Sir," he responded, showing a scowl as he prodded them along with his musket.

"And Sergeant?" Patrick called after him. The Sergeant paused and looked at him before he and the other Marines led the brigands below decks. "If any one of those bastards gives you trouble, gut him like a fish."

Bowyer restrained himself from smiling but let a wry smirk break through. "Yes, Sir."

After consulting with Harvey, the two ships agreed to go their separate ways. The *Enterprise* would escort the prize schooner back to San Juan to be delivered to the Spanish authorities, while the *Athena* would go ahead and patrol the waters surrounding Saint Thomas until the Americans returned.

The Spanish merchantman was repaired and went on her way, and once Latimer's repair party was recovered the ship got underway. Transiting back to San Juan would take the remainder of the day, arriving off San Juan in the dark, at which point they waited until dawn before entering the harbor. Once again, the Enterprise anchored offshore, though Spencer nimbly maneuvered the schooner into a prime spot along a wharf.

Patrick made his way ashore in the ship's longboat, the two women they had rescued along with him. Spencer was already at the dock waiting for him, along with a cadre of Spanish soldiers.

"The prize has been successfully delivered to the Spanish, Sir, along with the prisoners," he eagerly appraised Patrick as he stepped onto the dock. "Capitano Alvarez is waiting at the fortress for us to report on the action." He then gestured to the Spanish soldiers. "These men are here to escort the ladies we found to the local hospital, Sir. Their testimony will be needed against the pirates and the Spanish governor wishes to see to their protection."

"Understood," said Patrick. He turned and gave the two women a helping hand from the boat and onto the dock. He then informed them in Spanish that they were to go with the soldiers. The pair gave each other a wary look, their leeriness of men understandable, but complied. As they started to walk away, Spencer unexpectedly began to sing 'Spanish Ladies' again.

> *"Farewell and adieu to you Spanish Ladies*
> *Farewell and adieu to you ladies of Spain*
> *For we've received orders to sail for old Boston*
> *And we may never see you fair ladies again."*

His choice of song, and the manner in which he sang was not intended as making an advance on the women, but merely a friendly gesture to see them off. The women appeared to appreciate the sentiment, smiling, and one blowing Spencer a kiss. Unusually, he blushed, and smiled back at them, happy he had cheered them up.

"Very kind of you, Mister Spencer," Patrick said to him. "We best be on our way. Capitano Alvarez will have been pleased we've brought justice to the pirates." The two men then began to walk along the dock together.

"Do you believe those brigands were responsible for the Spanish ships that were attacked, Sir?" Spencer asked.

"I believe one or two," answered Patrick. "But even Spanish accounts spoke of a ship that matched the description of the *Wasp*. That ship was clearly not a sloop and could not be mistaken for one."

They had only walked a few more paces when something caught Patrick's foot. He tripped, but not badly enough to put him on his face. He turned to see what he had stumbled over.

"Hello, Paddy."

Even in the balmy Caribbean, the voice chilled him to the bone.

"Carlyle," he hissed at the man standing before him with the sandy side-whiskers. Even though it had been less than two years since they had last seen each other, his nemesis looked to have aged considerably. His face had become creased with lines, and his sandy hair increasingly flecked with gray. More than that, he looked tired, his eyes now ringed and baggy, his shoulders drooping in a way Patrick had never thought a man as haughty as Carlyle would allow. He wore civilian clothes, which were ill fitting and weathered. *He's finally suffering*, Patrick thought as he looked over the man. After what Carlyle had done to him and his friends over the years, he could not be moved to pity however.

"What a misfortune that we should meet again now that the war is over," Carlyle sneered. "I've no legal means by which to kill you in peacetime."

"Hasn't stopped you from trying before," Patrick retorted.

Carlyle folded his arms across his chest and snorted. "You also rebuffed my challenge."

"And I'll rebuff it still," he answered. "Hurl insults at my honor all you wish."

"I needn't bother. You're an Irishman, you don't have any to begin with."

Patrick let out a smirk. Even as enemies, he could appreciate a witty riposte. *This is as close to a duel as he's going to get*, he thought.

"No, we don't. We have more important things to worry about," he answered, though Carlyle only raised an eyebrow in response. "And what brings *you* to San Juan?"

"Trade," he replied, gesturing to the dock. "I have two motherless boys to provide for, and a military career was no longer proving lucrative. I still know how to command a ship; you can see it just there," he nodded off behind Patrick to the ships in port. Patrick took a quick glance over his shoulder but had no idea which of them was supposed to be Carlyle's.

"And yourself?" he probed with malice in his voice.

"Pirate hunting."

Carlyle burst into a laugh. "The Yankees sent you?" He laughed a little longer, then paused to catch himself as it appeared he was about to say something further.

"Yes," said Patrick when Carlyle had finished sputtering. "It's gotten quite dangerous in these waters of late. You may want to be careful if you're heading east."

Carlyle ignored Patrick's sarcasm and waved him off. "After surviving you, pirates would be a mercy." He then walked past Patrick and Spencer heading in the opposite direction down the dock. "Enjoy your pirate hunting Paddy. May we never meet again!"

Spencer leaned in as Carlyle left. "Who was that, Sir?"

Patrick grunted. "Roger Carlyle. Late of the British Army and Royal Navy."

Spencer's eyebrows went up. "Army and Navy? You don't see that often. What history do you have with him, Sir?"

Patrick sighed. "It's a long story. I'll tell you in the wardroom after supper tonight."

They walked a little further and had almost reached the end of the waterfront when they heard the sound of running footsteps and a shout of, "Patrick!"

Patrick turned around to see Anna hurrying down the dock holding her skirts up. She bounded into his arms and kissed him.

"Anna what are you doing here?" he asked, totally bewildered. "You said you were headed to Kingston."

"I did go to Kingston," she answered. "Once I reported, I volunteered to deliver some correspondence to the Royal Governor here in San Juan. I knew you were sailing here, and I owed the British Admiral a favor, so I thought I might as well come."

"Would that be the new Admiral of the West Indies Squadron?" he questioned. She nearly laughed. "Yes, why do you ask?"

Patrick shrugged. "The British commander I'm working with mentioned him. Can you tell me anything about him?"

Anna tilted her head to think. "He's a tall, curly-haired Welshman who has a bad habit of clearing his throat in the most annoying manner. Fine man though. But that's not important." She then leaned close and whispered in his ear, "I also brought my payment."

Patrick's eyebrows went up. She grinned at him and said, "Come, I need to show you. I'd rather you hold it aboard your ship. I shouldn't be traveling alone with so much money."

She started to pull him by the hand, but he dug in his heels. "I need to report to the Spanish. We captured a vessel."

She turned back to look at him, a bit disappointed that he was not as interested in seeing the small fortune she had gone to such trouble to acquire. "Oh, alright. Will you at least be staying here for the night?"

He gave her a slight grin of his own knowing what she was hinting at. "I think it will be necessary."

She smiled and put her arms around his neck. "Good. You can tell me all about your pirate hunting over dinner. There's something I want to tell you of as well, but it can wait until after dinner. Could I have the money brought aboard your ship first thing though?"

Patrick nodded. "Of course. Phillip, would you please go with Mrs. Sullivan and assist her with delivering some valuables to the *Enterprise*?"

"I'd be happy to, Sir," Spencer answered with a smile and a tip of his hat. Anna then started off with Spencer in tow before Patrick called after them one more time. "Be on your guard. I just bumped into Carlyle on the dock."

Anna's head whipped around in an instant. "Good God, he's here?!" Patrick could only nod in response. Anna then rolled her eyes. "Damn that man," she cursed. "You said you saw him on the dock? I'll avoid the waterfront further. If he sees me, Lord knows what he'll do."

Patrick felt a small amount of anxiety at the thought of Carlyle discovering Anna was here as well. While working in his service as a spy, she had betrayed him by refusing to kill Patrick, to say nothing of her defection to the United States. Even with the war over and Carlyle seemingly a broken man, Patrick could not be sure he would not make some attempt at revenge.

"Be safe," he told her.

She grinned again. "You know I always am." She held up her hand and wiggled her fingers at him in a playful wave. "I'll see you tonight."

The couple then went their separate ways. Patrick continued on to Fort San Cristobal, daydreaming about how much money Anna had received from the British, and of the prospect of enjoying an unexpected night of romance with her. He was completely lost in thought, even when delivering his report to Capitano Alvarez. The only thing that caught his attention when the Spaniard spoke was that he would arrange for Patrick to receive a small amount of prize money for the capture of the schooner.

With his duty complete, he returned to the dock. When he arrived, he saw that the ship's boat was still there, the hands who had rowed it ashore loafing nearby on the dock. When they saw Patrick approaching, the Coxswain swatted the arm of the nearest man, and they stood up, but not before hiding some rum they had purchased from a nearby vendor behind a barrel.

The Coxswain opened his mouth to apologize for their lounging, but Patrick spoke first. "Has Mister Spencer not returned?" he asked.

"No, Sir," answered the Coxswain, puzzled. "We've not seen the young man since you left together."

"Where could he be?" Patrick wondered aloud. "I've been with Capitano Alvarez for over an hour."

Another hand pointed out to the harbor. "One of our boats approaching, Sir."

Patrick looked up and saw the other boat, Boatswain Barnes sitting at the tiller. He raised an eyebrow at the sight. He walked over to the end of the pier and put his hands on his hips as Barnes tied the boat up alongside. "Mister Barnes, I gave orders that no one was to come ashore unless on ship's business."

"I'm sorry, Sir," said Barnes, saluting Patrick as he got off the boat and stepped onto the dock. "You'd been ashore so long and we'd not heard from you. I knew I couldn't wait any longer."

Patrick shook his head, confused. "What's the matter, Mister Barnes?"

Barnes pointed to a ship under sail exiting the harbor. "Sir, that ship! It's the *Wasp*!"

Patrick's eyes went wide. "Barnes... you mean to tell me she's been sitting right here at the dock in front of everyone?"

Barnes frowned. "I know my ship, Sir," he said adamantly. "It's the *Wasp*. I'm certain of it!" He then handed over a spyglass to take a closer look. Patrick extended it and aimed it at the ship. It was indeed a sloop, though flying a British flag. Unlike a British warship however, she bore a white stripe along her sides instead of ochre. A longboat dangled off the stern of the ship, obscuring the nameplate. Patrick then nearly dropped the spyglass when he spotted a figure leaning on the aft rail.

"CARLYLE!" he screamed, startling both his men and civilians nearby. He needed no more convincing from Barnes. The instant he spotted those sandy side whiskers he knew in his gut what had happened.

He took a step, thinking he should run to the fort guarding the entrance and have them fire on Carlyle before he could escape. He dismissed the notion, as he knew even if he made it to the fort in time, it would likely take too long to explain everything and convince the fort's commander to fire on a British flagged ship.

"Mister Barnes, return to the ship," he ordered the Boatswain. "Inform Lieutenant Forester I will be returning shortly and tell him that we will be needing every inch of canvas aloft to chase that ship."

"Aye, aye, Sir," Barnes responded, and leapt back into his boat, ordering the men to begin rowing back. Before they left the dock, Barnes looked back and spotted a commotion at the opposite end of the pier. "Sir, is that Mister Spencer?"

Patrick turned around to look at what Barnes was talking about. At the end of the dock where it met the street, there was a small crowd of people. They were in a semicircle around a solitary figure who was stumbling along. Patrick realized it was indeed Spencer and broke into a run when he saw the younger man fall to the ground.

"Spencer!" he gasped as he knelt down beside the Midshipman, seeing a stream of blood running through his blonde hair. He rolled Spencer over and winced, finding his face beaten and bruised, blood running from both his nose and mouth.

"I'm sorry, Sir," he managed to mumble.

"Phillip, what happened?" Patrick asked, trying to cushion his head.

Spencer coughed, and his eyes wandered before he gathered himself to answer. "Some men, Sir," he rasped. "They were waiting for us when we reached your wife's boarding house. I recognized that Carlyle fellow you had words with." He then sniffled and looked as though he might cry. "I tried, Sir, I tried to protect her. There was too many of them. They took her, Sir."

Patrick hoisted Spencer up and slung one of his arms over his shoulders. He then helped the battered Midshipman back to the boat, setting him down gently. The hands rowed back to the *Enterprise* as fast as they could. Reaching the ship, they lifted Spencer out of the boat first, into Doctor Chartrand's waiting arms. The doctor then swiftly brought Spencer below to begin treatment.

Stepping onto the deck, Patrick strode up to Lieutenant Forester. Before the other man could even speak, Patrick said, "Get the boat in quickly, Mister Forester. Is the ship ready?"

"Aye, Sir," the Lieutenant answered. "What's happened?"

"Mister Barnes was right," said Patrick. "That sloop under the British flag is the *Wasp*."

Forester looked stunned. "How can you be sure, Sir?"

Patrick gritted his teeth. "Because I saw the man who is commanding it. He is an old personal enemy of mine. I know what the man is capable of." He then slammed his fist down on the rail beside him. "And now the bastard has my wife!"

Chapter 9

April 1815, aboard USS *Enterprise* near the island of Saint Thomas, Danish West Indies

Patrick had tried to wring every knot out of the *Enterprise*, but it had been to no avail. Carlyle and the *Wasp* had taken such a lead on them that they could not close the distance before nightfall. Using the straits between Culebra and Culebrita as cover, the *Wasp* slipped out of sight as the sun went down. Unable to locate the enemy in the darkness, Patrick ordered the ship to set course for Saint Thomas and to rendezvous with the HMS *Athena*.

"How is he doctor," Patrick asked as Chartrand entered the wardroom that evening.

The Cajun shrugged and sighed. "I won't know for sure for at least another day or two, but as of now I think he'll mend. No doubt he took a drubbing, but he doesn't seem to have suffered any permanent damage."

"I don't understand, Sir," said Forester. "If they didn't want anyone finding out your wife had been abducted, why didn't they simply kill him?"

"Because he *wanted* me to find out," answered Patrick. "He wants revenge for his wife's death, so he's targeted mine."

"If you'll forgive me, Sir," began Forester, "Then why not simply kill her also?"

"He wants me to suffer first," said Patrick, and he *was* suffering, even if he didn't show it to the crew. By now everyone had heard and understood, although most were ignorant of the details and could not fathom why anyone would have a personal vendetta against him.

"He wants to twist the knife," he continued, making a stabbing motion in the air with his hand, and then twisting as he had described. "He wants me to fear for her, to feel helpless. He likely wants to draw me into a confrontation," he reasoned.

"And then?" asked Forester.

"Then he'll kill her," Patrick said gravely. "He'll want me to watch her die. Then he'll hope he can kill me as well and complete his revenge."

The other two men remained silent at Patrick's words. There was nothing of comfort they could say to relieve the situation. As they sat gloomily contemplating, Boatswain Barnes appeared in the doorway and knocked on the frame.

"Almost eight bells, Sir," he informed them. "Would you like me to take the night watch in place of Mister Spencer?"

Patrick shook his head. "That won't be necessary, Barnes. I'll stand the night watch."

"Are you sure, Sir?"

Patrick paused before answering. "Quite sure, Mister Barnes." He knew the Boatswain was trying to be kind and take some responsibility off Patrick's shoulders, but it was not the sort of thing he needed at that moment. *No, keeping busy will do me good*, he thought. There was nothing in that immediate moment that could be done anyway, so it was best to find something to occupy his thoughts.

Barnes started to leave but stopped and turned around. "Sir," he began, "I just thought you should know that all the boys feel terrible about what's happened to your missus. They're willing to do whatever you need to help get her back. If we were just hunting pirates, it would be one thing, but you being singled out by that bastard that's got the *Wasp* just doesn't sit right with them."

"Thank you, Mister Barnes," said Patrick. "And tell the men I said thank you to them as well."

Barnes nodded, gave a slight smile, and saluted before leaving. Once he was out of earshot, Chartrand spoke up again. "There's more to this I don't understand," he said. "If this man is driven by personal vengeance against you, then why has he gone to all this trouble of roving the Caribbean like a pirate?"

"He hates all Americans, doctor," replied Patrick. "I may be the lightning rod for his ire, but if unable to strike at me directly, he'll look for any chance to cause havoc. The death of his wife will have only deepened his hatred."

"But still," interrupted the doctor, "If he was so committed to some grander plan, why risk it by abducting your wife?"

Patrick could only shrug. "It may simply be that he saw an opportunity in inflict more pain. How could he pass it up if he knew the two persons that he hated most were within reach?"

Chartrand nodded, seeing his point, and sipped from his glass of brandy. Soon they heard the tolling of eight bells. Patrick stood up and said to the others, "Thank you for your company this evening gentlemen. It is most appreciated after a trying day."

Both of the men nodded wordlessly in acknowledgement. Forester stood as well, stretching and then leaving to get in some sleep before the morning watch. Chartrand elected to stay, putting his feet up on the table and quietly sipping his brandy. Patrick then left and went up on deck.

The Marine guarding the hourglass touched his musket as he approached. Everyone on deck was quiet, giving him a wide berth as he walked back and forth. They all nodded or saluted to him as he passed, and he saw in their faces as strange look of admiration. *I'm not holding up nearly as well as they think I am*, he admitted to himself. He silently acknowledged each of them in turn, his spirits buoyed to know that in his short time in command he had been able to foster some sense of loyalty among the crew.

He went to the rail and looked out over the water. The moon had risen, a night before full, and it illuminated everything with a brilliant light. From its position in the sky, it blazed a shimmering path across the calm waters to the islands looming ahead. He took out his spyglass and extended it, but even with the moon's beams reflecting on the water and outlining the dark masses of the islands against the night sky, he saw no evidence of the *Wasp*. He closed the glass and leaned against the rail, observing that the *Enterprise* seemed to be following the glittering trail in the water. Not usually one for superstition, he had an odd feeling as if the glowing light were a path deliberately leading him somewhere ominous.

"I am a damn fool!" Harvey muttered under his breath. The hands in the boat who were rowing, did not react but all traded glances with each other.

"They sailed right past us!" he fumed as he and Patrick sat together as they were being rowed ashore. As soon as the Americans had arrived at Saint Thomas, Patrick had told Harvey of everything that had transpired, and asked if he had seen the *Wasp* during the night.

"I tell you they were not even two cable lengths away!" Harvey went on, anger rising in his voice as he came to realize how thoroughly he had been duped. "I hailed them, they answered. They gave the name of another ship in the West Indies squadron. They even gave the correct watchword. They were flying our ensign, so I thought nothing of it."

"But she had white trim instead of ochre," said Patrick.

"It was still dark," replied Harvey. "The ochre trim is hardly standard as it is. You're certain it was him?"

"I spoke to him on the dock in San Juan," answered Patrick. "I saw him leaning off the rail as they departed. It's him!"

Harvey shook his head, still in disbelief. "And you say the man now has your wife?" he asked, his eyebrow raised. It was a particular detail that had caused him no small amount of confusion. "What on earth was she doing in San Juan?"

"She came to see me," Patrick told him. Harvey remained unconvinced. "It's a long story," Patrick deflected before he could ask more. "What was her heading?"

"East," replied Harvey, motioning in that direction. "That's all I can tell you. We didn't keep a close watch on her. We thought she was an advance ship for the Admiral. He's scheduled to inspect the fortifications at Road Town on Tortola tomorrow."

"We should be continuing the pursuit!" urged Patrick. "He could be all the way to Virgin Gorda by now."

"I know," answered Harvey, still flustered. "The garrison commander at Fort Christian summoned us immediately. He did not say why."

The two officers cut off their conversation as they neared the shore. It had been a smooth ride from their ships, which were anchored together in the harbor at Charlotte Amalie on the southern shore of Saint Thomas. The town was not particularly large, settled on a narrow strip of land hugging the coast. Some buildings toward the rear of the town clung to the hillside, but not many as the incline proved much too steep past a certain point.

Their destination was unmistakable. Fort Christian, which protected the settlement, was a typical four-sided bastioned fort, complete with the cylindrical guard posts on the corners that has been added to every fortification in the Caribbean regardless of nationality. What caught the eye of Patrick, and every other visitor to Charlotte Amalie, was that the fort was painted the same vivid shade of crimson as the Danish flag.

While the islands may have legally belonged to Denmark, their allegiance to Bonaparte had brought the British swooping down to occupy them. Therefore, it was officers from the British army that were there to greet them when they reached the dock. As befitting the tropics, they wore white trousers, and tall hats with brims rather than shakos.

"Sorry Yank," said one of the red coated officers standing on the pier as Patrick stepped out of the boat. "But if you're here to take the islands from us, the war's over."

"We'd like to keep it that way," Patrick answered, throwing a casual salute. "Lieutenant Commander Sullivan of the USS *Enterprise*. We're assisting HMS *Athena* in tracking down one of our ships. Unfortunately, it appears the ship was captured by pirates."

"Good Lord! Is that what's been going on?" said the second officer, a tall man who Patrick could tell had been weakened by a bout of yellow fever. *I suppose downing Chartrand's concoction isn't so bad after all*, he thought, looking over the Englishman. The poor man had gone pale, even in this sunny climate, with the tell-tale yellow pallor affecting his eyes and skin. The disease regularly ravaged the Caribbean. It was common knowledge that men desperate for promotion in the stagnant officer class of the British army would volunteer for a posting in the West Indies, as the mortality rate among Europeans was so high it would cull the upper echelons of whole regiments, allowing men to advance rapidly in rank. Needless to say, plans were often upended when those same officers fell victim to it.

The first man gave the sickly officer an exasperated look at his outburst but did not comment. Turning to Patrick, he returned the salute. "I am Major Cassidy, this is Captain Winkler, commanding the detachment of the First West India Regiment here on Saint Thomas. Gentlemen, if you'll come with me." He motioned for them to follow, and the group of men walked briskly from the dock and then across the small lawn in front of the fortress, which they entered through a small sally-port instead of the main gate. The

Major then led them to a barracks building where an office was located.

"Thank you both for coming ashore so quickly," said the Cassidy. "We just received two men who came across the sound from Saint John. I think you'll want to hear what they have to say." The Major then flicked his wrist at a guard standing near the door. Patrick noticed the soldier was black, a local who had a better tolerance against the deadly fever and wondered if the men of the garrison were part of the same West Indies regiment that had fought at New Orleans.

Once the guard left, the sickly Captain Winkler turned to face them. "We've had strange goings on of late," he told them. "We'd seen an American flagged vessel prowling around our waters, yet she never made an attempt to attack any targets on shore. We tried hailing her several times, but she never answered."

"Yes," mused the Major. "Also, we've had very little contact over the last several weeks with the populace on Saint John. I believe we've discovered why."

There was a knock on the officer door. The sentry had reappeared with two other people. The first was a white boy in his mid-teens, the other an older black man. Both were dressed in only threadbare pants and shirtsleeves. The boy appeared frightened and looked around the room warily.

"These two arrived this morning from the west end of Saint John in a small boat," Cassidy informed Patrick and Harvey. Then looking to the teen, he said, "Go on then, my boy. Tell them what you told me."

The boy nodded uneasily. "I'm the son of one of the planters on the island," he told them, and Patrick was surprised to hear him speaking with an English accent. The Major detected Patrick's confusion and interrupted with, "Most of the landowners on the islands are English and have been for some time. Few Danes live in the territory." He then raised a hand to excuse himself and let the boy continue.

"This is my father's servant," he said gesturing to the black man. Patrick of course needed no translation that in the Caribbean, 'servant' would be a polite euphemism for saying slave. "There are some pirates that have taken Coral Bay on the eastern end of the island," said the teen. "They have been gathering ships in the bay.

No one knows why. Their leader has taken hostages. He's holding them in the old castle atop the Fortsberg."

"Fort Freideriksvearn?" asked Winkler. "That place is a derelict," he scoffed.

The teen did not know how to respond to the comment and continued speaking. "The leader threatened to kill the hostages if any word left Saint John that he has taken the fort. He also..." The teen paused, and glanced sideways warily at his companion. "He also threatened to raise a slave revolt if they did not cooperate."

The Major rubbed his chin. "No idle threat," he said. "Saint John already had a revolt back in the thirties. And everyone knows what happened in Haiti."

Patrick turned to Harvey. "That explains why the shipping has gone missing in the area. Carlyle's made himself a safe haven to strike out from."

Harvey looked to Cassidy. "Sir, how could he have taken control of the fort? I thought we had garrisoned every post?"

"We did," answered Cassidy. "The men stationed there began packing up as soon as word reached us of peace with the Yankees. We're due to return the islands to the Danes within a week or two as it is."

"I can't say I blame them for leaving," commented Winkler. "Frederiksvearn was a horrible place to try and live. The walls were crumbling to pieces. It had no interior amenities, and one had to climb up that bloody hill just to get to it." The man went a little pale, and began to fan himself, displaying a physical reaction to just thinking of the place.

"We should alert the Admiral," said Harvey. "If I set out at once, the *Athena* can reach Road Town by nightfall. He'll be able to send us help. More ships and men. We can blockade them in the bay and then storm the fortress."

"Wait," said Patrick holding up a hand. "If we make any attack, he'll simply kill the hostages. We need to find a way to get into the fortress and rescue them first. Then we can destroy his little flotilla."

The Major of the garrison nodded to the sentry and said, "Private, please escort these men outside." The solider touched his arm to his musket and opened the door. The boy hesitated as if he had something more to say, but exited the room without another word. Once they were gone, the Major leaned forward, placing his fists on his desk.

"This threat of a slave revolt adds another wrinkle," he said to the naval officers. "Even if you were to successfully infiltrate the fort and rescue the hostages, he could turn the enslaved population on the landowners in an instant. It could then spread to the other islands in the chain."

"Commander Sullivan," addressed Winkler. "You spoke as if you knew the man who is the leader of these pirates?"

Patrick nodded. "I know the man. He is a former officer of the Royal Navy, and I was responsible for him losing his commission. Our enmity predates the late hostilities."

The officer raised his eyebrows at the revelation. "If you have prior knowledge of the man, pray, tell us, is he a radical emancipator?"

Patrick shook his head. "No. He is not motivated by altruism. I surmise he is plotting some sort of revenge for what he sees as past transgressions, though I do not know what his final objective would be."

Cassidy put his hands on his hips. "I'll give you what supplies we can, but that is all the support I can muster. My garrison is spread thin across the island, and even so, about a quarter are ill with fever. I cannot lend any men to you for a strike at the fort."

"I think the fewer men the better," said Patrick. "Do you have charts of Saint John?"

The Major nodded. "We do. I'll send a man to fetch them."

Patrick saluted, followed by Harvey. "Thank you, Major Cassidy, we'll keep you appraised as best we can."

After a final exchange of salutes, Patrick and Harvey exited the office. Stepping onto the parade ground, the pair put their hats back on their heads and started walking for the gate. "I fully understand you wanting to be the one that undertakes the rescue," said Harvey. "I'll still set out for Road Town. You'll need support once you've returned to your ship. If he has collected a dozen or so armed merchants and a sloop, you'll be fighting uneven odds."

"I know," said Patrick gloomily. "We'll need to arrange some sort of signal for you to know if we've succeeded. I'm sure he'll have lookouts to warn him if your squadron sails to blockade him."

Before Harvey could answer, the teenaged boy from Saint John approached them. Patrick cast his gaze around and noticed his companion had been separated by the soldiers and was sitting against a wall behind two of the redcoats. He got to his feet quickly, looking alarmed as the boy approached them.

"That's a fine firelock you've there, Captain," the boy said to Harvey, who had a pistol tucked in his belt out of habit.

"This?" Harvey asked, pulling it out and showing it to the youngster. "Nothing special. It's rather standard make I'd say."

Glancing sideways, Patrick noticed the black servant had now taken a few steps forward and was reaching slowly behind his back. When he saw Patrick looking at him, he broke into a run, a knife now in his hand.

"Harvey!" Patrick shouted in warning. Harvey looked up and saw the man advancing on them at the run. He started to raise his pistol, but suddenly the boy grabbed it from his hand, cocked it, and spun around, firing into the servant at point blank range. The man dropped face-first to the ground at the boy's feet, dead.

"What in blazes?!" yelled Harvey, grabbing hold of the boy and wresting the weapon away from him. The two Redcoats now came running over, and leveled their bayonets at the boy while Harvey held him by the scruff of the neck. Behind Patrick, the door to the barracks building was thrown open and Cassidy appeared in the doorway.

"What the devil?!" he exclaimed, while behind him, Captain Winkler looked on, confused and dabbing his forehead with a handkerchief.

"Wait! Wait!" the boy shouted as Harvey threw him to the ground. The soldiers then pointed their bayonets at his belly, ready to skewer him if made another move. "He's not my servant!"

"What?!" Patrick and Harvey blurted out simultaneously.

"He's one of that pirate's men!" ranted the boy. "I swear!"

Patrick reached down and pulled the boy to his feet. "What's your name, boy?"

"John Williams, Captain," he answered, ignorant of proper military nomenclature.

"Well, Master Williams," began Patrick. "If this is one of the pirate's men, then why did he allow you to come across from Saint John to tell us where he is hiding?"

"Because he *wants* you to attack."

Patrick stared blankly at Williams and blinked.

"He does, Sir!" Williams pleaded, clasping his hands together if praying. "You must believe me! He's set a trap for you!"

Patrick and Harvey exchanged a look. "What sort of trap?" asked Harvey.

Williams' eyes darted back and forth between the two men. "If you come by sea up the mouth of the bay, he'll loose his ships on you. They're hidden in an inlet. Some are armed with cannon, others are loaded with gunpowder. If you arrive with smaller ships, he'll overwhelm you with the men-o-war. If you bring larger ships, he'll blow them up with the gunpowder ships."

"We'll have to go in overland then," said Patrick. He started to turn to ask Cassidy again if he were certain there were no troops he could spare, but Williams grabbed his arm.

"No! That would be even worse!" he claimed. "If you come by land he'll feint retreat to the fort and blow it up once you're inside. He'll also send all his ships out while you are distracted attacking the fort. He plans on sending some to Tortola to attack the Admiral that has landed there, and the rest to attack Porto Rico."

"By God!" gasped Cassidy. "The man's insane!"

Patrick shook his head. "He's no madman, Major. He's evil. I assure you he knows exactly what he's doing. Think of what would happen if he were to sink even half of a Royal Navy Squadron, or blow up a ship in the harbor of San Juan, while flying American flags from his ships?" Patrick paused as he realized the enormity of Carlyle's plans. "He's so hellbent on revenge that he wants to keep the war going. He doesn't care how many people he has to kill, or even if he has to attack his own countrymen in order to get his way."

Cassidy continued to shake his head in disbelief. "Madness. Utter madness," he said to himself, turning away.

"What of this man?" asked Captain Winkler, who had knelt down beside the black man Williams had shot.

"That pirate fellow had sent him with me to make sure I told you what he wanted me to," the teen stammered. "He thought sending a black man along as a servant would be inconspicuous. He was ordered to kill me if I tried to tell you the truth. When your soldiers separated him from me in the courtyard, I knew it was my best chance." Williams looked back to Patrick. "Please, Captain, you must rescue the people in the fort. He's holding my mother and sister in there."

Patrick put a hand on the boy's shoulder to calm him. "How old are you son?"

"Fifteen," he answered.

"That's a brave thing you did," Patrick told him. "You come along with me. I'll need someone who knows the island well." He turned the boy around to face the opposite direction as the soldiers picked up the dead man's arms and dragged the body away.

"It's imperative I inform the Admiral," said Harvey. "If Carlyle's going to attack the squadron, we can't allow them to strike while they're sitting helpless at anchor." Patrick nodded in agreement.

"Coral Bay looks out to the south," Williams spoke up again. "From the fort you can see all the way to Saint Croix. He also leaves a ship anchored near the mouth of the bay."

Harvey let a soft smile tug at the corner of his mouth. "Thank you, lad," he said appreciatively. "We'll keep round the north end of the island then. We can hide behind Great Thatch, or even go as far north as Jost Van Dyke if we have to, and then make our way east under cover of darkness," he advised, speaking of the British islands to the northwest of Saint John.

"Agreed," said Patrick. "Major, are you certain there's no men you can spare us?"

Cassidy rubbed his chin for a moment then looked around the fort. Despite the pained look on his face, he said, "The best I can do is to send a detachment to secure Christian's Bay on the west end of the island. We'll be able to act to protect the inhabitants of the island in the event that the threat of a slave revolt is true. Even so, I'll have to call out the militia here just to keep our posts garrisoned."

"Understood," replied Patrick, grimly. "We should get moving. We don't have much time."

I am a damn fool! Anna thought to herself. She struggled against the ropes that bound her wrists behind her back. Her ankles were similarly tied to the chair she was sitting on.

She had gotten careless, but she was at least willing to admit that to herself. Her exuberance at the chance to surprise Patrick and show him the gold sovereigns she had brought with her had caused her to let her guard down. The war was over, her payment was in hand and the British safely behind her. Even with Patrick's warning that Carlyle was in San Juan, it had not occurred to her that he might have been observing her before then.

Poor Spencer, she thought, recalling how he had gallantly tried to defend her from Carlyle's men. He stood no chance against four armed men in a tight corridor. After pummeling him with fists and pistol grips, they had left him bleeding in a heap on the floor whilst she had been gagged and bound into a rolled-up carpet. Unlike Cleopatra, she was not given a dramatic reveal, but roughly unrolled onto the hard deck of the ship. Carlyle had only given her a look of contempt and then had his men haul her below. Now she was here, tied up in a crumbling fortress awaiting what nasty fate Carlyle no doubt had planned for her.

The foremost reason Anna was angry at herself was not just that she had let her guard down, but that she had placed more than herself at risk. "No, not papa, little one. I mean you," she whispered aloud looking down at her belly. She was pregnant, and had known for about a month and guessed she had conceived in February. She had not told Patrick yet for fear that he would have refused to let her go to Kingston to collect her payment. But carrying a child had only made her more determined, knowing how much good for their new family that the money could do for them. It had pained her to keep it from him, and was hoping to tell him once she had the money and could deliver it safely to him. Hiding it had been especially difficult, as she had been overjoyed at being able to conceive, having feared until then she might be infertile. Now she was cursing herself for not telling him. *No, best I didn't*, she reconsidered. *He doesn't need any more worries. Me being in Carlyle's clutches is enough.*

She looked out a nearby window, what had once been an embrasure for a cannon. Outside it was a clear sunny spring afternoon. The shadows were closing on the hills surrounding the bay the fortress overlooked. It had grown hot and humid during the day, and there had been little breeze coming into the room, leaving her sweating profusely. The room was completely bare, aside from the chair she was sitting on, and was diamond shaped. The roof and upper half of the walls were made of wood, and looked to be a temporary addition atop a corner bastion. She was completely lost as to what island she might be on.

The door to the room she was being held in opened, and Carlyle entered. He wore a tan jacket of light material, and white breeches with tall riding boots. He still wore an officer's cocked hat, while she recognized that he still had the same sword with the lion head pommel.

"Anna. You've grown careless," he said smugly. "Admittedly, I was lucky. It was pure chance I happened to glimpse you when you arrived in San Juan. But when fate gives such an opportunity as that, I knew I had to take it. You may ensure my plans succeed beyond all expectations."

She looked away back out the window, trying to ignore him.

Carlyle laughed. "Expecting to see your bog dwelling paramour coming to the rescue?"

Anna turned her head back and looked into Carlyle's charcoal eyes. "Why yes, I am expecting *my husband* to come rescue me."

"Husband?" he repeated, his eyebrows going up. He then stepped closer and bent over so that his face was close to hers. His dark gaze pierced into her, and she felt her hairs stand on end. "You married him? You? He'd have you after all you've done?"

"You wouldn't understand," she sneered back into his face.

"I gather not," he said, backing away and circling around the room, throwing his hands up in the air. "For I cannot understand how you could betray everything you served, for him! You betrayed England, you betrayed me!" He advanced on her again. "Tell me, what was it? A slight against you I made? Money? Or was he simply that skilled at bedding you?"

Anna snarled at him for a moment. She then chose to let all pretense drop and gave him a snide grin. "You can't betray what you've never been loyal to in the first place."

Carlyle's eyes widened. She had spoken to him for the first time in her native Irish accent. Before now, she had never used it in order to hide her identity, but there was no point in continuing that.

"Irish!" he growled. He pulled his right arm back, about to backhand her across the face, but he stopped himself. "I should not be surprised," he laughed to himself. "All of Wellington's spies in the Peninsula were Irish, why should you have been any different? He always was too loyal to that accursed island."

Carlyle turned away and began to walk around the room again. "Well, my dear Anna, I too am expecting your beloved Paddy to come rushing here to save you. In fact, I would hope for nothing less." He then leaned against a wall and folded his arms while facing her.

"You see, when we arrived here this morning, I dispatched one of my men with a local boy to inform the garrison at Saint Thomas of my capture of this place. Word will no doubt reach Sullivan in short order. He will of course know that I am holding you. Typical Paddy that he is, he'll come charging recklessly in."

Saint Thomas, she repeated in her mind. *I must be on Saint John then. Good, at least Patrick doesn't have far to search.* "You take him for a brash fool," replied Anna. "He's far more clever than that."

"Even if he is, his choices will be limited," answered Carlyle dismissively. "There are only two ways to attack this fortress. If he comes by sea, I have a ship at the entrance of the bay standing watch. At their signal, my flotilla will sortie from the inlet."

"And if he's brought reinforcements?" countered Anna.

"You mean from the British squadron at anchor at Road Town? My lookouts atop the mountains can easily see Tortola and would give me fair warning if they sailed. By the time they reached here we would be long gone, and they would find only an empty fort."

"And if he attacks by land?"

Carlyle chuckled haughtily. "Better still. No matter which part of the island he chooses to land on, he'll have to come by the roads to get here. If he tries going over the hills, he'll have to cut his way through jungle. My men can either block his passage and whittle down his forces or fall back on the fortress. And when Sullivan, blinded by his desperation to get to you, storms the ramparts, I'll detonate the gunpowder left here by the former garrison in their haste to depart."

Carlyle unfolded his arms and took a few steps toward her. "And while he is here, dying for his love, I will have already sailed with my ships. From thence, I shall strike the Spanish at Porto Rico, and the British squadron at Road Town, my ships under American colors."

Anna shook her head. "If you're simply going to blow up the fort when he gets here, then why haven't you killed me already?"

Carlyle smirked wickedly at her. "Oh, I have no intention of killing you. No. You will instead be brought before the authorities in Kingston, where after I expose your treachery, you will be hanged by the neck until you are dead."

Anna rolled her eyes at Carlyle's posturing. "Just how do you expect to do that? Do you really think that Patrick hasn't told everyone he can that it's you who is pirating ships under an American flag?"

Carlyle chuckled in response. "And just who is going to believe the rantings of a dead man? Whose only evidence will be that he saw me on a dock and then went off to mistakenly attack an abandoned fort to save his wife. The very same wife I will have exposed as being a traitor to the crown, whom I captured by chance while delivering goods to the port of San Juan. After all, I still have a letter of marque granted to me to act as a privateer, so I would still have enough authority to arrest you. My testimony will be the events that transpired on the Lake Erie frontier two summers past, about how you dismantled my spy network after I was captured, which led to those agents being executed by the Americans, and that you intended to deliver the gold paid to you in Kingston to the American officer you married."

Carlyle leaned forward and looked her in the eye. "You see, no matter what happens, I win. Sullivan will be dead, you will be hanged as a traitor, and Britain will renew the war with the United States, alongside Spain. How could they not after having a squadron destroyed in blatant violation of the peace treaty, combined with an unprovoked and dastardly attack upon the Spanish?" He broke into maniacal laughter. "Now all I need do is await Sullivan's arrival."

Anna's lip curled. "Genevieve would hate what you've become."

Carlyle ceased laughing at the mention of his wife's name. "How dare you!" he spat. This time he did backhand Anna across the face. Her vision went grey for a moment and stars winked in and out in front of her. She also tasted blood in her mouth from sharply biting her tongue.

"She is dead because of you! Because you betrayed me and aided the Yankees!" he roared in her face.

Gathering her wits, Anna replied, "You have no one to blame but yourself. You should have stayed in the Peninsula to fight the French, the real enemy. But no, you were too obsessed with vengeance. Where has that gotten you? Look where you are! Genevieve is dead and you're an outlaw hiding in a crumbling ruin dreaming grand designs. You're in such thrall to your own hatred you're still trying to kill Americans rather than raise your own sons!"

"Enough!" he shouted. "I have suffered too much to allow them to go unpunished. I will not be stopped. Not by your words or Sullivan's blade."

He turned his back on her and stomped his way to the door. Before he exited, he turned to her one last time. "Killing Sullivan will only be the beginning of my revenge, but it will be the most satisfying." He then walked out, slamming the door behind him.

Anna sighed and shook her head. Swishing some saliva around in her mouth, she spit out the blood from her tongue onto the floor. With the room quiet again, her burgeoning motherly instincts began to take over and her eyes darted around the room, trying to think of something that could help her escape. She struggled against the ropes that held her, but knew it was futile. Looking out the old cannon embrasure onto the harbor she thought, *For God's sake Patrick, please be as clever as I think you are.*

Patrick looked up at the pale globe hanging in the night sky. "It just had to be a full moon," he said to no one in particular. He shook his head at his ill luck and walked aft along the deck. Thompson, the carpenter, had two of the ship's boats arranged side by side and was covering them with black paint. He and some of the other hands had already spent the day blacking out the ship's sails and the white stripe along her gunports while they had waited for sunset behind Great Thatch Island.

"I'm not sure it'll have enough time to dry, Sir," he said as Patrick passed him.

"It will have to do," Patrick said with resignation. "Thompson, are you any good with a knife?"

The carpenter stopped his task for a moment and looked up at him with his brow furrowed. "I may have a special job for you on this mission," Patrick explained, without giving away any details.

Thompson thought the answer was satisfactory and nodded. He looked around himself briefly for a sharp instrument but settled on the paintbrush in his hand. He held up the brush and twirled it with his fingers for a few seconds, not splattering a single drop of paint on his hand.

Patrick chuckled at the demonstration. "Very good, Thompson. Can you swim?"

"Aye, Sir," he answered.

"Perfect," said Patrick. "I'll brief you shortly." He then walked back to the hatchway and went below to his cabin. Inside were all of the officers, along with Barnes, Doctor Chartrand, Sergeant Bowyer, and John Williams. Passing by the bandaged Spencer, whom he patted on the should as a gesture to show he was relieved to see him up and walking, he went around to the rear of his desk.

"We've cleared the passage between Little Thatch and Frenchman's Cay," he told them. "The *Athena* has broken off and headed for Road Town under full sail. I told Harvey to advise the British admiral to wait until four o'clock in the morning before he led the squadron out." He then twisted around the chart of Saint John that Major Cassidy had given him and motioned for young Williams to step forward.

"We need you to tell us everything you know about Coral Bay and the fortress," Patrick told him. "Where is the fort and where are all of his ships?"

Williams leaned forward and looked at the map. "The fort is here," he said, stabbing his finger on a small peninsula at the base of the bay beside the actual town of Coral Bay. "It doesn't look it on the map, but the hill is very high," the boy went on to say.

"Can you draw the layout of the fort?" Patrick asked him, holding out a pencil to him.

Williams nodded. "Yes, Sir, we used to play up there when I was a boy before the British garrison came." He took the pencil from Patrick and began to make a quick sketch in an empty space in the chart. The outline he drew was a simple rectangular fort with bastions at the corners with a building in the center. "The center building is stone, I think it's where the officers lived," he explained. "The British put roofs over the corners where the cannons are. I think that's where the soldiers lived."

"Do you know where the hostages were being held?"

Williams nodded. "In the center building with the gunpowder. There were ten other people besides me."

"Was there a red-haired woman among them?" Patrick asked. The rest of the officers all exchanged knowing looks between themselves but said nothing.

Williams frowned. "No, not in the center building," he said. "But I did see the pirates bringing in a red-haired woman as I was leaving the fort yesterday morning. She was blindfolded and they took her up to one of the rooms on the corners with the cannons."

"Damn," Patrick whispered, rubbing his chin. "Where are the ships?"

"Over here in Hurricane Hole," answered Williams, pointing to two of the inlets on the eastern side of the bay. "Except for the one ship down here next to the little island," he added, pointing to a small island at the mouth of the bay that could not have been much more than a large rock.

"Thank you, Williams," said Patrick looking over the map. After studying it for a moment he said, "I don't see any alternative. We'll have to anchor the *Enterprise* behind the end of this eastern point and then row the boats in all the way to the base of the fortress."

"That's an awfully long way to row," pointed out Latimer, who had a look of apprehension on his face, knowing that he was going along for the mission.

"I agree, Sir," said Forester. "It's too far, especially on a night with a full moon. The picket ship will almost certainly see you."

"You could use Haulover Bay," Williams spoke up again. "Over here," he pointed out on the map, indicating a spot along the peninsula that formed the eastern side of the bay. "It's a small bit of land that some of the fishermen carry their boats over instead of going all the way around the point."

"What about lookouts, Sir?" asked Forester. "If he's as cunning as you say, he'll have men in the hills keeping watch. They may even see us already."

"I've thought of that," said Patrick. "We'll anchor the ship at Brown Bay," he said, pointing out a spot on the northern side of the island. "You will make a demonstration of landing men ashore while I take the boats and row down to Haulover Bay. Hopefully you can draw his men off by convincing him we'll be coming over land."

Patrick turned the map back around. "I'm bringing along Thompson. He'll take the best swimmers in the crew with him and board the ships hiding in the inlets. At the first sign of a disturbance at the fort, those men will set fire to the fireships. Destroying the rest of the ships would be easy if the fireships have powder in their holds, but I doubt he would risk storing it that way. Carlyle also won't want to lose any cannon by leaving them on ships meant to be destroyed, so the fireships will likely be unarmed. For the rest of the ships, Thompson will cut the rudder cables. We can let the British deal with them."

He pointed a finger at Forester. "You are to make sail exactly at four o'clock, the same time the British leave Road Town. Don't worry about outpacing them, we'll need you to sink the picket ship at the mouth of the bay to clear our escape route. If we are successful, we'll signal you with a blue rocket. Even if we fail, sink that picket ship anyway and wait for the reinforcements. At that point, stopping Carlyle takes precedence above all else. Understood?"

Forester silently nodded in the affirmative.

Looking once again to Williams, Patrick asked, "Is there a suitable beach in the bay where we can place a rocket?"

Williams thought for a moment then pointed to a location near the inlets. "There's a small beach here. There's an old Danish cannon laying there, you can't miss it."

"Very well. Mister Latimer, you will wait there until you can see that we are returning to launch the rocket."

"Aye, aye, Sir."

Patrick looked around the cabin one final time. "Are there any questions?" Everyone shook their heads. "Good. Mister Forester?" The Lieutenant perked up at his name being mentioned. "I have one last command for you. Pray."

The others laughed softly, and Forester went a little red in the face. "I don't jest, Mister Forester," said Patrick. "We'll need all the help God can give us."

The Lieutenant gave a chuckle. "Aye, aye, Sir. I'll make it the best praying I've done."

"Thank you," Patrick said to him. "Dismissed."

The officers began filing out through the cabin door, but Spencer held back until they had all left. "Sir, I want to volunteer to go along with you."

Patrick frowned at him. "Phillip, you were just beaten within an inch of your life. I'm surprised you can walk."

"I'm not bad off, Sir," he blatantly lied. "Please, Sir, I –"

"No," Patrick said bluntly, raising a single finger. "You do not have atone for letting them capture Anna. I don't blame you for it, Phillip, I sincerely hope that you don't think I do."

Spencer shook his bandaged and bruised head. "No, Sir, I don't. I feel I owe it to her though." He stepped forward and gripped Patrick by the arm. "You are my friends. I can't stay here resting while you're both in danger. Please, Patrick, let me do this."

He stared intently at Spencer for a few moments. It was the first time the Midshipman had ever called him Patrick. "Alright," he answered. "Have Chartrand give you some laudanum for the pain."

Spencer shook his head. "No, it dulls the senses. I'll work through it."

Patrick smiled at him, silently admiring both his dedication and that he was made of sterner stuff than he had ever given the impression of. "Go up on deck then. I'll be along."

"Aye, aye, Sir," Spencer answered, saluting with a grin.

Once he left, Patrick looked over the map one last time. "Storm the fortress, save the damsel, kill the villain," he summarized to himself. "Sounds like a cheap work of fiction."

Chapter 10

April 1815, Coral Bay, the island of Saint John, Danish West Indies

Patrick's arms were already tired by the time they had beached their boats at Haulover Bay. To aid moving swiftly and undetected, Thompson had cut the boats' oars in half to allow them to paddle as if they were in canoes rather than longboats. Going around the outer edge of the island's northern shore was difficult work, as the prevailing winds kept pushing them toward the rocks. Pulling their craft ashore was a welcome relief.

"Take a few minutes to rest," he told the men. His party numbered only a dozen in two boats. Patrick was in the lead boat, along with Spencer, Sergeant Bowyer, and three other Marines. Latimer was in the other boat with Thompson, Henderson, and a trio of hands that were good swimmers. Every one of them was wearing dark shirts and trousers and had rubbed bootblack on their exposed skin. Spencer wore a knitted hat to cover his blonde hair and bandage, but the rest were bareheaded.

Looking ahead, the low-lying saddle of the ridgeline allowed him to see into Coral Bay. There was plenty of scrub brush between the beach they had landed on and the one on the inner side of the bay, but not the thick tangle of jungle that covered the slopes of the hills. He estimated the distance to be less than two hundred yards across to the other beach. *Not too far to drag the boats*, he thought.

The entire scene was bathed in moonlight. It was brilliantly bright, affording them little cover, and the white sands nearly glowed in the dark. From his vantage point he could plainly see the picket ship, a brig, at anchor near the small island at the mouth of the bay. It would have been beautiful had it been any other night, and even then, he could not resist soaking in the scenery for a moment.

"Mister Latimer," he spoke quietly. The Midshipman stood up and walked over to him. "Take one of the hands and walk ahead. See if there's a path to the other beach."

Latimer nodded silently. He then whispered to one of the nearby seamen, who got up and followed the Midshipman as he walked in the direction of the opposite bay. After a few minutes of waiting, the pair returned with good news.

"The way is clear, Sir," reported Latimer. "No sentries. There's a small path we can follow to the next beach."

"Very good," Patrick said to Latimer. He turned back around and waved to the men to get back to their boats. The group picked themselves off the sand and grabbed hold of the sides of their boats.

"Ready?" he asked them, and they all nodded back without a word. "On three. One, two, three, heave!" All twelve men grunted and groaned as they picked up their boats. They did not get much clearance off the ground, and more often than not were dragging the back ends through the dirt, but they set off as quickly as they could across to the other beach. The path Latimer had spoken of was barely wide enough for them to pass through, and the men often caught their clothes on the foliage. At one point, Patrick winced as he felt a sting on his upper arm and looked to see that a cut had been torn in his jacket by a tangle of snake cactus.

Finally reaching the beach on the inside of Coral Bay, they set their boats down again and Patrick motioned with his hand for them all to crouch down. Taking a look around, he saw no sign of activity from the picket ship, nor any on the hills surrounding them. "Alright, into the water," he said, and the men glided their craft off the beach.

Jumping in as each man touched the water, the last man gave an extra hard shove and hopped in as the boat drifted away. They took up their oars again and paddled into the bay. The water here was much calmer, the bay being shielded from the wind and currents. There were still hazards, as Patrick could see in the dark to his right, a rocky point they needed to round that the waves were crashing against. Seeing that it was connected to the shore by thin spit of land like the one they had already traversed at Haulover Bay, he waved at Latimer's boat to follow him, and they beached again on the shore behind the point. Here they portaged the boats again, having an easier time as the spit of land was little more than a sandbar, and there was a stagnant pond through which they could float the boats along.

With the rocky point behind them, the men clambered back into their boats and started paddling again. Now Patrick could clearly see the entirety of Coral Bay with an unobstructed view. In the center was the Fortsberg, a tall conical hill, on top of which he could see the flickering of torchlight emanating from the embrasures of Fort Frederiksvaern. To the left, set further back were more lights, the little village of Coral Bay itself. On the right, down in the furthest inlet, he spotted a bonfire on a beach, and could make out figures moving about around it. He heard noise coming from that direction, but it was not distinct enough to tell if it was Carlyle's men carousing, or just locals enjoying a late night on the bay.

Paddling to the first of the three inlets, they found the thin beach Williams had indicated on the map. Exiting the boat into water a little past his ankles, Patrick found this beach was rocky, the gravel made of broken coral. As they began pulling the boats in, he heard a shout of pain, and saw Henderson picking up one foot and hobbling to the beach.

"Henderson, quiet!" he tried to half shout, half whisper at the man. The cook did not make any further loud noises but continued to hiss through gritted teeth. As soon as he was clear of the water, he collapsed onto his backside and ripped his left shoe off. He then started inspecting the bottom of his foot and picked something out of it, which caused him to wince and seethe even more.

"Sea urchin. Right through my shoe," he managed to get out, followed by a hasty, "Sorry, Sir," for having called out so loudly.

Patrick knelt down beside him and picked up his foot trying to get a look at it. He held it up to the moonlight and could make out some discoloration. "Can you walk?" he asked.

Henderson shook his head. "Not a chance, Sir."

Patrick reached into the nearest boat and retrieved a pistol, along with a few cartridges and handed them over. "Stay here with Mister Latimer and guard the boats. Don't load it until the shooting starts, understood?"

Henderson nodded. "Aye, Sir," he rasped, still in pain. "I'm sorry, Sir."

Patrick put a hand on his shoulder. "It's not your fault, Henderson," he said to convince the man he had not let him down. Inwardly, Patrick now worried that his party to burn the boats was now short a man.

"Sir, here's that cannon Williams spoke of," whispered Spencer, who was a few yards away. Looking up, Patrick saw him standing next to what could have been mistaken for a log sticking up out of the ground. As he got closer, he saw it was indeed a cannon, rusting away and buried halfway into the ground. He gave it only a cursory inspection and briefly wondered how it had gotten there, particularly at such an odd angle.

"At least we know we're at the right spot," he said. Turning back around, he went back to the boats and pulled out the rocket for Latimer to shoot off, along with a spare, and pistol to light them off. Originally, they had been British rockets recovered from the battlefield at New Orleans, but fortunately Commodore Patterson had let Patrick have them for the *Enterprise* thinking they might be useful.

With a final reminder to Latimer not to set the rocket off until it was clear that Patrick's party was returning from the fort with the hostages, and a word to cheer up a dejected Henderson, the remainder of the group set off, this time with only one boat. While Patrick, Spencer, and the Marines paddled, Thompson and his group were towed along in their wake by a rope, kicking in the water to not make themselves too much of a burden. They cut across the first inlet, rounding a small cliff face they had to keep their distance from to keep from being crashed against a few sharp rocks at the bottom. Once past that obstacle, they crept by the entrance of the second inlet, where five ships of various rigging were anchored.

"Ready now, Sir," whispered Thompson as he clung to the aft end of the boat.

"Make it so," answered Patrick with a quick two fingered salute. "Stay close to the mangroves on the shoreline. If need be, hide among them. The watchmen might mistake you for flotsam."

"Aye, Sir. Good luck," he replied. The Carpenter then began swimming toward the ships, the others silently following.

"On to the fort," Patrick then said, and they began paddling as quickly as stealth would allow. They were now at their most vulnerable, moving across the clear open waters in the center of the bay. The entire way as they paddled, Patrick kept looking over his shoulder at the ships in the inlets, certain someone would see them on the moonlit water. *If not the ships, certainly someone in the fort*, he thought, looking up at the edifice high above them. At any moment he expected a shout of alarm, a bell ringing out, or a cannon firing at them. He felt his pace quicken, beating in his ears, and he paddled faster. The others in the boat must have noticed and quickened their own pace.

Despite all his fears, nothing happened. They reached the shore at the base of the Fortsberg Hill, climbed out, and hauled the boat ashore. Patrick then had the men turn the boat around, with the bow facing out to the bay so they could make a speedy escape. The Marines gathered up their muskets and cartridge boxes, while Patrick and Spencer tucked cutlasses and pistols into their belts.

"Remember, cold steel until I give the word," he told Sergeant Bowyer.

"Aye, Sir," he replied.

The party then began to make their way uphill through the undergrowth. It was tough going, as Patrick had feared. All manner of sharp protruding plants jutted out at them, cutting exposed skin and tearing uniforms. Trying to find footholds in the dark was an even more difficult task, and each of the men tripped and fell multiple times, one of the Marines almost sliding downhill. The air became denser the moment they entered the jungle, the humidity trapped by the vegetation, which also prevented the coastal breezes from penetrating. As such, they rapidly tired and began sweating. Their misery was compounded by a lack of canteens or water bottles, left behind so they did not encumber the men. The only reassuring aspect was that the cacophony of sounds coming from critters would mask their approach, and likely prevented anyone on shore from hearing Henderson's earlier cry of pain.

After what had to Patrick felt like hours, but was surely only about fifteen minutes or so, he broke through the brush onto a wide path. He immediately assumed this was the road up to the fort. "Stay to the sides," he whispered, and the six of them dispersed, three to a side. They then began heading uphill, Patrick trying to keep his ears open for the sound of anyone approaching. Sergeant Bowyer brought up the rear, watching their backs.

After following the road for a few minutes, it abruptly turned a corner, creating a switchback. Patrick waved them forward and they continued on around the corner. The fort, which had been obscured from view by the thick foliage, could now be seen again, the flicker of lights coming from within giving them a point to judge their progress by.

As they approached another switchback, Patrick heard voices coming from up ahead. Patrick motioned to get off the road and they scurried into the bushes. Breathing slowly, he watched as two men stepped into view, one white the other black. Their posture was casual, which relieved him, indicating they had so far achieved surprise. As the two men neared, he overheard their conversation.

"It burns when I piss," the black man said in a thick Caribbean accent. Patrick also noticed the man was walking a little oddly.

The white man laughed in turn. "What did you expect?" he replied, his voice marking him as Scottish. Patrick noticed he was wearing a British Army Redcoat turned inside out, the mark of a deserter.

"The brothel on Lovango Cay isn't known for the quality of its whores!" The Scotsman continued laughing and thumped the black man on the back as they continued down the hill.

No, most definitely not on the alert for intruders, thought Patrick. He waited until they were well out of sight down the trail before he stepped back out into the open. Once he did, the others emerged as well, and they continued on up the path.

When they got to within roughly fifty yards of the fort, Patrick called them to a halt, and they crouched low. Looking ahead, he could see two figures standing guard at the gate to the fort, located on the shorter western wall. Turning around, he pointed into the brush, and the group reentered the jungle, this time making their way around to the side of the fort.

Through the trees, Patrick could see a light flickering in the southwest bastion, so they continued farther east along the crown of the hill. Seeing that the southeast bastion was dark, he paused. Looking to the others, he jerked his head at the fort and said, "Follow me."

Anna rolled her head around to one side as she woke. She thought she had heard something outside, a scratching noise, but she couldn't be sure. *Probably some animal*, she thought, and wondered if there were any predators in the Caribbean that could climb the fort's walls. He primary fear though was that might be hallucinating. She had barely been given any water since arriving at the fort, and the heat had been taking its toll on her all day. She had sweated so much she had only called out to guards to relieve herself only once the entire day. *And they still blindfolded me*, she recalled, still sour over the indignity.

She heard another noise, more scraping against the stonework of the fort's bastion. Then came a human grunt. She realized someone was climbing the wall. For a moment she began to panic, thinking some of Carlyle's more lascivious men had decided to go around the guards and climb into her room to have their way with her.

A head then popped up over the edge of one of the embrasures, outlined by the glow of the moonlight outside. Anna gasped in surprise, but then froze in terror. The man hoisted himself up a little further, and upon seeing her, put a finger to his lips. She then recognized he was wearing the uniform of a United States Marine, his musket slung over his back, and she breathed the happiest sigh of relief in her life.

"Sir, I've found a woman," the Marine whispered back over the edge of the window after pulling himself through. He then unsheathed a knife from his belt and cut her ropes. She slumped against him and the Marine helped her to her feet.

"What ship are you from?" she asked, bewildered.

"USS *Enterprise*," another voice said from the window. Patrick appeared and pulled himself over the wall. He rushed to her as she staggered forward, and she collapsed into his arms.

"I'm here," he told her, pulling her up and giving her a firm kiss.

"I knew you'd come," she replied, feeling safe again in his arms. She looked up at him with fright in her eyes. "It's a trap, Patrick."

"I know it is," he said. "And we're about to spoil it. Did they harm you?"

"No," she said, understanding what he meant, then turned her face so he could see her chin. "Carlyle did hit me once though."

She heard a pained grunt and saw another Marine helping a fourth figure over the wall.

"Spencer!" she whispered with joy. Regaining her strength she went over to him, put her arms around him and gave him a friendly kiss on the cheek. "I feared they'd killed you," she said to him.

"Oh, not to worry. My head's rather thick," he joked.

The last two Marines climbed through the embrasure and unslung their muskets. Patrick went to the door and slowly cracked it open. Peering through, he saw a slovenly looking guard at the base of the bastion's steps, snoring. Over in the northeast corner of the fort's interior, several men were sitting around a small campfire, at least one also sleeping, though two were passing back and forth a bottle of liquor. There were a pair of torches mounted on the wall near the gate, and he could see the backs of the sentries standing there.

Backing away from the door, he asked Anna, "Do you know how many guards?"

She shook her head. "No. They kept me blindfolded the whole time."

Patrick sighed and shook his head. "There's too many in the courtyard to try and sneak past," he said to Bowyer. "We'll have to rush them before they can harm the hostages or set off the gunpowder in that stone building. Fix bayonets and load your weapons." The four Marines all did as ordered, while Patrick and Spencer also loaded their pistols.

Going back to the door, he took another look around, formulating a hasty plan. "Sergeant, you stay with me," he began. "We'll run past this guard at the bottom of the stairs and straight to the door to the center building." He then pointed to the three Privates in the group. "The first man behind the Sergeant is to run through the bugger at the bottom. There's a group of men on the right around a fire. Charge them with cold steel then fan out keeping a watch on the other bastions. Shoot anyone who opens a door."

To Spencer he added, "Bring up the rear and cover the Marines. Keep Anna behind you."

"Aye, aye, Sir," they all whispered back.

Patrick returned to the door, extracting his cutlass from his belt and cocking his pistol, and now opened it fully. He paused, did one last quick look around the fort, and took off running.

Sprinting down the steps, he leapt clear over the sleeping guard. He thought he heard Bowyer doing the same but there was a shout of, "Oi!" to his right. He ignored it and kept running. More shouts of alarm came from the men near the fire, and he heard the other

Marines running at them. The calls for help soon became screams and the sounds of a deadly hand to hand struggle.

Ahead of him, the guards at the gate turned around, their faces lit by the nearby torches showing complete confusion. Just as Patrick neared the corner of the central building, another guard he had not seen came walking around the corner. The man's eyes went wide as he saw Patrick coming at him. Before he could raise his musket, Patrick slammed into him shoulder first and shoved him to the side. He heard a scream from the man as Bowyer bayoneted him.

Rounding the corner, he saw the door. The guards at the gate now took aim at him. One fired first, the ball zipping past Patrick and ricocheting off the stone building. Patrick leveled his pistol and fired back, also missing. Sergeant Bowyer was now beside him and dropped to one knee. The Marine fired, striking the guard in the head. The second guard saw his companion get his brains blown out and decided to run for it. As he turned tail, another shot rang out, hitting him in the back, and he fell face first into the dirt.

"Good shot, Sir!" called out a Marine, and Patrick figured that Spencer had managed to make the shot with his pistol.

"Sergeant, get this door open," Patrick said to Bowyer, pointing to the door of the stone building. Just as Bowyer began to kick it down, the door of the room on the northwest bastion opened up. A confused and shabby looking pirate walked through, then dived backward into the room as a pair of musket balls ricocheted off the stone next to him. A few moments later, a flash and a bang emanated from the room as the man set off a cannon.

Well, that will have alerted this whole half of the island, Patrick thought. *At least Thompson should now begin burning the ships.* He then shouted to the Marines, "Get him!" while pointing to the bastion. The two Marines that had fired dashed forward and up the stairs to bastion. Recklessly charging through the door, the only other sound that came from the room was a man's scream that was cut off partway through.

He then heard the door to the central building fall off its hinges and a few screams from women inside. Going to the door, he looked inside, but could barely see inside the darkened room. "Outside, quickly!" he urged.

The ten civilians Williams had spoken of spilled out into the courtyard. Almost all were women and children, aside from a single man who appeared to be in his forties. Most were white, though there was a mulatto woman clutching whom Patrick assumed to be her children, who were even more mixed than her.

"Who are you?" asked the middle-aged man.

"Lieutenant Commander Sullivan, US Navy," he answered. "We're here to rescue you. Follow us, quickly, we have a boat at the base of the hill."

He started to walk toward the gate and spotted Anna kneeling down next to the sleeping guard he had jumped over. She was taking deep swigs of water from the man's canteen, the man still sleeping. Beside him were several empty bottles of spirits.

"Private, I thought I told you to run him through?" Patrick said to one of the Marines. The Private shrugged innocently back. "Sorry, Sir. I didn't have the heart to stab a sleeping man. He's stone drunk anyhow."

Patrick rolled his eyes. *I'll chew him out later*, he thought. Approaching the gate, now with the civilians in tow, he noticed the sentry Spencer had shot in the back was still alive and trying to crawl away. Walking up to him, Patrick pressed the heel of his boot into the man's wound, causing him to cry out in pain.

"Where's Carlyle?" he demanded, rolling the man over and putting his cutlass against his throat.

"In the hills to the north," he whimpered. "He thought you were landing there."

Patrick released the man, knowing in his wounded state he was no longer a threat. He waved to everyone behind him, repeating, "Follow me."

As they exited the front gate of the fort, Patrick turned around as he caught the glimmer of something out of the corner of his eye. In the nearest inlet below him three of the six ships there were now on fire, burning uncontrollably. The other ships anchored there were very close to the ships already on fire and the flames could leap to them at any moment. There was movement on the beach nearest the inlet where the bonfire had been, and figures were running about, with small boats rowing out to get men back aboard the untouched ships to try and save them.

"Good man, Thompson!" Patrick yelled out with an elated smile, while behind him the Marines gave subdued cheers and patted each other on the back.

"Sir, behind us!" alerted Spencer.

Patrick looked down the back of the hill to the north. Along a path descending from the hills above them was a line of torches snaking its way toward the village. The lead torch made a turn before getting there and now started moving in their direction. With Carlyle and his men now approaching there was only one thing to do.

"RUN!"

Chapter 11

April 1815 Coral Bay, the island of Saint John, Danish West Indies

Patrick and his party started flying down the hill along the path from the fort. With the women and children following they could not run as fast as they normally would. It was impossible for the children to keep up, and the Marines each picked one up and carried them over their shoulders.

The moon had by slunk down behind the hills to the west, and the path had become darker. Worse still, Patrick could already see the faintest sign of dawn to the east. Daylight would not come before they had reached the bottom of the hill and would be useless on their descent. It would however rob them of cover on their return across the open waters of the bay.

Hurrying down the path, Patrick rounded the first switchback. About thirty yards ahead, he saw the two brigands who had been discussing venereal disease walking back up the path towards the fort. Unsure if they were armed, Patrick decided to attack before they could harm the others. He broke into a sprint, wailed like a banshee, while swinging his cutlass over his head. The two men abruptly halted, turned tail, and fled at full speed down the hillside.

Patrick stopped running after a few yards and paused to catch his breath. Laughing as he watched the men retreating, he thought, *That should not have worked.* The rest of the group now came around the corner. Anna hurried to him and asked, "Why were you screaming?"

Patrick pointed his cutlass down the path. "Don't you see the two...?" he trailed off, realizing the men were now out of sight. He shook his head chuckling. "Never mind. Hurry along now!"

With Patrick still in the lead, they continued running down the hill. The sky had begun turning grey now, and the path was better lit. As they got close to the bottom of the hill, Patrick spotted the beach below them through a clearing in the trees. He skidded to a halt and pointed to the beach with his cutlass.

"Spencer! Through there, lead the way!" he ordered. Spencer stopped and walked off the path, hacking at some foliage with his cutlass and starting to make his way through it to the beach. Anna followed, then the civilians, with the Marines reloading as they paused there to bring up the rear. One by one, they followed as well, until it was just Patrick and Sergeant Bowyer.

"Sir! Down there!" the Sergeant called out, and he leveled his musket to take aim. In the gathering light, Patrick saw men coming up the path toward them.

"No time, go!" he said to Bowyer, and pushed the Sergeant along the makeshift path they were carving to the beach.

Going downhill was easier, particularly with daylight dawning, but the civilians slowed their pace as they tried to carefully trudge their way through the jungle. Patrick could hear the shouts of Carlyle's men behind the, and the Marines tried to urge the women and children on. One Private prodded too hard, and a young mother tripped and went sliding down the hill, pulling her son with her by the arm, until she impacted a tree. Bruised but not seriously injured, she moaned in pain but nevertheless continued on, picking up her son who started to cry from scrapes he had gotten in the fall.

At last Spencer broke through to the beach. The boat was only a short distance away and he ran over to it. He then started helping the women and children into the boat. Once clear of the jungle, the Marines likewise ran to the boat as well, unslinging their muskets and taking up the oars.

Bowyer then climbed in and sat at the rear, covering Patrick with his musket as he started to push the boat off the beach. "Here they come!" the Sergeant shouted, and fired a shot over Patrick's head. He did not pause to see if Bowyer had managed to strike anyone and kept pushing the boat off the beach. Spencer and the Marines pushed down off the sand and coral with their oars and the boat finally started to float. Patrick grunted and gave one more hard push, finally sending the boat gliding into the water. He kept pushing as he waded into the water up to his knees then jumped in.

Patrick picked up an oar and started furiously paddling with the others. Beside him, Bowyer picked up another musket and discharged it at the men who were now on the beach behind them. Taking a quick look over his shoulder, Patrick saw half a dozen men on the beach where they had been aiming muskets at them.

"Get down!" he urged as the pirates fired at the boat. Musket balls went flying overhead, one he heard strike the side of the boat, and another went past his arm hitting one of the women between the shoulder blades. She collapsed forward into the boat on top of one of the children who started screaming in terror.

Bowyer fired another discarded musket, then picked up the last of the Marines' weapons and fired it as well. Patrick handed over his pistol, and Bowyer fired one last shot for good measure. With every firearm available now empty, the Sergeant picked up the last remaining oar and started paddling.

Patrick took another look over his shoulder and saw one of the men starting to wade into the water after them. It was Carlyle, a pistol in each hand and two more in his belt, looking every inch the pirate he now was.

"Damn you, Paddy!" he shouted, then fired off both the pistols in his hands. Fortunately, they were far enough away by that point that scoring a hit would have been unlikely, and the balls plinked into the water beside them. "Damn you!" he shouted again, tossing aside his pistols into the water and drew the remaining pair, firing them haphazardly in their general direction.

Patrick let out a smirk seeing that Carlyle was too enraged to even bother aiming at them. "Make for Latimer and the old Danish cannon!" he called ahead to Spencer at the front of the boat, as Carlyle's shrieks of rage pierced the air behind them. Spencer now tried to steer, but the boat had become heavier with the civilians aboard and less maneuverable, not to mention slower. The middle-aged man and two of the women made themselves useful by picking up the Marines muskets and using the butts to paddle.

Looking back to his left, he saw that in the furthest inlet, all of the unarmed ships were now blazing hulks. *Damn fine job, Thompson*, he thought as he paddled. The ships in the second inlet gave him pause though. They were once again in the center of the bay, a sitting duck for any of the ships lying at anchor. He saw the *Wasp* was nearest to them, its pirate crew now on deck. They were clearly confused by what was going on, and it did not appear that they were cleared for action. He heard someone aboard shouting out orders in Spanish, and the seamen began running to and fro.

"Faster!" he yelled out, knowing someone had finally realized what was happening. Everyone paddling strained to keep the boat moving and get behind the cover of the small rocky cliff that separated the second inlet from the cove where Latimer was waiting with the rockets.

Out of the corner of his eye, Patrick saw a man on the *Wasp's* quarterdeck aiming a swivel gun at them. "Down!" he hollered as the gun fired. Everyone ducked down as far as they could, the women throwing themselves on top of the children. The small boat was raked with musket balls. Patrick felt a searing pain across his back as a ball grazed him. The middle-aged man was sitting in front of him and took a ball in the thigh that had punched through the hull of the boat. One of the Marines was peppered with three balls hitting him in the arm and chest and he slumped forward.

Patrick picked himself up, and despite the burning pain in his back kept paddling. "Keep going! Faster!" he urged. "We're almost there."

Those that could picked up their paddles and kept rowing. Anna pushed aside the fallen Marine and started paddling herself. Someone, he thought perhaps Sergeant Bowyer beside him, started praying rhythmically, trying to set a pace. Looking back to his left, he saw the *Wasp* inch out of view behind the cliff just as the first cannon was fired at them. The round shot impacted the side of the cliff, spraying chunks of rock and dirt into the boat, but passed overhead into the bay.

It would take the pirates some time before they could get any of the ships moving, so Patrick was able to let out a temporary sigh of relief now that they were out of view or out of range of anyone that could shoot at them. He did not let up paddling, knowing that they could not afford a moment's rest. Looking ahead, he now saw the beach where he had left Latimer. The Midshipman was standing upright, waving to them. Henderson sat in the second boat, an oar already in his hand ready to start paddling. Thompson and his four swimmers were sitting in the surf, looking tired, no doubt exhausted from their long night in the water.

"Fire the rockets!" Patrick shouted to Latimer as they approached. The Midshipman cupped his ear, causing Patrick to shout again. He then nodded and quickly went over to the two rockets he had set up. Placing the end of the fuse of the first rocket in the pan for his pistol, he pulled the trigger and the fuse caught. A few seconds later, the blue rocket streaked into the sky with its characteristic screech, until detonating overhead. For good measure, Latimer then set off the second rocket in case the first had not been seen by the *Enterprise*.

Spencer guided the boat onto the rocks a few feet short of the beach. "Mister Latimer, get the wounded into your boat!" Patrick ordered. Latimer and the rest of the men splashed into the water and started to lift the wounded out. When he got to the Marine, Latimer took a quick look at him and said, "He's dead, Sir."

Patrick shook his head. "Damn. Pull him out and place him on the beach. We'll come back and bury him later."

"Aye, Sir," answered Latimer, and though he did pull the dead Marine out of the boat he looked thoroughly unnerved at touching a corpse. Thompson then came alongside the boat. "All present, Sir," he reported. "Did we managed to burn all those ships in the far cove?"

Patrick nodded. "You did. Fine work Thompson. What of the others?"

"We cut the cables just enough that they won't notice at first, but one good turn hard over and they'll snap," said Thompson.

"Very good," answered Patrick. "Shove us off and get to your boat."

"Aye, Sir," replied the Carpenter, and he pushed the boat back off the rocks before running back to the other boat.

"Sir, you're hit!" Bowyer said, noticing Patrick's wound. Anna's head spun around, with concern in her face at hearing the words.

"Don't mind me, Sergeant," Patrick brushed him off. "I'll be alright. Keep paddling."

The boats now started off together again, heading for the open water at the entrance of the bay. Looking behind him again, Patrick saw more boats plying the waters of Coral Bay, all of them heading for the inlet where the remaining ships were anchored. He knew that they would not have much more time to escape, as once the pirates were able to get their ships moving, they would quickly intercept them. Up ahead of them, the brig still lay at anchor guarding the entrance to the bay. They had gotten lucky getting past the *Wasp's* guns, but if Forester was late, there was no way they could hope to evade its cannon fire.

In his mind he quickly tried to think of alternatives. He could instead take to the hills and try trudging through the jungle to the town on the opposite side of the island, but he knew the terrain was too unforgiving and Carlyle's men too numerous for them to get very far. He considered portaging the boats over Haulover Bay again and making for one of the British islands that were near, but even with the extra time Carlyle would take to wear around the eastern point, his ships would still run them down. His brief moment of doubt was allayed when a pair of masts crept into view around the hills of the eastern point.

"Sir! It's the *Enterprise!*" an elated Spencer cried out. The men in the boats let out a cheer at seeing their ship coming to their rescue.

The *Enterprise* swung around and opened her gunports. The picket brig had evidently been taken by surprise, as they still had their guns trained on the two ship's boats. Fire rippled along the side of the ship, and a second later the rumble of cannon fire echoed across Coral Bay. Even at a distance Patrick could see the brig take multiple hits, and he guessed from the number that Forester was double-shotting his guns. The brig began to turn on its anchor, and soon it was floating free, with either the anchor being raised or cut loose. Before they could train their guns on the *Enterprise*, she fired again. The brig was staggered, and she continued to turn, now on a collision course with the small island she had been anchored nearby. The crew was unable to recover in time, and she crashed against the island, her bow being pitched upward on the rocks. The gunners on the *Enterprise* showed no mercy, dropping anchor and pounding their helpless foe at point blank range until it was clear that no gun aboard could fire on the returning boats.

The remainder of their journey back to the ship was uneventful. Latimer's boat had outpaced Patrick's and got to the ship first. The wounded were slowly lifted out of the boat as tenderly as possible, before Latimer, Thompson, and the rest of the hands went up the ladder.

"Get the wounded below to Doctor Chartrand immediately," Patrick called up to Forester as the latter looked down at them over the ship's rail.

"Aye, Sir, already done," he answered.

Patrick's boat now pulled alongside. The civilians were helped aboard first, followed by Anna. Sergeant Bowyer and the surviving Marines went next, with Patrick bringing up the rear after Spencer.

Boatswain Barnes then had the boats tied on the coast along in the ship's wake.

"Your prayers worked, Mister Forester," Patrick said as the two shook hands.

"A hundred Our Fathers, Sir. I made sure to count them off." Forester then leaned closer and whispered, "And I threw in one of your Papist Hail Mary's when no one was looking, just for you, Sir."

Patrick smiled and gave a chuckle. "I'll make a convert of you yet."

Forester looked past him to Anna. "Good to see you safe, ma'am," he said.

"Likewise, Lieutenant," she answered.

Patrick turned to Spencer. "Phillip, escort the civilians below to Doctor Chartrand. Make sure to get them into a safe location until the action has been concluded."

"Aye, Sir," he answered, and started ushering the women and children below. Anna waited until the rest had started below before walking up and giving Patrick a quick kiss. "Thank you, love. Stay safe." She then departed below with the others.

Patrick looked around and saw the men all staring at him. *It's not every day they get to see the Captain being kissed on the quarterdeck by a pretty woman*, he thought. Noticing that he was looking back at them, they all hurriedly returned to their tasks.

"Shall I have the Doctor dress your wound, Sir?" Forester asked.

Patrick shook his head. "No, he has his hands full below. I can wait." The wound still hurt, but he was getting used to bearing the pain, and it was assuredly minor compared to the wounds the others had suffered.

"Weigh anchor," he ordered Barnes, and the Boatswain piped out the order on his whistle. "Where is the British squadron?" he then asked of Forester.

"Not far behind us, Sir," the Lieutenant answered. "They should be rounding that headland at any moment. In fact, I see one just there on the other side of that saddle you crossed the boats over."

Patrick turned around and saw a schooner passing by the gap between the hills where Haulover Bay was. He could tell they had a following wind out of the northeast and were making good speed.

"Very good," said Patrick. He then looked into the bay. The *Wasp* was leading five other ships out of Coral Bay. Their sails were just beginning to catch the wind and would soon be bearing down on the *Enterprise*.

"Mister Forester, I believe we've outstayed our welcome," said Patrick. "Get the ship moving. We'll draw them off until the British are able to come into action."

"Aye, Sir," Forester replied. He then barked out in his booming voice to Barnes, "Bosun Barnes! Loose the main and topsails!"

The hands above did not need to wait for Barnes to relay the order, and they dropped the sails from the spars, which filled with wind in an instant. The ship began moving again, the wind carrying them southwest away from Coral Bay. Behind them the *Wasp* closed rapidly, outpacing the ships behind her, who were exiting the bay in a classic line-ahead battle formation.

"She's gaining on us, Sir," said Barnes. "She's a faster ship."

"We don't have to outrun her, Mister Barnes," said Patrick. "We only have to get them to chase us for a bit."

A hand in the tops above then called out, "Sail ho! On the starboard quarter! It's the British, Sir!"

Around the tip of the headland came the British squadron, led by a forty-four-gun frigate. The *Athena* was behind them, followed by another sloop and three schooners. The British were also arrayed in battle formation.

Carlyle must have been alerted that the squadron was coming up behind them as the Wasp then began to turn. His other ships started to turn as well, and Patrick surmised he was attempting to cross the enemy's 'T', to bring all of his ship's guns to bear to rake the enemy battle line while they were unable to fire back. It was a bold move against a superior force, something Patrick would have expected from Carlyle.

Patrick saw Thompson look at him nervously. Patrick in turn held up his hand with his fingers crossed. This would be the moment of truth to see if Thompson's cutting of the rudder cables worked as planned.

The ships entered their turn, helms hard over. Everything at first seemed fine, that they would complete the turn and then cross the frigate's bows. It soon became clear something was wrong however. The ships reached the point where they should have steadied their course, but instead they kept turning. Soon they were facing bows-on to the incoming British squadron, the wind backing their sails to where they were now immobile.

Barnes let out a whoop of excitement at the sight. "We've got them, Sir! They're in irons!"

One by one, the frigate overtook the first of Carlyle's ships. As they passed, the frigate unleased a full broadside at the hapless schooner. The smaller ship was shredded, her hull shot through with holes and her masts collapsing, and she did not return fire. The frigate continued on to its next victim, the *Athena* close behind, further pummeling the stricken ship. The next ship in the line fired off a few shots, but the frigate was much too large for any substantial damage to be done. As the frigate floated on by, she let loose another barrage of cannon fire, with similar results, leaving the frail converted merchant a shattered wreck.

The crew of the *Enterprise* was so taken with the lopsided encounter they did not immediately notice the *Wasp* starting to maneuver again. Patrick saw the ship starting to turn back to pursue and wondered, *How the hell is he doing that?* It then occurred to him that Carlyle must have immediately sent men to manipulate the rudder by hand, swinging the tiller beam back and forth. *Crafty bastard*, he thought. *He's quick thinking if nothing else.*

"Helm, come about to larboard!" he ordered. The Quartermaster hesitated, confused by the sudden command, then complied and spun the wheel hard over. "Mister Forester, have the larboard battery ready to fire on my order."

"Aye, aye, Sir," he answered, now aware of the danger.

The ship swung about, and Patrick now realized he was in a position to cross the *Wasp's* 'T' as Carlyle had intended to do to the British squadron. He waited for the opportune moment when he could rake the Wasp from stem to stern, and then ordered, "Fire!"

The *Enterprise* shuddered as her cannons fired. Rolling from one gun to the next, each cannon spit out its charge of two, twelve-pound, iron round shot. The shots impacted the bow of the *Wasp* and tore across the ship's deck. Still the sloop kept coming.

"Bring us about back to starboard before she crosses our stern," Patrick said to the Quartermaster, who sent the wheel spinning back the other way. The *Enterprise* now returned to its southwesterly course, with the *Wasp* soon to come even with them on their starboard side. The gun crews all ran to the other side of the ship to reload and run out the guns before the *Wasp* came alongside.

Patrick started walking forward along the deck. "Load double shot and keep steady," he told the men. Reaching to where Latimer was stationed amidships, he looked out the center gunport, watching as the Wasp's bow crept into view. Only a mere fifty yards separated the two ships.

"Fire as you bear!"

The ship's guns fired their rolling barrage from the stern forwards. The shock from each blast rippled across Patrick's body, the noise, even with his hands covering his ears, numbed his hearing, and he felt each strain on the ship's deck as the cannons jerked backward on their carriages. Beside him, Latimer stepped up to take a look over the hammock nettings above the rails.

"Sir, I think –"

The next moment seemed to slow in time as Patrick watched it play out. He did not hear the guns aboard the other ship firing, but saw the instant that Latimer was struck. Only three feet away from him, a grape shot ball came hurtling in, hitting Latimer square between the eyes. The Midshipman's face caved in at the ball's impact before the top half of his head exploded. Latimer's lifeless corpse then flopped backwards onto the deck.

"Jesus Christ!" a hand on the gun beside Patrick blurted out after having been sprayed with the Midshipman's blood and brain matter.

Forester turned around to berate the man for his blasphemy, then went pale at the sight of Latimer's mostly headless body. He took a step backward, and for a moment Patrick thought he might suddenly breakdown, but the Lieutenant regained his composure. "Reload!" he ordered, his voice cracking.

Patrick took a quick look up and down the length of the ship to survey the damage. Some rigging and been shot away, and there were plenty of holes in the ship's rails, but altogether the *Enterprise* herself looked fine. A few other men had been felled by the enemy's counterfire. One man was seen running down the hatchway, his hand missing. Another sailor pulled a wounded comrade who had been hit with splinters into cover behind one of the masts. Otherwise, casualties appeared minor.

From the tops above, Sergeant Bowyer and the Marines were keeping the pirates' heads down with accurate musket fire. Someone on the *Wasp's* deck fired back at them. The ball missed Bowyer, and hit Seaman Wilhelm, one of the topmen that had been reloading for them. Wilhelm let out an inhuman shriek as he tumbled off the fighting top and into the water below.

"All gunners, fire at your discretion!" Patrick shouted above the din, and the cannon beside slammed backwards against its ropes as it fired. Several more of the guns fired as well. The *Wasp* had shortened sail and was running at roughly the same speed now as the *Enterprise* and fired back at them again. All around, seamen dove to the deck as iron round shot crashed through the ship's sides, sending splinters scything through the air.

We're going to have to slug it out, Patrick thought. The notion did worry him, as the *Wasp* outgunned the *Enterprise*. Still, no matter what Carlyle's expertise, he had faith that a trained and dedicated US Navy crew could best a polyglot collection of pirates.

"Sir! She's turning in on us!" called out Forester.

Patrick looked through the nearest gunport. The *Wasp* had now turned to larboard, intent on ramming the *Enterprise*.

"All hands brace!" shouted Patrick.

The two ships collided with a halting smash. The deck of the *Enterprise* lurched upward for a moment as the starboard side of the ship was momentarily lifted out of the water by the impact.

"All guns fire!" Patrick ordered one last time. The starboard battery thundered into the side of the *Wasp* at point blank range, shattering timbers and upending cannon. From the other deck came screams and wails of pain, while Carlyle's booming voice ranted and raved, calling on them to keep fighting.

"Mister Thompson!" Patrick called out, pointing to the Carpenter. "Get below and assess the damage."

"Aye, aye, Sir," he answered, and started crawling back to the hatchway as musket balls zipped through the air overhead.

There came a chorus of battle cries, and a fusillade of gunfire. Patrick looked up and saw a bearded pirate jump over the rail, musket in hand. He dodged out of the way as the man tried to club him down, then grabbed the man by the back of his jacket and threw him against a cannon. More pirates swarmed over the rails and onto the *Enterprise's* deck, and soon the entire crew was locked in a furious melee.

Grabbing a bucket off the deck, Patrick threw water into the face of the pirate he was tangling with, momentarily blinding him. He then grabbed the pin used to clear out the vent hole from the nearest cannon and jammed it straight through the man's eyeball. The pirate screamed as the pin was driven into his skull. He fell to the deck, clawing at his face for a moment before he expired, though his body still continued to twitch. That foe dispatched, Patrick picked up a rammer and swung it at an unsuspecting opponent who was grappling with Forester. The blow caught the man in the back, stunning him. Forester was then able to deliver a solid punch to the face, grabbed the man and drove his head into the ship's bell. Whether the man survived that or not was irrelevant, as half a dozen sailors then beat his prone form with any object at hand.

The Marines now descended down the ratlines, led by Sergeant Bowyer, who decided to get into the action more quickly by sliding down a loose line. The blue coated Marines charged into the fray with bayonets fixed and skewered the final remaining pirates who had made it onboard.

Just then another group of boarders started to jump over the span between the two ships. The Quartermaster jumped over to the swivel gun mounted near the wheel, and fired it into the mass of men, spraying them with musket balls. As the pirates collapsed backward in a heap, Carlyle now came into view, bounding over the rail onto the quarterdeck.

"WHERE IS HE?!" Carlyle raged, wildly swinging his saber at the Quartermaster. The man backed away and ducked for cover behind the ship's wheel. "WHERE IS SULLIVAN!?!" He swung his saber again, swiping a handgrip off the wheel.

"Carlyle!" Patrick shouted from twenty paces away. Carlyle stopped and looked at him, allowing the Quartermaster to retreat to safety.

"It's over, Carlyle," he said, the crew now looking on behind him in curiosity at what was playing out between the two men. "The war is over. Your flotilla is sunk, your men are dead, and the island will soon be secured by Redcoats. All this needless death has gotten you nowhere."

Carlyle chuckled. "That may be so. But I can still kill you!" In a flash, his hand went to his belt and drew his pistol. Cocking on the draw, he fired it.

Patrick winced, expecting to be hit, but he felt the ball go past him. Forester let out a cry of pain, and spun to the deck behind him, gripping his arm.

"DAMN YOU!" Carlyle roared. "What sorcerer's charms or curses have you placed upon yourself to make you untouchable?" he ranted, throwing aside the pistol.

Patrick knelt down next to Forester to see how badly he had been wounded. After seeing it was only a flesh wound, he stood back up and faced his nemesis. "If it's charms, it's only the sort that come from being an Irishman. But no, I think it's simply your terrible aim."

Carlyle seethed and brought his sword to bear. "I'll just have to do it with cold steel." He started forward but then a single pistol shot erupted from the hatchway. Spencer stood there partway up the steps, pistol smoking, having reappeared from below. Carlyle staggered backwards from the hit to his shoulder. He shook the blow off and started forward again.

"Marines," Patrick coolly called out. "Shoot him."

Sergeant Bowyer and his men aimed and fired their muskets in unison. Carlyle was struck by three balls in an arm and both legs and was thrown backward against the ship's wheel, his saber flying out of his hand and clattering to the deck. Even this did not kill him, and he stared at Patrick in complete shock. He slumped over to the side and started crawling toward his saber.

"Bosun Barnes," Patrick said quietly. "Fetch me a thick cord of twine about three feet long."

Barnes gave him a puzzled look and went to go search the deck for something suitable. Patrick then slowly walked across the deck. He sidestepped the crawling Carlyle and stooped over to pick up the fallen saber.

"No," he told Carlyle simply, and handed it off to Spencer. He pulled Carlyle off the deck and shoved him face first against the ship's wheel.

"Well go on, Paddy," he rasped. "Just shoot me or hang me and be done with it."

Patrick picked up some loose bits of rope lying on the deck. "Both are too good for you," he said, then used the rope to tie Carlyle's limp arms to the wheel.

"What are you doing, Sir?" Spencer asked with trepidation.

"Giving the bastard what he deserves."

Barnes came up to them, a thick bit of cord in his hands that matched the description of what Patrick was looking for. Patrick took the bit of cord, and then using Carlyle's own saber, cut open the back of his jacket.

"Sir, is this necessary?" Spencer began to say, but Patrick cut him off with a curt, "As you were, Mister Spencer."

Carlyle's eyes went wide as he realized what was about to happen. "No, no!" he pleaded weakly.

Patrick's lip curled in disgust at his begging. His answer was the first lash across Carlyle's back. He whimpered at the first blow, which caused Patrick's blood to boil. In response, he whipped him even harder, raining blows down in the man in a fury. Carlyle began to scream in agony, coupled with tears of humiliation.

"What's wrong you bastard? After all the men you flogged! Can't take it?" Patrick shouted, continuing to flog him harder and faster.

With every lash he recalled every wrong done to him by Carlyle, and the many that others had suffered at his hands. It was not just his own flogging, or beating Spencer, or abducting Anna, there was far more. From his friend Bixby, who Carlyle had executed during the mutiny, to Private John Wilton whom he had shot at Derna while aiming at Patrick. Captain Somers and the crew of the *Intrepid*, blown to pieces when Carlyle's gunboats found them entering Tripoli harbor. The countless American soldiers on the Lake Erie frontier, massacred by Indians at his urging. The murders of Johnston Blakeley and the crew of the *Wasp*.

As every one of them crossed his mind, he flogged harder, eventually letting out a primeval cry of rage. Blood streamed down Carlyle's back as new rents and sores were opened in the skin. Chunks of flesh came flying off and splattered the deck.

"Patrick, enough!" Spencer finally shouted, grabbing his arm to prevent him from striking again. Beneath him Carlyle whimpered like a wounded dog.

Patrick looked up, dazed. Spencer looked back at him, his expression a mixture of terror and confusion. Looking over his shoulder, he saw the crew all staring at him with the same petrified look. Nearby, Barnes was similarly speechless, his jaw hanging open.

Patrick threw down the twine and started walking back along the deck. With the crew's eyes still on him, he paused and said, "That bastard is the reason I've never flogged a man, until now. And I'll never flog another." He then jerked his thumb over his shoulder and said to Barnes, "Clap that piece of excrement in irons."

Chapter 12

April 1815, aboard USS *Enterprise* in the Caribbean.

Once the ship's deck was clear of dead pirates, the crew had to see to the safety of their own ship.

"The hull's not been breached, Sir," reported Thompson, back from his inspection below the waterline. "The other damage is superficial. I can make repairs to most of it while we're underway."

Patrick nodded, only half hearing the man. He was still too distracted from the desperate action to fully give his attention. He looked around the battered deck, seeing debris and carnage strewn about. "For a moment, the fighting became so hot, I thought we might lose her," he admitted.

"Oh, don't worry, Sir," said Thompson, knocking on a beam. "She's a tough lady. A week or two in the yard and she'll be good as new. Even if they did manage to sink her, the Navy would just build another. I don't think history will forget the name *Enterprise*."

Patrick smiled at the man's optimism. "What about the *Wasp*? Can we get her under tow back to a safe harbor?"

Thompson shook his head. "No, Sir, she's had it. That crash did more damage to her than us. Her bow was weakened after that first broadside we hit them with, and when she struck us her seams opened. She was also holed twice by shot. She's already low in the water, and she'll go under in a bit."

"Understood," said Patrick. "Good work today, Thompson. All around. I'll be making special mention of you in my report."

"Thank you, Sir," the Carpenter replied, giving the knuckled saluted. Patrick returned it, and the man went back to his duties.

Patrick then ordered that they give the foundering *Wasp* a wide berth. Spencer, now taking over for the wounded Forester, relayed the order and the topmen loosed the sails. Once clear, they took up a position near the British frigate.

He heard the sound of Boatswain's whistles coming from the frigate. Looking up, Patrick saw the ship's company, her officers, men, and Marines all lining the rails. The officers doffed their hats, and the fifes and drums of the Royal Marines began to play the American national song, 'Hail Columbia'.

"They're rendering 'passing honors', Sir," said Spencer with a surprised smile on his face.

"Let's return the favor," replied Patrick. "On my command, have the men sing 'Rule Britannia'."

Spencer tilted his head and raised an eyebrow.

"Well, I'm certainly not singing 'God Save the King'," Patrick said, anticipating Spencer's next question.

Spencer laughed. "Aye, Sir," he said simply. He then gathered the men alongside, Barnes piping the call to man the side, and when Patrick nodded, they belted out the chorus of 'Rule Britannia.' The British responded with a rousing three cheers.

The men returned to work, clearing the deck, tending to the wounded, and preparing their dead for burial at sea. They almost took no notice of Commander Harvey's boat approaching from the *Athena*.

"I'm sorry we're a little short on ceremony," Patrick told him as helped the officer aboard.

"I'm not one to trifle over such a thing, especially after what you chaps just went through," Harvey said, stepping onto the deck which was still awash with blood. "We saw it all. A grand fight. What were your casualties?"

"Fortunately light," Patrick answered, though he could not shake the image of Latimer's head being blown apart in front of his eyes. "Two dead, one overboard, several others wounded but not severely. I also lost a man ashore."

"If you tell me where he fell, I'll send a boat to retrieve the body once I'm back aboard the *Athena*," Harvey told him, placing a comforting hand on Patrick's shoulder.

Patrick nodded his thanks silently. "Would you care to stay a moment? We're about to bury the dead."

"Of course," answered Harvey, and he removed his hat.

Barnes piped the call for all hands on deck. The wounded, and even the civilians came up the hatchway. Forester, his arm bandaged, opened his Bible and read the traditional prayer for burial at sea. He then handed Patrick the short list of the dead and missing.

"Richard Wilhelm, Able Seaman," he began reading. "Charles Norwich, Gunner's Mate. James Latimer, Midshipman. United States Navy. John Reese, Private. United States Marines."

Forester then led an Our Father. When it was concluded, the flag draped bodies were tipped over the side and into the water. Patrick then went over to the rail. "In nomine Patris, et Filii, et Spiritus Sancti," he recited, making the sign of the cross over the water. "Amen."

"Amen," the rest of the crew said in unison. The brief service concluded, they returned to their duties.

As Patrick continued to look down at the water, he felt someone touch his arm. Anna came up beside him, and hooked her arm around his. She said nothing, only leaned against him.

Harvey now came up on Patrick's left side. "I must assume you are Mrs. Sullivan?"

"I am," she answered. "And you are Commander Harvey."

"Indeed, I am," he said, tipping his cocked hat. "I am glad to see you safe and unharmed. I can't imagine what Carlyle was thinking when he abducted you." Harvey turned his attention back to Patrick. "He is dead then?"

"No," Patrick shook his head gloomily. "I shall release him into your custody. He's been hunting your ships, not ours. We'll let you deal with him."

Harvey nodded, satisfied. "We'll deal with him in short order. The Admiral will be pleased. He sent me to express his compliments. I daresay, if you were in our Navy, they would have given you a knighthood for this."

Patrick straightened up. "I'll settle for prize money," he joked. "Do tell the Admiral, I am grateful for his sentiments, and for his timely arrival." He then extended his hand to Harvey. "I am glad we have been able to work together, Commander Harvey."

"I feel the same, Leftenant Commander Sullivan," he replied, shaking Patrick's hand. "Hopefully with our own family squabbles concluded our countries can work together more often."

Patrick smiled. "I should look forward to that."

"Bring up the prisoner!"

Drummers from the *Enterprise, Athena,* and the British frigate all beat in unison. The Admiral had convened an immediate court martial following the action. As a pirate, he could have summarily executed Carlyle, but chose to at least give him the legal veneer of a trial. The proceedings were of course brief, and the outcome never in doubt.

From the hatchway came two red jacketed Royal Marines, dragging the wounded Carlyle who could barely walk. Patrick stood next to Harvey on the quarterdeck of the *Athena*, silently observing as the Marines walked Carlyle over to the gangway and stood him on top of a plank stretched out over the water. A line hung down from a yardarm, a noose at the end.

"Roger Carlyle," Harvey now spoke up. Carlyle looked over, a scowl on his face. He had said nothing in his defense at the trial, or indeed anything at all since being taken into custody.

"You have been found guilty of murder, piracy, and treason against the United Kingdom of Great Britain and Ireland, and his Majesty, King George the Third. Your sentence, handed down by a court martial, is that you are to be hanged by the neck until dead. Do you have any last words?"

Carlyle stared at the two officers for a moment. "A decade ago, you both conspired against at Malta. I should have executed you both when I had the chance."

Patrick shook his head, infuriated that Carlyle still could not come to accept the fact that his misfortune lay in his own actions.

"Very well," said Harvey dispassionately. He then motioned with his hand to the Marines. The two guards bound Carlyle's hands behind his back. One offered him a hood, but he declined. The noose was then pulled down and placed around his neck. A Marine then leveled his musket, ready to push him off the plank with his bayonet.

Silence fell over the *Athena's* crew as they waited for Harvey's command. After a few moments, Harvey cleared his throat. "Hoist him!"

Carlyle's eyes went wide, and his head whipped around to look at Harvey in shock. Before he could do anything else, a group of seamen hauled on a line, and Carlyle was lifted into the air.

"A cruel trick, Commander," Patrick whispered to Harvey. The Englishman shrugged slightly. "I want to see him dance a jig." Normally one would drop the condemned over the side and let gravity snap the neck, resulting in instant death. Harvey had instead chosen to let Carlyle dangle and slowly suffocate.

Carlyle gagged and sputtered as he twisted around in the air at the end of the rope. His legs kicked and thrashed wildly. His eyes and tongue bulged, and his face turned purple. The spectacle dragged on unrelenting for minutes as he struggled for air. Some of the other British officers became disgusted and looked at Harvey, silently asking his permission to end it by pulling his flailing legs and breaking his neck, but Harvey shook his head. Eventually, his spasms ceased, and he hung limply from the noose, dead at last.

By that evening they had made their course back to San Juan. The civilians had been placed back ashore, the lone Marine's body returned by the British and buried at sea, and what battle damage that could be had been repaired. After finishing the dog watches, Patrick retired below to his cabin. Anna was waiting, sleeping in an extra hammock that Henderson had hung from the ceiling. She had discarded her tattered dress and was wearing some sailor's smocks that a few of the men had donated. He pulled a chair over and sat down beside her, taking her limp hand and caressing it gently. She stirred, and groggily look at him.

"Are we on our way?" she asked. He nodded back silently.

Anna smiled at him then yawned. "You should get some sleep. You've been up all night and all day."

His eyelids began to sag as she spoke of sleep. He was tired, but not quite ready for bed. "I asked Henderson to bring us some food. After dinner, then I'll sleep." A thought came to his mind, and he asked, "What happened to the gold you were paid in Kingston?"

Anna sighed. "Carlyle took it. He was keeping it aboard the *Wasp*."

Patrick put a hand to his face as he realized three thousand dollars in gold was now sitting at the bottom in the wreck of the *Wasp*. "All that trouble for nothing," he said, shaking his head.

"I wouldn't say that," replied Anna. "If I'd not gone to San Juan, Carlyle wouldn't have made the mistake he did in capturing me. Without any other lead to go on, he could have carried out his attacks on San Juan and the British squadron."

Patrick shrugged. She was likely right, but after what he had been through it did not give him any solace.

There came a knock on the door, and Henderson walked through holding a tray, hobbling on his injured foot.

"That's alright, Henderson, I'll take that," Patrick said, relieving him of the tray of food. "How's your foot?"

"Still smarting, Sir," he answered. "Doctor Chartrand doesn't think it's poisonous, so it'll mend. Fish tonight, Sir, if you don't mind. Fresh caught," he added, pointing to the food.

"Thank you, Henderson," said Patrick. He gave the man a friendly pat on the arm and said, "You're relieved until morning, Henderson. Get some sleep and rest that foot."

Henderson saluted Patrick, responded, "Aye, aye, Sir," and departed the cabin, closing the door behind him.

Patrick began to disperse the plates off the tray and onto his desk, shifting aside Carlyle's saber which he had taken as a trophy. He looked up at Anna and asked, "In San Juan, on the dock. There was something else you wanted to tell me later that night, what was it?"

Anna rolled out of the hammock so her feet were touching the floor. She looked out the cabin windows into the darkness and started counting off on her fingers. Her face brightened with another smile. "We'll be needing a third seat at the table for Christmas."

Patrick raised an eyebrow. "You want me to invite Spencer over for Christmas?" he asked. "Besides, we'll need four. He'll bring Martha. He said just a few hours ago he's going to propose to her. That brush with death made up his mind."

Anna laughed. She stood up and walked over to him. "They can come if they like, but that's not what I meant." She put her arm around his neck, then put his hand on her belly. "We'll need a third for Christmas, because November comes nine months after February."

Patrick stared blankly at her for a moment before he finally caught on to what she meant, and his eyes bulged.

Anna laughed at his expression. "Tom and Sam were right. You really can be dense at times." He opened his mouth to speak, but she held a finger to his lips. "I know, I should have told you sooner. It's why I wanted the money so badly. I wanted to wait until I had the money because you wouldn't have wanted me to go if you'd known."

"You're damn right I wouldn't have let you go," he answered, a bit distressed to know she had been an expectant mother the entire time she had been in danger. He sighed and took her head in his hands and kissed her on the forehead.

"I think we've both had enough adventures for the time being."

She smiled at him. "Agreed."

He kissed her again and said, "Mo ghra thu." He then looked down to their hands pressed together against her belly and added, "Both of you."

Captain Porter set down Patrick's report on his desk. "Well, that was a ripping good yarn," he said to Patrick, looking up. "Still, the important thing is that a further outbreak of war has been averted. I cannot fathom how a man could be so enraged that he would go to such lengths for petty revenge."

Patrick shrugged. "He believed that the world had wronged him but could not see that he was the cause of all his troubles. I think it was just his nature, Sir. Whether born or raised that way."

Porter's eyebrows went up. "Be that as it may, the threat has been dealt with. I received word from the British Admiral that the Danish West Indies have now been safely transferred back into the custody of Denmark. The battle itself will be buried in his reports as being just another clash between local pirates. No word of any hostages, or seizing a fort need be mentioned. Likewise, thanks to your capture of those escaped criminals, the Spanish authorities can tell Madrid that their lost ships fell victim to bandits as well. This entire incident can now be safely forgotten."

"And what of the men of the *Wasp*, Sir?"

Porter hesitated. "They will be considered missing, presumed dead, and the ship to have been lost in a storm." He saw the disappointment in Patrick's face, and added, "I know it's a sordid business, Lieutenant. But I think it is better for all our sakes if the matter is laid to rest."

"Understood, Sir," he answered, knowing that the shroud of secrecy over the incident would prevent the families of the dead from ever knowing the truth.

"We do have other concerns," Porter stated. "We may have put an end to one scoundrel with grandiose machinations, but piracy is exploding again all over the Caribbean. The British have the only navy with enough strength to even try and patrol those waters, and there's not nearly enough ships now that they've reduced expenditures. I'll be traveling to the capital soon to ask Congress to approve an expansion of our own West Indies Squadron here on the New Orleans station."

"I wish you luck, Sir, but you know how tight Congress is with the purse strings when it comes to the Navy," Patrick said.

Porter nodded several times while rolling his eyes. "I do not need to be reminded of Congress's intransigence regarding the naval budget. Fortunately, I'm not asking for massive ships-of-the-line like the other naval yards. No, we need schooners, sloops, small and fast ships that can travel up rivers and inlets to strike pirate havens set back away from the shore. We can act as a swarm of insects prowling the seas and ridding them of marauders. A 'Mosquito Fleet' as it were."

I'm sure the men aboard the ships would think the name came from having to fight off the swarms of insects they'll encounter in the Caribbean jungles instead, Patrick thought.

Porter noticed the slight grin tugging at the edge of Patrick's lips and asked, "Does the prospect of chasing down pirates hold an appeal to you?"

Patrick cleared his throat to buy himself a few seconds, realizing Porter was trying to recruit him for duty in the new squadron. "I believe I've had my fill of pirate hunting for the time being, Sir. Perhaps in the future. In the meantime, I would like to request shore duty at the Washington Navy Yard. You see, my wife just informed me that she is expecting our first child..."

Porter held up a hand. "Say no more, Lieutenant. I understand completely. I'll draw up the orders and you can be on your way."

Both Patrick and Porter then stood up and shook hands. "Fine work out there, Lieutenant. I hope that once you're ready, you'll return to sea duty. I would still like the chance to have you serve aboard my ship."

Patrick saluted the Captain. "I intend to request your ship, Sir. Thank you."

Porter returned the salute and Patrick exited the cabin. He made his way on deck and then down the gangplank back onto the dock in front of the Place d'Arms. Anna was sitting on a bench in the shade of a tree on the square, in a new white dress and a parasol shading her from the sun. He walked over to her and sat down, taking her hand and intertwining his fingers with hers.

"My request for transfer was granted," he said, giving her a kiss on the cheek.

"I'm glad he gave it without a fuss," said Anna. "Sam will be so glad to see you again. I can't wait to see her new little one."

"I'm sure she'll be glad to hear our good news as well," Patrick replied.

There came a sudden cry of joy from the center of the square. They looked over and saw Spencer down on one knee in front of Martha. She pulled him to his feet and kissed him, spinning around and making quite a scene.

"It's looks like we're not the only ones with good news," Anna quipped. She looked back to Patrick. "Who would have ever thought of Spencer as marriage material?"

"Her, obviously," he joked. He then looked into her hazel eyes. He was about to say something more, but completely forgot. Anna smiled at him. She also said nothing, and simply kissed him.

Historical Note

I have jumped the gun somewhat in the timeline by entitling the book "The Mosquito Fleet" and speaking of the US Navy West Indies Squadron. In reality, the West Indies Squadron was not officially formed until 1822, though anti-piracy actions had been undertaken by the Navy and Revenue Marine (precursor to the Coast Guard) as early as 1817. The squadron was first commanded by Commodore James Biddle, with David Porter returning to the Caribbean to assume command in 1823.

As might be expected, there is much more fiction in this novel as compared to some of my previous titles. The USS *Wasp* did indeed disappear during the autumn of 1814, presumed lost during a hurricane or tropical storm near Bermuda. However, the prospect of a missing ship proved too tantalizing a story-telling device to pass up, and I opted to have the ship commandeered by Carlyle for his nefarious purposes.

The section dealing with the Battle of New Orleans I have tried to render as faithfully as possible. Almost all the characters mentioned in this portion by name were real persons, including former French General Humbert who had commanded the French troops at Castlebar in 1798. I chose my focus to be on the underappreciated contributions of the US Navy during the battle, as the famous climatic ground assault has been well covered elsewhere. Even so, many details were left out simply for the sake of time, as to tell the story of just the battle alone could have required an entire book. I deliberately shied away from the contributions of Jean Lafitte, as I felt his myth has been added to enough, although I did want to at least point out he was not the swarthy mustachioed rogue of pop culture. The battlefield at New Orleans on the Chalmette Plantation is still preserved to this day by the National Park Service, albeit surrounded now by an industrial area.

The War of 1812 itself officially came to a close on December 26th, 1814. However, due to the technology of the era, it continued until all combatants had learned of the Treaty of Ghent. Thus, the Battle of New Orleans was fought almost two weeks after the war had ended. Despite the fact that the terms of the treaty were 'status quo ante bellum', essentially a draw, the news of the peace treaty reaching the United States came on the heels of the victory at New Orleans giving the American public the view that the war had been a glorious victory. In Britain, when it is remembered at all the war is viewed as a sideshow to the Napoleonic Wars, whereas it is seen almost as the founding struggle of Canada. The final shots of the war were fired in June of 1815 by USS *Peacock* when attacking a British merchant vessel off the coast of Java in the Dutch East Indies.

The USS *Enterprise* was chosen as the ship for the heroes not just for the character's previous association with the ship, but also the ship's involvement with the West Indies Squadron following the War of 1812. There was a small gap in available Navy Records as to where the *Enterprise* was during the Spring of 1815. She departed in July for the Mediterranean to assist with the Second Barbary War, several months after the rest of the squadron had departed. I used the odd delay to explain where the ship was in the interim. When she returned to the United States, she was posted to the West Indies Squadron, having considerable success as a pirate hunter.

Capitano Alvarez of the Spanish Navy is fictional, as are of course Commander Harvey and the HMS *Athena*. Puerto Rico would remain a Spanish colony until 1898, one of the country's few remaining bastions of the old empire following the revolutions and wars of independence in Latin America during and after the Napoleonic Wars. The island has been a US Territory since the end of the Spanish-American War, and San Juan has grown quite large, encompassing the entire bay it is located on. Roughly half of Fort San Cristobal was razed as the city grew beyond the boundaries of its walls, but most of the other fortifications of the old city remain, now a National Park Service site and arguably the island's leading tourist attraction.

I have my wife to thank for using the island of Saint John as the setting of the climax for this book. She was insistent on a vacation to the US Virgin Islands (the property of Denmark at the time of the story) and a kayaking excursion to Coral Bay gave me invaluable inspiration. My initial thoughts were to have Patrick storm an abandoned Spanish fort on one of the smaller islands east of Puerto Rico, but when I learned of the abandoned Fort Frederikvaern I reasoned, "Why not use the real thing?" The ruins of the old

Danish fort are now located on private property and difficult to access. Much of the area surrounding Coral Bay, as well as portions of the bay itself are under the protection of the National Park Service as part of either Virgin Islands National Park, or Virgin Islands Coral Reef National Monument. The upturned Danish cannon does indeed exist on the shoreline, rusting away and accessible to anyone willing to paddle out to it.

General Andrew Jackson

Following his victory at the Battle of New Orleans, Jackson was feted as a national hero, riding his fame and glory all the way to the Presidency in 1828. He was such a larger-than-life figure during the period, it is collectively referred to as 'The Jacksonian Era.' The anniversary of the Battle of New Orleans itself became a national holiday for several decades, as a sort of winter Independence Day, until its celebration died out during the Civil War.

Commodore Daniel Patterson

Following the Battle of New Orleans, Patterson remained in active service the rest of his life, eventually taking command of the famed USS *Constitution* as well as the Washington Navy Yard. He died in 1839.

Captain David Porter

Porter would go on to command the West Indies Squadron from 1823-25, successfully putting an end to the second wave of Caribbean piracy. Court-martialed for an unsanctioned action in Puerto Rico, he resigned his commission and became commander-in-chief of the Mexican Navy. He later had his reputation restored, and was appointed ambassador to the Ottoman Empire, dying on assignment in 1843. His son, David Dixon Porter, and adopted son David Farragut, would become the US Navy's first Admirals.

USS *Enterprise*

Named in honor of the first American warship, the third ship to bear the name had a storied career during the First Barbary War and War of 1812. In July of 1815, she joined the Mediterranean Squadron during the Second Barbary War, after which she was assigned to pirate hunting duties with the West Indies Squadron. During this time, she captured numerous pirate vessels, as well as fighting off an entire pirate flotilla in 1821. She wrecked on a small island near Curacao in 1823, though her crew survived without loss. Her descendant ships are the most revered lineage in US Navy history.

About the Author

Andrew Costa is a part-time teacher and historian living with his wife in Ohio. His area of expertise is US and military history, with a particular interest in obscure and forgotten military conflicts. In his spare time, he is a volunteer interpreter for the National Park Service.

Works by the author:

The Sullivan Saga
1. *"For Right and Freedom"* – Seaman Patrick Sullivan and the Barbary War 1803-05.

2. *"Meeting the Enemy"* Lieutenant Patrick Sullivan and the Lake Erie Campaign, 1812-13.

3. *"Conquer We Must"* Lieutenant Patrick Sullivan and the Burning of Washington, 1814.

4. *"The Mosquito Fleet"* Lieutenant Commandant Patrick Sullivan and the West Indies Squadron, 1815.

5. *"Gone to Fight"* Lieutenant Thomas Sullivan and the Seminole War, 1836-37. (Coming Soon)

Printed in Great Britain
by Amazon